All She Ever Wanted

Marissa McQueen

For my father.

Contents

ALL SHE EVER WANTED

1

Eulalie

Greenwood 1910

Sixteen-year-old Eulalie Hopewell skipped along, making her way to the back of the church. Her eighteen-year-old beau, Vernon Jackson, had promised her two things. First, he'd sneak her a milkshake from Wallace's. Her mother had been harping on her about keeping a "girlish figure" and had forbidden Eulalie from imbibing. Since she and her sister Cassidra were almost grown, they had to put their childish ways aside. They were to look prim and proper at all times, and that included a trim waistline. They couldn't attract a husband if they didn't look the absolute best they could.

Eulalie didn't care about attracting a husband, since she'd already found one. Vernon had her heart and she, his. He didn't care what size she wore or who her father was. He loved her for her.

Second and most importantly, Vernon had promised to have the "talk" with her father. Even though they were young, Vernon said he'd marry her and give her a passel full of babies. He'd said he was going to ask for permission to marry her. He would meet with her daddy man-to-man, promising to love, honor, and respect her.

Vernon had said it wouldn't take too long. He'd only be a moment with her father, then he'd meet her in the expanse behind the church.

She sat in the grass with her back along the hot brick building, waiting.

One hour passed then another.

When droplets of sweat soaked into the dress she'd picked specially for the occasion, she stormed into the church to find it empty. Her father's office was locked, and no one else was around.

Fueled by frustration, Eulalie stomped all the way to Vernon's house. Surely something had happened to him.

Just inside the picket fence, Ida Jackson was hanging clothes on the line. Vernon's mother had always been kind to her, but for some reason, Eulalie felt a pull in her stomach. Something wasn't right.

"How are you, Mrs. Jackson? Is Vernon home?"

Mrs. Jackson dropped the patchwork quilt she'd been holding, letting it fall into the wicker basket at her feet. She inhaled deeply then let out a long breath. "Baby, I don't know what Vernon promised you, but you're going to have to find someone else. He won't be bothering you anymore." She barely spoke above a whisper, but her words punched Eulalie in the gut.

"Bother me? He doesn't bother me."

"He may not, but don't come back around here. It's not proper for the reverend's daughter to be asking after my son." Mrs. Jackson returned to the line, obviously done with the conversation.

Hot tears pricked Eulalie's eyes as she walked away.

It took her twenty minutes to walk home. She thought the tears would have subsided by the time she hit the front porch, but she was wrong. Hiding her face, Eulalie pushed open the front door to find her mother and father standing in the entryway.

They turned in unison to look at her.

"Eulalie, is everything okay?" Mama asked.

She nodded. "Everything is fine." Eulalie took the stairs up to her room and cried until she fell asleep.

2

Vernon

Greenwood District 1920

The noise level was almost too much for Vernon to bear. He was used to being in loud juke joints, where sweaty musicians played their horns for hours on end. He'd been around trains, their loud engines and whistles announcing every arrival and departure. But something about the vibration of Al's Supper Club was bothering him. The patrons were laughing too loudly and seemed to be having too much fun.

Vernon laid his trumpet in its case on the floor and stepped through the crowd, past the kitchen, and out the back door. He pulled a pack of cigarettes from his front pocket and tapped the bottom, needing the calmness of a break.

A warm summer breeze blew across his face, making it difficult to light his smoke. He cupped a hand around the end and turned his back to the wind. Pausing, he took a long drag and let out an even longer exhalation, grateful for the crisp evening. All he needed was a breath of fresh, quiet air.

"What's wrong, Vern? You had too much to drink?" A heavyset man standing in the shadows guffawed at his own joke.

"Naw, your old lady just asked if she could stay at my house. I told her no, I don't need no more women in my life. That's why I came outside to get away from her."

"Damn, man, why do you always gotta take it too far?"

"I thought we were telling jokes. That's all. Ain't nothing to it, Clyde." Vernon had probably been harsh, but he wasn't in the mood for jokes. He hadn't had any alcohol in months, but for some reason, that was the only thing that people brought up. It was starting to get old.

The last time he'd drunk with Clyde had been about six months ago, when the trees had just lost all their leaves and the evening breeze blew much colder. They'd been down at Mr. Denman's billiard hall and spent the entire evening drinking and shooting pool. They ran the billiards table for hours, collecting dimes from everyone they'd beaten. Vernon had been drunk on corn whiskey when he told Mr. Denman that he was making more money working the tables than they were at the bar. He and Clyde had promptly been muscled out the door and told to come back when they "knew howta act."

Clyde got sick while they walked home and emptied his stomach all over the roots of a bare tree, spilling coins from his front pocket as he bent over. Torn between picking the coins up and leaving them there, Vernon watched Clyde trample over the pinkish mixture with his boots. He had never left money anywhere and would never forget leaving good dimes to go to pot. Hell, he could have gotten some bread or eggs with that money.

As drunk as Clyde had been that night, he would have thought the man wouldn't have remembered. It didn't seem like he was going to let Vernon forget, though—forget that he'd been a wild man, a drunk, a gambler.

But the past didn't make the present. Something had changed between the time he and his sister had fallen out and now. He'd been a terrible brother, almost losing the person who mattered to him the most, Pearl.

Since then, he'd pledged to get his life together. He stopped drinking and gambling out of fear Pearl would never speak to him again. Once he stopped all that, he found he had a good amount of money and time freed up to pursue whatever else he wanted.

"Aren't you about to go on stage?" Vernon reminded Clyde. He inhaled the last few drags before dropping the end to the ground. He'd come outside for peace, but Clyde was there, reminding him of his past life.

"I'm headed in now. Don't be mad when I set the ladies' panties ablaze."

Vernon ground out the glowing butt before returning to look for Pearl.

Inside, the kitchen was just as busy as the dining room had been. A wave of heat encapsulated the room, making Vernon want to remove his suit coat.

Alfred, his best friend and soon-to-be brother-in-law, stood over a deep pot. He stirred with all his attention focused on the bubbling contents. Two line cooks were at the counter behind Al, chopping vegetables and slicing fresh cornbread. Al carefully ladled the brown soup into bowls and placed each bowl on a plate.

One of the line cooks, Ezekiel, broke away from his chopping to lay a few roasted root vegetables next to the soup. The second man plated a large helping of bread then covered it with a dollop of fresh butter. Vernon watched in amazement while the well-orchestrated process happened in silence.

As if she'd been called, Pearl rushed through the kitchen door and headed toward the filled plates. She noticed Vernon standing in the corner and sidled up next to him.

"What's wrong, Vern? What done crawled up your behind and died?" She stood with her hands cocked on her narrow hips and focused all her attention on him. His sister was tall and thin like he was, the same color brown and everything.

"There ain't nothing wrong with me, Birdie." He uncrossed his arms and leaned, leg cocked, on the wall. He was just in a foul mood. That was all. *Can't a man have a bad mood every once in a while?*

"Boy, when's the last time you ate? It's probably why you're so grumpy. Let me fix you something to eat before you go back on stage."

"I'm not hungry."

"Yes, you are. I can tell." Pearl turned her back to him, ignoring his shaking head. She moved quickly, reaching for one of the waiting plates and pulling it away from the others to the corner where he stood.

"I need another starter," she called over her shoulder to the three men working. The line cooks didn't say anything, instead keeping their heads down, focused on their work. Al, on the other hand, grumbled but filled another bowl.

Despite what he'd said, the plate Pearl sat in front of him made his mouth water. She'd been right. He hadn't had much to eat, but he hadn't had time. The band was supposed to go on in a few minutes, but they could wait. Pearl had forgotten a spoon, but before he could say anything, she'd piled the plates of food on a large tray and rushed out of the kitchen. He picked up the bowl, letting the heat warm his fingertips, and sipped the rich broth. Small bits of onions, garlic, and peppers mixed with pieces of chicken made him feel better immediately. The fragrant soup warmed his throat and made its way down to fill his stomach. He took a bite of the crusty bread before letting it soak in the broth and then ate a softened bite. After inhaling the roasted potatoes, turnips, and carrots, he slurped the rest of the soup and bread.

Al's Supper Club had been open for only a few months, but business was booming. Almost overnight, it had become one of Greenwood's premiere experiences.

His friend had gone from working long days in the fields to owning his own business. Al had been able to employ men and women to work in the kitchen, bar area, and band.

Vernon was happy to see Al's success and be a part of the experience. The dinner club's popularity had led to his own exit from working in the fields. Now Vernon could play his horn and figure out what he wanted to do to secure his own path. For the moment, though, playing his horn felt right.

"How big of a crowd do we have out there?" Al asked. He didn't look up from the stove, instead keeping his eyes focused on the different pots that bubbled.

Vernon moved his dirty, now empty plates toward the dishwasher and stepped closer to his best friend.

"It's all the way full, man. You made it. That soup was good."

"Was it good or great?"

"The best I've ever had." Vernon clapped Al on the back and popped another piece of cornbread into his mouth.

Then he left the kitchen, stood off to the side of the dining room, and watched the stage.

Clyde stood at the edge, telling jokes to the excited crowd. They laughed obligingly at his slick words, keeping their eyes focused and conversations to a minimum to hear what he was saying. His quips would be repeated all over town, everyone talking about the performance. Clyde pointed out a woman's large, flamboyant hat, comparing it to the size of his manhood. The crowd roared with laughter at his inappropriateness as he gesticulated sexually. Once he'd gotten all the men riled up, he motioned for Tommy, the piano player, to join him on stage so he could sing and tear the hearts out of all the women. Vernon crossed his arms and waited.

Pearl hustled among the tables, serving fresh plates of food after clearing out the dirty ones. A dishwasher followed behind her and the other waitress, Loretta, and shuttled plates from the dining room to the kitchen. Vernon's eyes followed Loretta's curves as she worked the dining room. She was pleasing to look at, but her mouth was more than he cared to deal with. Loretta was a pretty woman, the color of the early-morning sun, but his sister's best friend. Not that he should care about their friendship. Pearl and Al hadn't cared about his feelings when they started seeing each other. They were the perfect couple now, but there had been a mountain of controversy when he'd found out.

Tommy played a light jazzy number as Clyde started to sing, his falsetto echoing around the room. It sounded nice, he had to admit. Clyde had a certain stage presence that drew the crowd in. Vernon took notes, noticing when the women paid attention and when they looked away.

Stepping away from the dining room, he moved through a closed side door, into the holding room with the rest of his band. Three men lounged, waiting for their turn to entertain the crowd. Big Mike, a tall teddy bear of a man, sat behind the long bass instrument. Ronnie, the band's drummer, sitting next to Mike on a wooden box, leaned back, his arms resting easily behind his head. Ricky, the saxophonist, lay across an old couch. Individually, they'd been playing music since they were children. As a foursome, they'd been playing for about half a year as a means to make some extra money. The group had been Vernon's idea, one of the many he'd had over the years.

He'd disappeared for a few weeks the previous year, when he got the opportunity to travel to make music. Vernon had made money and had fun playing stages all across the Midwest. For a few weeks, he was on the stage, albeit in the background, playing for white folks and people of color. He saw Oklahoma City, Kansas City, St. Louis, and Nashville before they replaced him with someone else. Then he'd gone home, the fire for music burning in his blood. He vowed he would start his own band, which would travel everywhere, stay in motels, and make plenty of money. It wasn't as if he didn't have the talent. He had plenty of it. He just needed to do it.

So far, the band had only made it around Greenwood, but at least it was steady work.

"We got about five more minutes until Clyde's done with his set. Then we're up next, boys. Time to wake the crowd up," he said.

The band members reached for their instruments to make sure they were tuned up. Vernon paced back and forth in the doorway, waiting for the cue from Clyde.

Most evenings went exactly the same way for Al's Supper Club entertainment. Clyde was the introductory act, the man who began the experience. He got the crowd interested by telling a few jokes and singing while the patrons had their first course. By the time Pearl and Loretta cleaned up the starter plates, the band graced the stage to play as dinner came out. It had happened like that for months, every weekend night, twice a night, everything going without a hitch. Sometimes, only two of them could play because of other obligations, but for the most part, the quartet was a consistent fixture at Al's. Vernon hadn't missed a night and didn't plan on missing one.

"Thank you. Thank you. Y'all have been a beautiful crowd. Now enjoy your food as the band makes its way out here to grace you with a bit of entertainment. Vernon, Ronnie, Ricky, and Mike, otherwise known as the Good Notes. Come on out."

Clyde joined the dining room in applause as he vacated the stage to make room for the men.

The saxophonist, drummer, and bassist made their way to the stage, while Vernon pulled his horn to his lips and let out a long, low note. The patrons watched, entranced, as he played a few sad, bluesy notes while walking to the stage, calling everyone's attention to him before the others joined in. Together, they started a cacophony of upbeat music, in a complete juxtaposition of what Vernon had initially started. A jaunty melody filled the air as dishes of roasted hen appeared on the tables. They played for an hour straight, melding one song into another, over the hum of hushed conversation and silverware scraping.

As if they'd been timing their performance, the band brought their instruments to a standstill as dessert was served. They bowed to the crowd's applause, making room for Clyde to once again take the stage. Clyde would talk them through dessert and a nightcap before the lights were turned up. The first dinner patrons, who'd arrived at six o'clock in the evening, would be turned out by seven thirty so the eight o'clock dinner would start on time.

"Hot damn, boys we did it again," Vernon boasted.

"We did it," Ricky said, pointing to himself and Vernon. "I couldn't even hardly hear you back there Ron."

The band members argued and made their way to the side room as the dining room emptied.

The early patrons found their coats and socialized their way out the door. The young parents would be headed home to get back to their children before the sun set and the veterans were off to have another drink. Either way, Vernon had finished one performance and had one more to complete. Then he could go home and relax.

3

Eulalie

"Lalie, I know that's not my dress. I told you to stay out of my closet." Cassidra frowned, pulling off her shawl and handing it to the waiting attendant.

Eulalie smirked at her older sister, focusing on the very round, pregnant belly Cassidra sported. Cassidra couldn't fit in the dress if she wanted to.

Besides, it had always looked better on her anyway. Sidra had been busty before she got pregnant, and now, her chest had exploded in width and girth. Eulalie's smaller chest was better suited for the fitted A-line dress, since her sister's body expanded the fabric to its limit. The emerald-green satin fit perfectly over her hips and waist.

Eulalie handed her overcoat confidently to the attendant and shrugged. Sidra had already seen her, so she wouldn't have to sit in her coat all evening. She'd been eyeing the dress ever since Cassidra had brought it home from the seamstress and reveled in wearing it. The dress had been left in the closet of their parents' house, where Eulalie still lived—one of the many items Sidra hadn't taken with her when she'd gotten married and moved into a house of her own.

Her husband's a doctor, Eulalie reasoned. *She can afford whatever new dress she wants.*

"I thought you said I could have it, since you couldn't fit in it."

"I said nothing of the sort. I won't be pregnant forever, even though it certainly is starting to feel like I am." Cassidra turned sideways and ran her hand over the curve of her belly. She was only about seven months along, but her stomach looked like she could pop at any time.

"Don't you think it's a little late to be having dinner? Surely that can't be good for the baby," Eulalie said.

"When did you become such a spoilsport? Lord, it's only eight o'clock. You'd think I'd dragged you out of the house at midnight."

"I'm not a spoilsport. I'm only looking out for you."

Eulalie and Cassidra followed a shapely woman to find their seats. They weaved through the fifteen or so tables to one that sat on the far left of the restaurant, just in front of the stage. Eulalie had heard Al's Supper Club was the best dinner in town, but she hadn't had the chance to see what all the fuss was about. Hell, she wasn't even supposed to be there. Cassidra was supposed to be having a private dinner with her husband, George, but the good doctor had a patient call in the afternoon that was going to take up the rest of his evening. Even if the surgery was finished before dinner started, George wasn't going to be in the mood for a loud band accompanying his dinner.

Cassidra had shown up at their family home that afternoon, wanting to know if her sisters, Eulalie and Leona, would accompany her. Leona didn't want to be bothered, instead wanting to stay home with her books. Eulalie, on the other hand, couldn't say yes fast enough. She didn't care how long it would take to curl her hair, iron a dress, or paint her face. She was going out on the town.

Eulalie helped her sister settle into her chair then took the seat across the table. Al's was everything she'd been daydreaming of. Their table was covered in a thick, dark tablecloth that had been pressed and starched bone straight. In the middle of each table sat a tall, thin glass vase holding three long-stemmed blue irises. Tea lights surrounded the vase, adding a bit of glimmer to the table. The cloth napkins were artfully folded in front of each seat, with polished silverware flanking each napkin. It was the fanciest dinner she'd ever attended. She'd joined Mama at the hotel for the ladies' luncheon, but that had been during the day. At the hotel, they'd dressed up and socialized at an affair meant to raise money for the school.

Al's was something completely different. At the luncheon, Eulalie felt pretty, like a lady who spent time with other ladies. At Al's, she felt sexy, like a woman who spent evenings out in the company of dapper men who smoked. As a teacher and preacher's daughter, she never felt sexy. The grown atmosphere evoked something sensual in her. She pushed her shoulders back and sat up straighter.

Well-heeled women and men alike made their way to their assigned tables, catching up with their neighbors as they passed. The crowd was a flurry of floral perfume, feathered hats, and fur coats that exchanged hands from Greenwood's fashion elite to the waiting staff. Champagne glasses were ceremoniously filled to the brim to celebrate life. A waiter came around to their table with a tray covered in tall flutes of the bubbly liquid, offering one to each of the ladies. Cassidra shook her head, but Eulalie accepted, taking the drink and placing it on the table.

Cassidra raised her eyebrows in question. "Since when do you drink champagne? Or any alcohol, for that matter?"

"When did you become such a spoilsport? Besides, I'm old enough to drink." Eulalie teased her sister with her same words.

Cassidra rolled her eyes then focused on the gold bubbly liquid. "It's not about you being old enough. Nothing good comes from drinking alcohol, and you know Mama and Daddy would have a fit if they saw you."

"Good thing Mama and Daddy aren't here." Eulalie sipped a bit of the champagne and managed to keep her face straight. It was awful. The gold liquid looked like sweet manna, but it was nothing of the sort. The bubbles expanded up her nose and down her throat, trying to assault her senses. The drink itself was not sweet at all, instead almost bitter. Determined to enjoy herself, she took another infinitesimal sip before pushing the glass back toward the center of the table.

"Oh my goodness, Cassidra, you look great! I can't believe you're having a baby."

The sisters turned to find Pearl Jackson standing over their table. She was dressed in an all-black ensemble, a long-sleeved crepe shirt and a matching skirt. They yelped in excitement, jumping from their seats to embrace the tall, brown-skinned woman. They'd grown up with Pearl, attending school and church together for most of their lives. Pearl pulled Cassidra into a deep hug then turned to give one to Eulalie.

"Pearl, we heard you're engaged to be married. When is the big day?" Sidra asked.

"We've been so busy I don't even have time to plan anything. The dinner club has been so backed up we can't get a weekend off. I wouldn't change it for the world, though. We've been thinking about sneaking down to the justice of the peace just to make it official. It's not about the ribbons and rice. We just want to be married." Pearl waved off the question with a shake of her hand.

"If you did that, Mama and Daddy would chase you out of town," Sidra said. "There's nothing the good reverend loves more than a wedding celebration. Whatever help you need, we will jump in and plan."

"I appreciate the thought. I may call on you. Your wedding was so beautiful, Sidra. How's our Dr. George?"

Eulalie stood awkwardly as the two women chatted about men and married life. After a few minutes of polite conversation, Pearl turned to Eulalie. "How is everything with you? Are you ready to join the old married ladies' club yet?"

"Maybe not yet but soon. Teaching is keeping me very busy."
"I know those children are keeping you running, bless your heart."

A waiter walked up, interrupting Pearl to whisper into her ear. She nodded before turning back to the conversation.

"It's been good catching up with you both, but I have to go. Enjoy dinner, and I hope to see you both again soon." She followed the man away from them toward the back of the restaurant.

Reseated at the table, Sidra focused on Eulalie's naked ring finger.

"Why didn't you tell her about Samuel? Where's your ring?"

Eulalie snatched her left hand away and let it rest under the tablecloth, out of view.

"He hasn't given me a ring yet. Besides, nothing is official. I told Samuel I would let him know."

"You would let him know what?"

"I would let him know if I would marry him or not."

"Eulalie, what is there to think about? He's a handsome accountant. He works hard and has his own business."

Cassidra opened her mouth to discuss her thoughts further, but a man dressed in a pinstripe suit walked past their table and stood in the middle of the stage. He let out a long, angelic note, sending a hush over the crowd. All eyes focused on the elevated platform as the waitstaff brought out the first course, a bowl of soup and fresh cornbread.

"Good evening, ladies and gentlemen. My name is Clyde Woods. Do you mind if I sing a little something for you?"

The crowd clapped appreciatively, dividing their attention between the food and the entertainment. Eulalie dipped her spoon into the steaming velvety liquid and slurped appreciatively, keeping her eyes on the singing man. He was no more than a few feet away from their table, his presence a formidable fixture. Eulalie felt like the queen of Sheba, like he was singing only for her. She ate and enjoyed as he spoke, made jokes with the audience, and sang songs that would make any woman fall into his arms.

The servers came to the dining room, weaving through the tables to clean the dishes from the introductory course. Clyde took a bow and exited the stage, making way for a band to set up. The hum of a trumpet played off the side of the stage as a second young man returned to the table, carrying two plates.

"For dinner tonight, we're serving roast chicken with a side of root vegetables. Please enjoy." He placed a plate in front of each of them, gave a small bow, then departed.

The quarter of chicken had been arranged artfully in the middle of the plate. Turnips, carrots, and cooked beets had been cut into long matchsticks and placed alongside a mountain of mashed potatoes covered in gravy. It was a simple meal presented majestically. The large bite of potatoes melted in Eulalie's mouth and made her want to dance.

"When are you going to give Samuel your answer?" Sidra asked over the building music.

The burly bass player had stationed himself right next to their table, making Eulalie strain to hear. She didn't even want to talk, let alone about Sam. She wanted to enjoy the atmosphere, her champagne, and dinner in peace. Her real-life problems could be solved another time, when she was in the mood for thinking.

"I don't know, Cassidra. I'm not entirely sure I want to marry him."

Cassidra set her fork down and pursed her lips tightly. "What do you mean? You two have been courting for months. What else is there to be sure about? Does he hit you? Is there something going on that I don't know about?"

Eulalie stuffed chicken into her mouth to avoid her sister's question. That was the funny thing—there was absolutely nothing wrong with Samuel. He was perfect in every sense of the word. He was brown skinned and handsome. He dressed well if a little stuffy, but that was to be expected from a bookkeeper. Sam didn't wear flashy clothes or buy things on credit. He had his own apartment, which he took care of and kept as clean as a corner of heaven. He was serious and responsible. Sam escorted her to church and was the picture of respect. He gave her chaste kisses and didn't press her to do anything sexually that she didn't want to do. He was kind and helped her mother. He was perfect.

"No, Sidra, he doesn't hit me. He doesn't drink or smoke or gamble. There's nothing wrong with him."

"So then what's wrong with you?"

"I just don't know if I'm ready to be married yet. I only just started teaching. I want to get my feet under me before I look to get married. I'd like to be settled first."

"Well, don't make him wait too long. You know how men can be. And remember, I'm always here to talk if something is going on." Cassidra reached across the table and patted Eulalie's hand. Somehow, her sister knew something was wrong, but Eulalie would never speak the words. They sounded so silly to her.

How can I say that Samuel is... well, boring? He had no passion or fire. Well, he did have passion—for numbers and his books. To Samuel, Saturday evenings were for reading and relaxing in the house. He would never spend the money to have dinner at Al's, especially when there was food in the house that he'd already spent money on.

Eulalie nodded at her sister and returned her focus to her dinner. She might as well enjoy the experience while she was there.

"I want to do something special for y'all. Something a little different. That is, if you're okay with that," a raspy voice called over the crowd.

The music stopped as a cheer went across the dining room, but a small chill ran up the back of Eulalie's neck. The deep, gravelly voice launched into a heartfelt song that vibrated from the base of the singer's soul.

"Since my baby left me... my life ain't been the same. All my love is gone... and I lost all my brain..."

Her dinner forgotten, Eulalie turned all the way around to find Vernon Jackson walking toward the head of the stage, singing. His sweet song entranced the crowd. He had their full attention, singing without any accompaniment. He finished the song about losing the love of his life before bowing to thunderous applause.

Eulalie, on the other hand, couldn't breathe.

"I don't usually sing, so thank you for being receptive. Now back to the music." Vernon took a small bow, turned to the right, bowed again, then turned to the left. He rose slightly and, while turned toward Eulalie, made eye contact with her. Eulalie's cheeks warmed instantly under his direct gaze. She tried to smile, letting the sides of her mouth curl only slightly. Vernon's face remained impassive. He turned to face forward, brought his horn to his mouth, and started to play.

"Why didn't you tell me Vernon was going to be here?" Eulalie hissed.

"How was I supposed to know who was going to be here?" Cassidra turned her head, looking around at the patrons seated at the tables.

Eulalie discreetly gestured to the stage, where Cassidra turned to focus her attention.

"Wow, I didn't even realize that was him. It's been years since I've seen him. He sings well."

Eulalie crossed her arms and tapped her foot impatiently. She'd been having fun, but now her head throbbed, and she was ready to go home. It was getting late, and they had church in the morning.

"Have you had enough to eat? I think we can skip dessert and get out of here."

"Oh my Lord, girl, grow up. Vernon Jackson isn't thinking about you." Sidra sighed.

"He's mad at me. I know he is."

"Why would he be mad at you? It was only a teenage infatuation. You're both adults now, and you've moved on with your lives." Cassidra knit her brow in confusion.

"The last time I saw him in Cleaver's, he walked past me like he never even knew me."

"What a blessing. Why would you want to talk to him anyway?"

Eulalie shrugged to avoid continuing the conversation. Dinner was almost finished. All she had to do was make it through dessert, then she could hightail it out of the dining club.

4

Vernon

"Let's take it from the top one more time."

The next afternoon, Vernon stood in his living room with his horn at the ready. He brought his trumpet to his lips and steadied his fingers. Ronnie counted the time with his drumsticks then gave a soft tap-tap on the golden hi-hat. After a count of five, the saxophone, trumpet, and bass joined in harmony, the music ringing throughout the Jackson family living room.

Since Pearl had moved out to live with Al, he had the entire three-bedroom single-family home to himself. Over time, the band had migrated to practicing at his home in their free time. In the course of six months, the men had gone from drinking and making noise for fun into pursuing a serious venture. The front room was the perfect place for them to play to their hearts' content, until the wee hours of the morning.

The group played for an hour straight, riffing off one another's cues. When Vernon was tired, he stopped and let the instruments go on without him. They practiced sounds, tempo, and beat, molding the distinct sound of their band. Without speaking, each man took a turn to play alone to highlight each individual instrument. Vernon stopped along with Ricky and Mike to let Ronnie's drumming take center stage. Ron started calmly, letting the regular beat take over the room. He pounded harder and faster, the rhythm rebounding through Vernon's bones. After the drumming had continued for an indeterminate amount of time, Ricky stepped in with a slide of his saxophone. Ronnie slowed down his fury as the sax ramped up, the *beep-boop-bop* punctuating the slow beat of the drum. When it felt like the right time, Vernon added the heavier melody of his horn to the bebop beat. Ricky lowered the saxophone and let Vernon play alone to the imaginary crowd.

For a moment, Vernon closed his eyes and imagined he was on stage in a theater, playing for an audience of two thousand. His hands moved from memory, a song no one knew by name but a melody that sounded strangely familiar. He felt the warmth of the spotlights on the stage, the bright bulbs trained on him and the group. Gorgeous women yelled in pleasure, waving their handkerchiefs in time with the music. Couples swayed together in the aisles, moved to amorous connections all because of the sound—the music he made. If he had his way, he'd play a slow number that he would dedicate to a beautiful woman in the audience. He would look at her, speak to the crowd, and claim her beauty was the reason he performed.

Mike's low pings of the bass pulled Vernon from his thoughts, returning him to his home in Greenwood, Oklahoma. He slowed to allow Mike to take over. The sound of the large bass plinked in the background as Vernon came to face the truth. There wasn't even a theater large enough to hold more than five hundred people in Greenwood. He had to really be dreaming if he thought they would be playing for a crowd that large.

The music stopped, each man looking at the other.

"Are you going to sing for us, Vern?" Mike asked. The large man mopped the sweat from his forehead with a small white towel.

Everyone laughed at Vernon, and even he cracked a smile.

"I wasn't expecting it, but I will say you didn't sound half bad." Ricky sat down with his saxophone on the flower-print couch to rest for a moment.

"Y'all just wish you could sing like me," Vernon countered. It was like he'd explained the night before—something had gotten into him. It had made him want to burst into song. Whether it was watching Clyde singing or the air in the room, he had a song in his heart.

"Man, if I could sing like you, I'd have ladies falling all over me," Mike said.

"You do have ladies falling all over you, but it's because you're a slob. They trip over them big feet and all the shit you leave everywhere," Ronnie countered.

Mike's face contorted, but he didn't say anything. Sometime during the afternoon, he had taken off his shoes. They were currently haphazardly forgotten in the middle of the room, along with his handkerchief and hat.

A loud pounding on the door kept Vernon from answering. The band members laughed together as Vernon opened the door to find a young woman standing on his porch.

"How are you, love? What can I do for you?" He looked the woman up and down. She appeared to be in her early twenties, her face unlined and fresh. Small and thin, barely tall enough to reach his chin, she wore a plain blue dress and carried a large cloth bag on her shoulder. She had a brown hat atop her head and sturdy boots that were covered in dust. She'd obviously walked to his home from somewhere and appeared to be alone.

"I'm here to pick up some tonic water. You know what kind of tonic water I'm talking about," she answered.

Late the previous year, Vernon and Al had learned how to brew corn alcohol and started selling it around town. The business had been slow to start but eventually gained traction in the Greenwood community. Instead of purchasing alcohol from elsewhere, Vernon, Al, and Pearl were able to convince business owners to try a spirit they'd called Tonic Water. Tonic Water was being sold in pool halls, juke joints, and of course, Al's Supper Club. The trio had gone from begging people to try it to selling every bottle they produced. Since Al and Pearl had their own supper club to manage, Vernon took over production and sales of the alcohol. He kept copious notes on how much each ingredient cost, how many bottles they produced, and how many they'd sold. He wrote down who'd bought bottles and how much they'd been charged. Business was going so well that Vernon had paid off the mortgage for the house he'd inherited from his parents. It was a far cry from the cotton fields he used to work in.

"Who sent you?" he asked.

The girl hemmed and hawed before cobbling together an unintelligible answer. "I don't know if I'm supposed to say."

"Well, I ain't gon' stand here with the door open all day. Either tell me what I need to know, or get off my porch and have a good day." The words came out a little harsher than he'd meant, but it didn't matter. She was interrupting his practice and his day.

"Lloyd Parrish. He's the one who told me to come over here."

"Why didn't he come over here himself and get it? Why did he send you to run his errands?"

The girl flushed with embarrassment as she turned her face to the floor. She spoke but without any conviction or volume.

"I can't hear what you're saying."

"He was supposed to come, but his wife called him home. Said he had some errands to run and he would meet me later."

A smile crept across Vernon's face as the truth was revealed. Lloyd had been in the middle of planning a date for him and the girl when his wife called. Vernon didn't know what the girl was being shy about. If she was ornery enough to be seeing a married man and bold enough to do his bidding, she should just speak up and say what she wanted.

"How much tonic do you need?"

"Only one. Just for the two of us."

He waved her forward. "Come on in."

The woman walked in behind Vernon through the crowded front room. She maneuvered around the music equipment, stepping high over Mike's shoes, and gave a quiet hello to the men watching her. They nodded politely, returning her salutation with cheery ones of their own.

"I'll be right back, gentlemen. Continue without me." Vernon sauntered to the back room, gesturing for the woman to follow him deeper into the house.

One of his bandmates let out a low whistle, making the other two snicker. Vernon ignored them and hoped she did also. The bass played in the background as the trio started up again.

He walked to the empty bedroom next to his, pushed open the door, and stepped aside to let the woman enter. As she swept past him, the hint of perfume following her, he glanced down to look at her backside before closing them both in.

The room was bare, with the exception of a simple wood desk and three chairs, one large one behind and two in front. A framed portrait of Jesus hung on the wall, silently judging their transaction. Vernon walked around the desk and took the large cushioned seat.

"What did you say your name was?" He reached into a drawer and pulled out a ledger and a pair of old spectacles.

"Velma."

"Pleasure to make your acquaintance, Velma. I'm Vernon." He fit the glasses on his face and opened the ledger, fumbling to find the correct page. Once he found where he'd left off, he penciled in her name along with Lloyd's and added a one to indicate the number of bottles she wanted.

"Did Lloyd give you money to pay?"

She reached into her bag, counted out a few dollars, then handed it to him. He left the money on the desk and made another annotation in his book.

"I'll be around later on to deliver your bottle. Where would you like me to bring it?"

"I can't have it now? What did I come all the way over here for?"

Vernon pursed his lips. "Velma, you must understand that I can't keep an inventory of grain alcohol here in this house. One of these knock-kneed, nappy-headed goons would tear my house apart, trying to separate me from all the product I work so hard to create. Not to mention the police would take me to jail and probably burn down this house." He removed the glasses and placed them and the ledger back into the drawer.

"You don't have one teensy bottle I can take with me?" She looked around the empty room like one would fall out of the wall.

"That's not how this works. I'm surprised Lloyd didn't explain it to you. I'll deliver it later." Vernon didn't mention that Lloyd had sent a different young woman to pick up Tonic Water the previous week. It wasn't his place to be in Lloyd's business. He only wanted to sell the alcohol.

Velma gave the address, and together, they walked out of the back room. She waved goodbye to the band and left with a click of the front door. Vernon returned to his horn and the awaiting stares.

"Who was that?" Ronnie asked.

The other men nodded.

"Some lady named Velma. She was here to drop off something for Lloyd Parrish."

Vernon didn't want to divulge all of his business to the men, even though they were his friends. His bandmates weren't stupid, but that didn't mean they needed to know his business dealings. It was part of the reason he went to the back room—for a bit of privacy. All they needed to know was he didn't have any liquor in the house. He'd be supplying all of their liquid dreams if he did. It was better to keep the band and business separate.

"Introduce us to Velma next time," Mike said.

A cloud of laughter rose as they discussed Velma's assets.

"That's between you and Lloyd. I'm sure he'll have something to say about you pushing up on one of his girls."

"I thought Lloyd Parrish was married," Ronnie interjected.

Vernon shrugged, avoiding an answer. Far be it for him to try to understand what another man did with his time. Vernon wasn't interested in married women. He would never share his lady with another man.

A loud knock sounded at the front door, interrupting for the second time.

"Damn, what is it now?" Vernon set his trumpet back down and stomped toward the front door again.

Instead of Velma, another woman stood on the porch. She was several decades older than Velma and a foot taller, almost his height. Unlike Velma, who was clad in a plain dress, the woman wore a fancier silk dress, a matching hat, and a pair of high heels.

"How are you, love? What can I do for you?"

The woman frowned at his greeting and crossed her arms. "I'm not your love. I'm here to talk to someone about hiring the band."

"Why don't you come on in? You came at the perfect time. The band is all here." He opened the door wide to allow the woman to enter.

She found a seat at the dining room table, opting to avoid sitting next to Mike on the couch. Vernon followed her, throwing Mike's shoes from the middle of the room over to the side wall. The woman settled in, removing her hat to sit next to her purse on the table.

"Madam, what did you say your name was?" Vernon stood in front of her as the rest of the band members looked on with curiosity.

"Mrs. Edith White. I come from Greenwood Holy Baptist Church. I do believe I've met some of you before today. I'm looking to hire your music group."

The men rushed to their feet at her announcement, moving to acknowledge and shake her hand. They introduced themselves individually and noted the instrument they each played.

"Would you like us to play something for you?" Vernon asked.

"If you don't mind, that would be lovely." She folded her hands primly on her lap, waiting as if she had nowhere else in the world to be.

They spoke for a moment, agreeing on what they wanted to play, a light and jazzy number. If one of the church mothers wanted to hire them, slow, sultry music wouldn't do. Vernon positioned his horn as Ronnie let off an eight count to start the tempo.

The trumpet's sound rang out in a series of jaunty beeps in what he hoped was a simple, yet colorful tune.

When she'd heard enough, Edith waved her hands to stop the music. "I could stay all day to listen, but I can't. As you all may or may not know, the church is having a celebration."

Greenwood Holy Baptist was the largest, most visited church of the community. It had been the church Vernon had grown up in, the one his parents had dragged him and Pearl to several days a week. He hadn't set foot in that church for more than ten years, since his parents passed away.

"We are celebrating the church's and the pastor's anniversaries. There will be food and games and music, if you all are able to play," Edith continued. "The church has allotted twelve dollars for your band to play at the event. It will be outside on June 19. We start just before noon and will conclude sometime around five in the evening."

Vernon kept his face passive as he thought through the offer. Three dollars a man was much less than what they were accustomed to, especially for an all-day event. If he agreed, it might set the precedent for others to pay him lower wages. He should've consulted with the other band members, but instead, he answered, "Yes, ma'am. We'll play at the celebration."

5

Eulalie

Eulalie stood in front of the large blackboard and turned to face her class. The room held eighteen five-year-old black and brown faces, both boys and girls. At some point in their schooling, most of the children would stop coming. It would be a few short years after they left her class, so it was imperative she got through as many lessons as she could. Miss Hopewell was one of the first teachers they'd have before they officially started their schooling in the fall. Eulalie's parents had been ecstatic when she went away to university and came back with a teaching certificate. She'd only been teaching for about a year, pleased to take the sweet younger children, teaching them letters and how to read.

The one-room building that she'd been assigned had just enough space to hold single wooden desks and chairs for each of the students. She had a desk and a filing cabinet in the front corner but spent most of her time up at the chalkboard, having the students turn their scribbles into writing.

"Miss Hopewell, are you going to be at the church celebration?" A young girl missing her front teeth raised her hand while simultaneously asking the question. She sat with her feet swinging, her legs too short to reach the floor.

"Of course, Dorothy. I'll be there. My father is the reverend, you know. Will you and your family be there?"

Dorothy nodded as the young boy seated next to her, Ernest, raised his hand.

"I ain't never been to no celebration before. What will they have there?"

"'I haven't ever been to a celebration before.' Please repeat that after me."

The boy huffed at the correction but did as she asked. She wouldn't move on until he'd spoken correctly, and she knew he wanted to keep her talking.

"Thank you, Ernest. That was very good. I've been going to the church celebration every year probably since I was born. Each year, at the beginning of summer, we celebrate the season when the church was started here in Greenwood. We go outside and have fun on the land, just like our parents did before there was an actual building."

A curious murmur waved over the class as the students all talked excitedly.

Eulalie fluttered her hands to reclaim their attention. "We only have a few more minutes, so I'd like to go over the words again." She pointed at the board, where she'd spelled out the ones they'd been practicing all week.

"Miss Hopewell, we already know all the words. Will you please tell us more about the celebration?" Dorothy asked.

"Well, there will be music, food, and games. When I was a child, we skipped rope and had footraces."

"I'm the fastest in the class. I'll win a footrace against anyone." Ernest hopped up from his chair, daring someone to contradict him.

Eulalie laughed at his boldness as the other boys argued against his claim.

"I'll race you, Ernie, and we'll see if you're really the fastest," one challenged him.

Dorothy raised her small hand again, waiting to be acknowledged as the class quieted. "What about your husband, Miss Hopewell? Will he be there? We sure would like to meet your beau."

The girls screeched with excitement. Although they were barely off their mother's hips, they were already enamored with the boys in the class. Much to her pleasure, the boys didn't care one whit about the girls. They didn't want to play with them, didn't want to sit next to them, and certainly didn't want to be seen doing anything that could be considered lovey-dovey.

"I'm not married, Dorothy, but I would love to see you there. Where would you get the idea that I have a beau?" The words came out of her mouth a bit choppy. After teaching for a while, she knew children were apt to say anything. Eulalie'd had many conversations with the children over the years about things that happened in their homes, good and bad.

"My mama said she saw you and a man walking alongside Main Street. She said she wouldn't be surprised if another one of the reverend's daughters was married and with child soon." Dorothy used a mocking voice, which only served to rile up the class more.

Good Lord, why don't their mothers watch their mouths around these young and impressionable ears? Why was Dorothy's mother even talking about me anyway? Eulalie scanned her recent memories of walking down Main with Samuel. Surely that was who she was talking about. She hadn't been out walking with anyone else.

"This is not an appropriate conversation for school." Eulalie did her best to try to calm the children, but she'd lost control.

As if he'd been conjured by Dorothy's words, Eulalie looked toward the classroom doorway to find a man standing there watching her. Samuel filled the doorframe, grinning at the wild class. Her face warmed at his sudden presence. Of course he'd come at the end of the day, when the children were giddy and rambunctious. She wished he could have seen them all poring over chalkboards and readers. Their behavior had been spot-on except for the last few moments, when she'd let her guard down.

"I hate to say it, but it's the end of the day."

The clock above the door showed three on the dot, punctuating her statement.

A loud whoop went up as the students jumped from their seats to collect their belongings.

She tried to scream over everyone, but they were intent on getting out of the classroom as fast as they could. "Try to practice your spelling over the weekend! We will be testing next week. Don't forget your things, and Ernest, help your mama out. I don't want to hear about you getting in trouble. I will see you all at the celebration."

Samuel stepped into the classroom, which was like standing in front of a firing gun. He waved the children out the door then turned to face Eulalie.

"What are you doing here? I thought you had to work." She walked around the room, cleaning up scraps of paper and trash that had been forgotten.

"I did, but I took off a few minutes early. I wanted to know if you'd like to go for a picnic."

"Help me clean up things here, and yes, I would love to get outside."

They walked around the room together, resetting it before her weekend could start. Samuel dutifully rearranged the tables and benches to their appropriate spots. At her own desk, she gathered papers and cleaned the blackboard. The erasers would have to be beaten next week, first thing in the morning. She was eager to get out of the school and hoped to avoid being seen by Dorothy's mother.

"Are they always like that?" Samuel asked as he pulled the classroom door shut behind them.

"Like what?"

"You know, loud and wild."

Eulalie let out a short laugh. "They are children, and yes, they have more energy than us. It's not wild. It's just how they are. You were a child once."

"Yes, but I don't remember running like that."

They made their way to his Model T, and he held open the door for her. Eulalie got comfortable in the front seat, spying a large wicker basket and checkered blanket that waited in the back seat.

Samuel's surprise was thoughtful. She'd planned to go home to lock herself in her room with a novel and a glass of lemonade, a quiet retreat from all the noise she'd dealt with that day.

He hummed lightly as he drove down the dusty roads outside the school, toward their neighborhood lake on the edge of town. When they arrived, she carried the blanket and he, the basket, deciding on a perfect spot several feet from the shoreline. He helped her spread the blanket then insisted she sit and relax as he unpacked everything.

Tufts of green grass grew all around, undisturbed. A lazy breeze skimmed across the top of the water, small peaks forming. It was like all the underwater creatures were coming to the surface to witness the majesty of the summer day.

Not another soul was around for miles. Eulalie lay back on the blanket and watched the fat clouds roll by, trying to decipher what each of them looked like and what they were trying to tell her.

"How was your day?" Samuel asked, his gaze focused on the basket.

Eulalie looked for guidance from the sky before answering. *How was my day?* Like most other days, she'd gotten up early. She'd been asked a million questions and hadn't eaten much or received much of a break. She'd walked to the schoolhouse that morning and was looking forward to going home.

"My day was wonderful. The class was a delight, and everything went well. How was your day?"

"Do you remember when I told you about the Jones store account? Their books were in disarray when I took over the account, off by hundreds of dollars. As you know, the Jones store is very popular, so I wasn't sure if someone was stealing or not. Could you imagine having an employee steal money every month?"

He droned on for a few minutes, the softness of his voice mixing with the grasshoppers' chirps. She stretched out farther than the edge of the blanket, letting her arms and legs unroll to their full length. It felt good to tense each of her muscles for a few seconds before letting them relax again. She crossed her ankles then covered them with the fabric of her skirt. For a moment, she considered taking her shoes off but thought the act might elicit a familiarity with Samuel she wasn't sure she wanted.

The sun rays warmed her, turning her brown skin golden. She listened as he spoke of the Jones store, Greenwood's oldest department store. They sold a mix of home goods, clothing, and sundries that women of certain means cared about. Eulalie hadn't spent much time in the Joneses'. She didn't have a household to furnish or any additional money to spend on clothing. Her mother and sister hand made most of their clothing or had items that were handed down from other women who'd gotten new items. Eulalie daydreamed about what it would be like to have new silky underthings. She closed her eyes to imagine what the inside of the store looked like.

"Eulalie. Eulalie. Are you awake?"

Samuel's voice cracked the edges of her dream, making her awaken with a start. She sat up straight up and looked around, trying to shake off the cobwebs.

"I'm so sorry. I must have fallen asleep. The sun has gotten the best of me. Please continue with your story."

"As I was saying, it turns out they had a small error in their accounting practice. They'd forgotten to account for the petty cash. Every day, Mr. Jones put away money in coins and bills to be able to make change. It is astounding how easy it is to get your books off track when you don't count everything properly. Would you like a sandwich?"

He offered her half of a tuna salad sandwich, which she accepted with thanks. The bread was soggy in the middle, and the tuna needed salt, but she ate it anyway.

"Have you given any thought to my proposition?"

"Samuel, I've been so busy—"

"Wait, wait, wait. I don't want to upset you. I just want to make my intentions known. I like you, and I want you to be my wife."

"Don't you think we're a little young?" As soon as the words left her lips, she wanted to take them back. She was almost twenty-seven years old. By everyone's account, she was an old maid, threatening to spend her life on the shelf.

"Darling, my own mama was married with three children by the time she was your age. We're old."

"I suppose being around all the children makes me feel younger than I really am. I only just started teaching." Her eyes drifted from the water to the man seated next to her. For the first time that day, she took a long, hard look at him. Samuel's dark-brown skin gleamed in the sun streams. He reminded her of a large barn owl with his wide-set, questioning eyes and small ears pinned close to his head. He was of middling height and weight, not too big or small.

"Why do you want to be married? Most importantly, why do you want to marry me?" She shifted in her seat and reached for a few grapes, waiting for his answer.

"You come from a great family. Your father is a great man, and I know he's raised you and your sisters well. You work with children every day, so I know you'll be a wonderful mother. Most importantly, you're beautiful. You have a nice petite frame and a pretty face. I could see us being very happy together."

Eulalie nodded at his answer. They sat in silence for a moment, only their chewing filling the air.

"May I ask you a question, since you've been asking me everything?" He grinned, the action brightening his face.

She nodded, wondering where the conversation would take them.

"Do you want to spend the rest of your life in Oklahoma? Wouldn't you like to see Chicago? A real city? We need teachers up there also."

Eulalie looked out over the lake in an effort to digest his words. It was easier to let the calm wave of nature soothe her than it was to face his questions. She'd never considered leaving Greenwood, let alone the Oklahoma territory. It had been her home for her entire life. Her family was there. Her niece or nephew hadn't even been born yet. The thought of leaving before meeting the new baby made her stomach roil.

"Isn't Chicago cold? I don't know if I could get used to that type of weather."

"Oh, yes, ma'am. Chicago gets very cold. Did I ever tell you about the time there was so much snow it stood taller than me?"

She turned her head in disbelief, pursing her lips. "There's no way there was that much snow. I've never even seen that much snow before in my life."

"Gal, you wouldn't believe it. The temperature on that day was negative degrees, and the wind was so strong it would have blown a small thing like you away." Samuel's countenance brightened as he spoke of his home city with passion and fervor, and suddenly, she felt silly. Samuel was fine. He wasn't flashy or exciting, and that was okay. He'd set everything up to surprise her to try to make her happy. He'd be a nice husband, one who'd take care of everything. Everything was fine. Perhaps she just wanted too much.

6

Vernon

Somehow, the preacher must have had a special relationship with the Lord. He couldn't have picked a more beautiful day for an outdoor celebration if he tried. The sky was a light shade of blue, and fluffy white clouds floated along, keeping the sun from cooking the people and souring the meat. The thunderstorms and high winds of the spring had passed, giving way to the pleasant days of early summer, before the heat sent everyone inside.

Vernon led the band down the dirt path that ran along the outside of the brick church. Each man carried his own instrument, Ronnie sweating with effort at toting the large bass. They ambled out of the shadow of the large building, into the back acres the church had accumulated over its decade of existence.

Two young boys ran underfoot before peeling off the path toward a grassy area, reminding Vernon of his own childhood. Women set up games that visitors would play, everything from knocking over milk cans to potato-sack races. On the far side of the building, a group of men argued beside a stack of wood about the best place to set the spit. One didn't want it to be so close to the church. There was no reason to put it in danger of catching fire. The other argued they needed to be next to the building for the shade it offered. In less than an hour, the sun would be high in the sky, and by the late afternoon, it would be setting on the other side. They wouldn't be as hot, and the fire was going to make everything even warmer.

Vernon was walking about, looking for someone to direct them, when he locked eyes with Mrs. Edith. She carried a large basket of apples, resting it on her hip while she directed with her fingers.

"Welcome, gentlemen. I'm so glad you could make it." She dropped the large carrier onto the ground and rushed toward the band. "I'll show you where you can set up." She waved for them to follow her before a girl about ten years old ran up and stopped her.

"Mother Edith, they need you in the kitchen."

"Baby, I'll be right there. Give me just a minute."

The girl persisted. "Elder Charles said if you don't get there right away, Georgetta might lose some fingers." The little girl waved her hands, trying to impart the importance of the message.

Edith huffed then looked around before screaming toward a group of women stationed around a large tin washbasin. "Eulalie. *Eulalie*, come here please." She turned to the child, saying, "I'll be right there. Let me get Eulalie to help the band."

The girl ran off toward the kitchen as Eulalie turned at the sound of her name and walked straight toward Vernon.

His heart started to beat out of his chest, and suddenly, the day felt too bright. He'd known she was going to be there. Hell, her father was the most important man in the church. At some point in the day, he was bound to run into her. He just didn't realize it was going to be so soon.

He allowed himself a genuine once-over. Eulalie wore a light-blue dress that fit along her top half while simultaneously swinging loosely around her calves. She had to have a hat somewhere to keep the sun off her face, but it must have been forgotten some-where in all the preparation. Her hair had been straightened and curled, and it flowed around her shoulders as she walked toward them. She looked vibrant, like she was in secret competition with the sun. She was different from the girl he remembered, more sure-footed and confident. Before she even made it over to him, a rush of familiarity swept over him. He wanted to reach out to see if she felt the same, but he kept his hand gripped around the handle of his horn's case.

"Yes, Mother Edith, you called?" She stepped close, and boldly, Vernon looked her in the face. She avoided his gaze, keeping her eyes trained on the older woman.

"Will you show the band where they can set up? Up on the small hill where everyone can see and hear them." Mrs. White started to walk away before turning back to the group. "Do y'all think we can wheel the church's piano outside? I feel like hearing the tinkling of the ivories."

Ronnie exhaled loudly and walked away, unwilling to assist in carrying anything. He was already sweating, and they hadn't even started to play yet.

"I suppose we could get a few men on the job. I'll take a look at it and see if we can move it once we get settled," Vernon answered.

With a nod, Mrs. Edith moved in the opposite direction, walk-ing as quickly as her large legs would carry her.

"Follow me, please."

Eulalie's voice was barely above a whisper, but that was fine. They all knew why she was there and what they needed to do. Truly, Vernon didn't even need her to lead the way. He'd played on the church grounds when he was a boy and knew the land like the back of his hand. But it had been a decade since he'd been out there.

They made their way to the grassy hill, which stood about four feet higher than the rest of the land. From that area, the band could play, and families could sit or stand at the bottom to listen to the music. Nature had provided Vernon a stage. All he had to do was play.

Mike and Ricky huddled around Ronnie, helping him with the bass, while Vernon turned his attention to Eulalie.

"Did you enjoy Al's the other night?" He was cautious with his words, unsure of how to break the ice. He was certain it had been her sitting at the table with her sister. The moment he recognized her, he almost stopped playing.

"The evening was beautiful. The food, the dining room, the company. Everything was great." She still refused to look at him.

It would take some time. They hadn't seen each other in years. She didn't owe him anything, not even the conversation he was desperate to have.

"What about the music? Did you like the music?"

"The music was the best part of the evening. I could have stayed and listened for hours."

"Does your daddy know you were drinking champagne?" he teased, and by the looks of the smile that grew across her face, she understood.

"Why? Are you going to tell him?" Finally, she met his gaze. She had full cheeks and a gorgeous smile. Her eyes crinkled at the sides, making Vernon yearn to shade her from the sun.

"I was thinking about it. But I don't have time for a lecture today. If I tell him you were out drinking, he'll have me in the office, telling me I'm a community leader and I have to hold myself to a higher standard. I can't let the devil's drink ruin the neighborhood."

Eulalie let out a loud fit of laughter, causing the band members to look over in concern. If Vernon didn't do anything else that day, it would be fine. Making her laugh had made his entire day. She was an oasis and he, a thirsty traveler.

Vernon laughed with her, trying to memorize the sound of her breathy squeak of a laugh.

"My word, 'the devil's drink'? That is something he would say."

"You're lucky, Lalie. I don't have time today because I have to get the band set up. But I may tell him tomorrow."

Her nickname had fallen out of his lips before he realized. They hadn't spoken in a decade, but that one comment pulled him right back into a cloud of ease with her.

It made him recall when they were young and laughing was easy. On long summer days, he'd listened to that laughter. His only goal had been to make it continue for as long as he could.

****

Fifteen years ago, in the same patch of grass behind the church, Vernon Jackson and Alfred Harris had been thirteen-year-old boys. Full of energy, they'd spent the church picnic running with other boys as their family members socialized.

Reverend Hopewell had overseen the building of the church in the newly established Greenwood. When Vernon was a child, they'd started gathering to have services in a tent, praising the Lord on a tract of land that had been purchased with money collected from the members of the growing congregation.

The church celebration that year came a week before his fourteenth birthday, when they'd finally finished the building. When the services were finished, adults and children alike moved outside to celebrate with friendship and food, like they used to do.

Al stood across from Vernon, several feet back, focused on a rubber ball in front of him. In the game they'd created, each boy was supposed to kick the ball as hard as he could to make it go as far as he could. The runner had to chase the ball, grab it before anyone else could intercept it, and return to the field to take his turn as kicker.

Al reared his leg back and took a running start toward the ball before sending it soaring. Keeping his eyes on the ball, Vernon ran as fast as his legs would carry him, over the uneven terrain. The ball sailed high over the east side of the church and fell out of his sight on the other side of the building.

Vernon cursed. *Why didn't Al kick the ball the other way, away from all the happenings?* If either one of their parents caught them, the ball would be taken away immediately.

His heart pumped as he ran. After rounding the corner of the building, he passed a group of women, who yelled at him to stop running. Much to his surprise, the front of the church was empty, with all the activities happening at the back of the building.

Vernon searched frantically around the trees and bushes, trying to find the ball. The downward pitch of the church's roof would render it impossible for the ball to have gotten caught, so it had to be somewhere. He'd just spotted the ball lying in the grass, close to the inbound dirt road, when he heard sniffling.

Eulalie Hopewell sat alone on the white stone steps, crying. Vernon ran to pick up the ball before stopping in front of her. She startled at his sudden appearance, wiping the streaks of tears from her face. She looked so small and helpless that he had to stop. Her hair had been plaited back from her face, and she wore a white shirt and blue skirt decorated with thin white bows.

"Are you okay, Eulalie?" Vernon was tempted to turn back around. It was his turn to kick. Instead, he wanted to make sure she wasn't hurting.

"Leave me alone, Vernon. I'm not in the mood for teasing."

"I'm not trying to tease you. I'm just asking if you're all right."

"No, I'm not all right. I'm sick of you stupid boys." She twisted her body to the side and crossed her arms.

"What do you mean? I didn't even do nothing."

"All of you stupid boys are the same."

"No, we're not." Once, when he was younger, his pop had given him the beating of his life when he teased a girl because her hair was shorn like a boy's. After Pop turned his bottom blacker than it already was, he made Vernon sit on the couch and listen to his stern lecture.

Men are supposed to take care of women. What would you do if someone had hurt your sister's feelings? Is that the type of man you want to be? The kind of man who makes women cry?

The lecture stung worse than his backside. Vernon would have taken a hundred more beatings if it meant he didn't have to disappoint his father again. After that, he'd given most of the girls he knew a wide berth. From that day forward, he was the only one who could mess with Pearl. Anyone who made her cry would have to face his wrath.

Eulalie sat before him, tears streaming down her face. She wasn't his sister, but it wasn't right. Boys weren't supposed to make girls cry.

"What happened, Eulalie?"

"Gerald tried to look up my skirt." She crossed her legs, smoothing down the edge of the blue skirt over her knee.

Vernon took one look at her pitiful face and knew what needed to be done. "That ain't right. I'm sorry. Get up and show me where he is."

"Don't tease me. I'm not in the mood."

Vernon got close to her face, where she had no choice but to look at him. "Show me where he is."

Eulalie stared at him for a few seconds, her eyes wide, as she seemed to be trying to decide whether she wanted to trust him. She slowly uncrossed her legs and got to her feet. Then she led him around to the back of the church and stopped for a moment to shield her eyes from the piercing sun. They looked together, scanning the grounds for Gerald.

The picnic was in full swing. Long rows of wooden tables with benches were filled with congregation folk. Plates were piled high with roasted chicken, salted pork, fresh corn, and slices of watermelon. A group of teenage boys had started a baseball game on one side of the yard. Men huddled together over a stack of cards, playfully arguing over who was going to win the hand. Women everywhere were in motion, chasing children, cleaning messes, and laughing together. Everyone was having a great time—everyone except Eulalie.

Alfred ran up. "Vern, where have you been? Are you going to kick the ball or what?"

Vernon had just turned to answer his friend when Eulalie interrupted. "There he is over there." She pointed toward the thicket where he and Al had originally been playing.

He scanned in the direction she'd indicated, looking over everyone until he found the one he was looking for. Gerald Jones stood with three other boys, all of them bigger and older than Vernon. He started toward the pack, but Al pulled at his arm.

"Whoa, where are you going?"

"I need to speak to Gerald."

"Gerald's fifteen now. You ain't gotta go messing with him."

Al's eyes were taut with fear, while Eulalie's were wide with expectation. It didn't matter what Al said. Vernon had made a promise to Eulalie.

Ignoring Al's pleas, he marched toward Gerald, his heart thumping.

"Look, it's Eulalie with the holes in her bloomers!" Gerald said in a singsong to the other boys.

The pack cackled at the joke, fueling Vernon's anger.

Without a word, Vernon balled up his fist, cocked it back, and punched Gerald right in the side of his fat head.

7

Eulalie

Eulalie froze. For a moment, the world stopped.

She hadn't expected Vernon to hit him. She thought maybe he would just go tell Gerald he was being mean and that he should leave her alone.

Everyone watched, stunned, as Gerald fell back to the dirt. He hadn't been expecting an attack and hadn't prepared himself to be punched in the face. Vernon stood over Gerald, his chest heaving. Gerald lay unmoving for a moment then emitted a low whine and rolled over. At least he wasn't dead.

When the bubble broke, everyone remembered where they were and whose side they were on. Beanie, one of Gerald's friends, rushed toward Vernon and pushed him hard on the chest, knocking him onto his behind. Alfred stepped in to help his best friend, as did one of the other boys. The last ran away from the group and melded into a crowd of adults.

Eulalie didn't move. She couldn't. She wasn't about to jump into the tangle of swinging arms and kicking legs, but she wanted them to stop, so she did the best thing she could. She screamed. "Boys, stop! *Stop!*"

None of them seemed to hear.

"You think it's okay to mess with a girl? Mess with me!" Vernon swung wildly, but Beanie kept his face away. Vernon's face scrunched with seriousness.

Gerald regained his breath and stood, catching Vernon around the back. Vernon, who'd been so focused on Beanie, was caught unaware.

"Are you mad because I saw your girlfriend's panties? I didn't know you liked dirty drawers." Beanie pulled his fist back and knocked Vernon square in the stomach.

"What in the world is going on over here?" Mr. Winston ran up and separated the melee. He yelled for backup, catching the attention of other men who were standing around. Adults surrounded them, pulling everyone in different directions. Vernon was yanked to his feet by his father, who grabbed Al with his other hand. Before Mr. Jackson led both of the boys away, Vernon turned and looked at her. They locked eyes, only focusing on each other. Vernon had stood up for her. He'd hit Gerald and gotten punched in the stomach for her.

A tight hand clamped around her upper arm and pulled hard, turning Eulalie face to face with her mother.

"What are you doing over here with these boys? Get your tail over here."

Eulalie kept her face trained on the wild group, which now included a bunch of adults, instead of watching her step. She stumbled over the uneven ground, making her mother's hand clamp down harder.

"I told you to stay away from those boys."

"I wasn't even messing with them," Eulalie said.

"All this fighting and carrying on at the church picnic," Mama continued, not even hearing Eulalie speak. "Y'all got the entire congregation looking at you."

Eulalie felt all eyes on her as she followed her mother from the harsh sunlit day into the darkness of the empty church. When they'd reached the hallway outside her father's office, Mama finally let go of her arm.

"Sit down and tell me why they were fighting like that." Mama crossed her arms and tapped her foot impatiently.

If Eulalie didn't give an accurate answer, Mama was liable to start swinging. Daddy didn't spank any of his girls. He was a man of God. That grace didn't extend to Mama, though, especially when she was angry.

"I can't tell you, Mama. I'm ashamed." She wanted to cry but refused. It would only make her mother angry.

"You'd better tell me something."

Sunshine from the window streamed into the long hallway, running across Mama's face and highlighting her round cheeks and tight jaw. It was just the two of them. If Mama got mad, at least she wouldn't be embarrassed in front of anyone else. She'd already told Vernon, so she might as well tell Mama what happened.

"Gerald looked up my skirt. I was going around to the kitchen to get more lemonade like you asked me to. I walked around the building, and there wasn't anyone there except me and him. He followed me and kept pulling up my hem to 'see if my panties were clean.' I told him to stop, Mama. I swear I did." At that point, she couldn't hold the tears in. Fat, hot droplets spilled down her face and landed on her shirt.

Mama's expression lightened, and she immediately pulled Eulalie into an embrace. "Oh, baby, I'm so sorry. I didn't know."

Eulalie let all the embarrassment and shame she held melt into her mother. Mama stood there for a moment, just holding her until the tears dried into soft sniffles.

"Stay here and don't move. I'm going to get your father." Mama strode off.

Eulalie sat alone, wishing one of her sisters were there with her. If she hadn't been walking around alone, Gerald wouldn't have bothered her in the first place.

Eulalie's few minutes of peace were interrupted by the cacophony of a large group. Her father, Reverend Hopewell, led the line in his upright, righteous manner. Vernon and his father followed Daddy, leaving Gerald and his grandmother to bring up the rear.

"Come on in here, Eulalie." Daddy's deep baritone echoed down the hall. He didn't sound mad, but he wasn't happy either.

Eulalie waited until everyone had passed, keeping her eyes directed to the floor. She couldn't look at Gerald or Vernon now that she'd told on both of them.

Each of the adults sat in a chair, leaving all the young people to stand behind their guardians. Since Eulalie had come in last, she stood awkwardly just inside the door. Her daddy settled behind the desk in his large pastor's chair. It didn't feel right to go back there with him, so she stayed a few feet away from Gerald.

"As I understand it, young man, the reason we're here is because you looked under Eulalie's skirt."

Eulalie's cheeks burned when every eye in the room turned toward her. She moved to speak, but she couldn't think of what to say. It was one thing to admit it to her mother but an entirely different situation to say it in front of everyone and their grandmama.

"That's not true, sir. I didn't look up her skirt," Gerald said.

Eulalie's mouth fell open, and she turned to face him. "Stop fibbing, Gerald. You did look up my skirt."

"Eulalie. Enough." Daddy's voice was serious and unyielding. He turned to Vernon. "How did you get involved, young man?"

"My father told me to take care of women, and that's what I did. I couldn't stand to see her cry, so I fixed it."

Daddy nodded before talking to the adults. Everyone apologized for the mishap, promising to attend to their child. Daddy smiled, said a quick prayer, and dismissed everyone to enjoy what was left of the picnic.

Everyone, that was, except for Eulalie. He closed the door behind the visitors and returned to his chair. She thought she was in trouble until her daddy's face broke into a big grin.

"Are you okay, Lalie?"

She thought she might start to cry but instead pushed her chin up and outward in defiance.

"You didn't do anything wrong, but do me a favor, baby. Stay away from those boys. Especially Vernon Jackson."

"Why Vernon? He didn't even do anything."

Daddy sighed heavily and sat back. "When you're older, you'll understand. For now, heed my words, and stay away from him."

"Yes, Daddy." Eulalie gave him a kiss on the cheek before she, too, was dismissed to enjoy the rest of the celebration. She walked down the empty hall and turned to exit the front door of the church. She stepped back into the hot sun and stopped on the top step to adjust back to the light.

"I can't believe you told on me, you little bitch. I was just having fun with you is all. Can't you take a joke?" Gerald was standing next to the bushes alone, waiting for her. His left cheek was swelling and turning dark.

She swallowed hard. For a few moments, she considered ignoring him, but she had a lot to say.

"I told you to leave me alone," she retorted. "You should have listened." She took a few steps down the front of the church and kept walking back toward the celebration.

"You're lucky your daddy and your boyfriend are here today. Next time, you won't be so fortunate." He leered at her, his lip curled up in defiance. He'd closed the distance between them, bending over to whisper into her ear.

Eulalie had two choices. She could scream and ask for help, or she could be like Vernon, bold and taking matters into her own hands.

Eulalie took a deep breath, pulled her fist back, and punched Gerald as hard as she could, connecting with his ear.

Nobody was going to tell boys she had dirty panties. Her drawers were very nice and always clean. Mommy made sure of that.

****

Eulalie snuck a peek over at the hill, where the band was in full swing. She found a shaded spot close enough to enjoy the music and sat down. Cassidra waved as she walked by with her husband, letting her stomach lead the way toward the food. Her younger sister, Leona, was busy helping Mama at the children's station. For a moment, she could relax and enjoy. She didn't have to run around and chat with the elders or fix anything.

Vernon, Ricky, Ronnie, and Mike played a few sharp notes, calling for the crowd's attention. Then Vernon brought his horn to his lips and blew a long, deep note, beckoning all of the congregation toward the stage. Most of them hadn't seen the band play together, unless they'd been lucky enough to dine at Al's Supper Club.

A crowd gathered around the base of the small hill, abandoning their conversations in favor of the impromptu concert. The longer the band played, the more attention they got. Couples wandered over from the tables to spin in one another's arms. Eulalie's student Dorothy swung around with each toot of the horn, the hem of her skirt flying in the wind. She laughed with the other little girls, enjoying her time in the sun.

Feeling brave, Eulalie gazed over the crowd until her eyes landed on Vernon. He'd arrived that morning wearing a navy-blue suit but at some point had removed his jacket. He stood performing in a crisp white button-down shirt with the first few buttons undone and his sleeves rolled up to his forearms. The metal rivets on his suspenders gleamed in the sun as he twisted and turned in time with the music.

Since she was alone, she let herself indulge in a bit of staring. Vernon had recently been to the barber, his hair cropped closely to his head. His long fingers danced over the buttons, and his full lips pouted perfectly over the mouth of his instrument. He looked good.

As if reading her thoughts, Vernon met her eyes. He stared and kept playing, like he played for her and only her. She warmed under his gaze, refusing to break eye contact first. Her heart beat erratically in her neck at his attention. She thought back to when he'd made her smile, teasing her about the "devil's drink."

Of course he made me scream with laughter, she thought. *Maybe he's not mad at me.*

Vernon was the first to break eye contact, turning to look at the band members. The tempo changed, and Rick, the saxophonist, stepped forward. Vernon stopped playing for a moment and let his trumpet fall to his side. That time, he looked pointedly at her, since he wasn't distracted by performing. He winked at Eulalie, licked his lips, brought his horn back to his mouth, and began to play again.

A small smile grew across her face before she could stop herself. No, he wasn't mad at her at all. She refused to look back up at him, instead giving only her ears the pleasure of music. That was why she was sitting there, to hear the music. She tried to stifle the glee that grew, since she couldn't show him that he'd made her smile.

Eulalie turned in the other direction to give herself something new to focus on. In the distance, standing next to the church, her father stood alone, watching everyone like a proud rooster. She was about to turn back to the band when Samuel walked up to her father and shook his hand.

God, why is he talking to my father? She knew he was supposed to be here, but why couldn't he just sit and enjoy the party like everyone else?

The two men laughed as if Samuel were the funniest man in the world. They made their way toward the crowd, and she tore her eyes away from them, suddenly tired.

"Everyone, please clap your hands for the band if you enjoyed their music," Daddy announced. He stood back while the quartet bowed at the rousing thunder.

"We're so blessed that they could come out and share their music with us on this beautiful day. While I have everyone's attention, I want to see if my daughter Eulalie will join me up here." Daddy looked directly at her and waved.

Fifty people stood between her and the hill, and every person turned around to look at her. Without feeling the ground beneath her feet, Eulalie shot up and floated to the front to stand next to her father. The crowd milled about, wondering what was about to unfold.

"As you all know, Eulalie is one of the sweetest, smartest daughters a man could ask for. She's a teacher, sings in the choir, and has always been helpful to her mama and me." Daddy placed a hand on her shoulder. It felt heavy and unwieldy, a boulder offsetting her balance.

"I have always been proud that she is one of my girls," he continued, "but it seems as if she will no longer be one of mine."

Eulalie inhaled sharply at her father's words. A murmur went over the crowd when Daddy pulled her into a deep hug, seeming to enjoy the attention they were receiving. He released her, grabbed her by each of her shoulders, and turned her around to face the opposite direction.

Samuel was on bended knee behind her. He held up a ring, a round sapphire set inside a halo of diamonds. It gleamed in the sunlight, blinding her.

"Eulalie, will you make me the happiest man on earth? Will you marry me?" Samuel grinned too widely, exposing his mouth full of teeth.

A crowd of expectant faces looked up at her. She felt the hopefulness they exuded, the happiness for her.

She couldn't say a word. Nothing would come out. *Nod. At least do that.* She brought up her hand to cover her mouth, feigning shock. She was forced to agree now, knowing at some point, she'd have to make a decision.

"Is that a yes?" Samuel asked tentatively.

"Mm-hmm."

"If y'all can't hear back there, she said yes!" Daddy yelled.

The crowd roared in delight, rushed to the top of the hill, and enveloped the couple in hugs and well-wishes.

8

Vernon

Vernon sat on the porch, watching the sun disappear behind a set of dark clouds. He wished he had a bit of moonshine to help enjoy the evening but knew that wouldn't end well. It felt better to sit and listen to the sounds of the crickets. The creak of the fence called his attention down to the edge of the yard, where Pearl was walking through the gate.

"What are you doing sitting out here like an old man?"

He smirked. He felt like an old man, one who'd lived through some things and wanted to spend his evenings alone.

"I'm just trying to enjoy the nice summer evening. Can't I get a bit of fresh air?"

"Didn't you get enough fresh air at the celebration today?" She pressed her lips together. "You got out of there pretty quickly. One minute, you were playing, and the next, you'd disappeared." Pearl made her way up the front steps and sat on the top one.

"It was too hot. I needed to come home and change." Vernon sat there as bold as sin, in the same suit he'd been wearing that afternoon, the buttons on his shirt half done.

Pearl didn't answer, leaving the two of them in silence for a moment. He knew she wasn't buying his story, but it didn't matter.

Vernon tore his gaze away from Pearl and looked back at the sky. The wind picked up, sweeping his desolate mood over the porch. Heavy clouds approached, bringing in a storm that matched Vernon's gloomy mind.

"Are you hungry? I have a few chops in there I can heat up for you." He shifted awkwardly in the chair, hoping to change the subject.

"Naw, I've eaten already. I just came here to check up on you. Are you doing all right?"

"Birdie, I'm fine," he answered. "You don't need to check on me. Why wouldn't I be fine?"

Pearl crossed her arms and turned around on the stoop to face him. "So seeing Eulalie get engaged today didn't make you feel anything?" She cocked her head to the side.

"I haven't spoken to Eulalie Hopewell in ten years. I've been living this long without her. What difference does today make?" The twinge in his gut made a liar out of him, but Pearl didn't need to know.

"Hmm. That's a good answer but not really what I asked. I asked if what happened today made you feel anything."

He considered her question, deciding whether he wanted to answer truthfully. If he was being honest, the entire situation had affected him more than he cared to admit. Seeing Eulalie brought back so many memories he'd thought he'd pressed down and locked away. She looked good, like she'd been taking care of herself, like she was happy. Every time they'd run into each other, she scurried away before they could speak.

"Was I pleased to see her engaged? Naw. But I knew the day would come. I was expecting it sometime before now."

"I know she meant a lot to you," Pearl said.

"Birdie, I was a teenager. It wasn't that serious. I've bedded so many women. I don't even think about her."

As soon as the words were out of his mouth, they both knew it was a lie. Eulalie had been the first girl he'd ever cared for and wanted, the only girl he couldn't have. It didn't matter anymore, though. She was in love with someone else.

"Truly, she's gotten so pretty. She used to be such a scrawny little thing." Pearl laughed.

"I know you ain't calling nobody scrawny."

"Well, yes, we were skinny but always tall. Eulalie was the smallest kid out there. No meat on her bones and not tall enough to play with anyone." Pearl continued with her musings. "She's still short, but now she's as thick as cream. In a good way, of course."

Pearl stood abruptly, putting an end to the conversation. "Anyhow, I wasn't staying. I just came over to see how you were doing." She gave a concerned look at the storm clouds approaching.

"I can't let you go alone in the dark. The wind's pickin' up. You'll get blown away."

Vernon locked the door of his house and started down the street with his sister. He was glad she'd shown up, glad she'd taken the time to check on him. She was the only person in the city who knew how he'd once felt about Eulalie. They'd always had their differences, but Pearl was one of the few people who'd always been there for him, no matter the mess he'd gotten himself into. Now that she was marrying his best friend, his two favorite people in the world would be creating a new life. He felt good knowing they hadn't forgotten about him.

"How's wedding planning going?"

"It's going, I suppose. We wanted to be married by the end of summer, but everything is so busy with the club."

"Al's not having cold feet, is he?"

"I don't think so. He still wants to marry me." Pearl smiled shyly.

"You aren't having cold feet, are you?"

Pearl pursed her lips and rolled her eyes. "I know it ain't sitting right that your sister and best friend are getting married, but you gon' have to get over it."

The wind whipped as they neared Pearl's place, carrying the heavy smell of rain. Although they hadn't married yet, Pearl and Al were living together in the small apartment above the supper club.

Vernon's shirt flapped in the wind. He buttoned it up, trying to shield his chest. It had gotten dark since Pearl's visit, but from what he could see, storm clouds were gathering in the distance.

"It's about to pour. You'd better get on home," Pearl said.

"I left my trumpet at the church because..." He paused to think about his words. "Because I needed to get home. I'm going to stop by Ricky or Mike's place while I'm out to see if someone has it."

"Vernon, just go home. You can get that trumpet tomorrow."

"Did you hear the radio?" a heavyset woman called over to them. She had been passing by and somehow eavesdropped on their conversation. Lord, he couldn't stand a nosy woman.

"A thunderstorm is on the way, and there may be a twister that comes along with it. Don't be surprised if the siren sounds tonight." She wished them well and ran off, holding her hat on her head.

"Well, I gotta go. I don't want to be out if there's a tornado coming." Vernon hugged Pearl and waited until she stepped inside before he turned away. He'd promised his sister he was going home, but he turned toward Mike's house.

The winds picked up even more after each stop he made. His trumpet wasn't at Mike's. Mike said Ricky must have picked it up. Vernon hurried through the dark neighborhoods to Ricky's to find it wasn't there either. At his last stop of the night, Ronnie finally told him that his hands had been full, and he'd seen the church secretary take it with her toward the church.

The city bell rang in the distance as he turned toward the church, hoping someone was there.

If he was going to be stuck in the house alone, at least he could play a little to keep himself company. A lone drop of rain fell on the back of his head and rolled down his neck, but he figured he had plenty of time to make it home before the worst of the storm rolled through.

9

Eulalie

"Ladies, I hate to leave you like this, but I gotta get home and check on the kids." Mrs. White looked out the window at the darkened sky.

Eulalie, Mama, and Mrs. White had spent hours after everyone left, cleaning the kitchen and gathering trash. Daddy and Leona had gone home thirty minutes earlier after a long day. He needed to make sure he had his sermon together, and Leona had had enough. That left them to make sure the church was thoroughly cleaned for the worshippers to join in the morning.

A low rumble of thunder sounded in the distance.

"Mother Edith, I'll walk you home. There's no reason you should be going out in the dark by yourself. Especially with this weather coming." Mama pulled her apron over her head and hung it on the back of the door. "Eulalie, make sure all the lights are turned off, and I'll be back around to collect you."

Eulalie fought the urge to roll her eyes. She was twenty-six years old, and her mother was still worried about her walking the few blocks home. "Don't worry about me. I can see the house from the church porch. I'm only a few steps away." Eulalie exaggerated the closeness of her family home, hoping Mama would understand she would be okay. There were no fewer than twenty congregants' homes between the church and hers. If she showed up at their door, she could stay for the entire week if she needed. "I'll probably make it home before you."

Mrs. White said to Mama, "She's right, Orlene. She'll be fine. Let's get out of here."

"I'm just going to make sure I shut off the lights, then I'm leaving behind you." Eulalie escorted them to the front door then stood in the threshold. The rain was starting to fall, and the winds were as wild as wolves during a full moon. The women made their way into the darkened night, laughter following in their path. Eulalie watched them amble down the street until they disappeared into the darkness. She hoped the storm would pass quickly, and she could wait it out in the church.

Eulalie was enjoying the smell of the rain when a dark figure appeared in the opposite direction from where Mama had started walking. He walked with the swagger of a man on a mission, moving quickly in the dark, closing the distance between the two of them. Eulalie wasn't interested in helping anyone, especially a man. Yes, it was the church, and the doors were open to anyone in need but only when her daddy was there. She stepped back to close the door.

"Eulalie. Eulalie, wait."

Lord, she would know Vernon Jackson's voice anywhere. She looked around the door to verify that she'd heard correctly. Vernon walked up the front steps, drenched. His pants stuck oddly to his skin, and his shirt was so wet she could see his brown skin tone through it. She waved him into the vestibule and locked the door behind him.

"What are you doing here? It's almost nine o'clock in the evening."

Vernon moved stiffly to try to keep his soaking body from wetting the entire carpet. "I can't find my trumpet. I've been everywhere, looking for it, and no one has it. I thought I would walk past here to see if someone turned it in."

"Let's find you a towel. Then we'll go to the back room and look for it."

Eulalie made her way back to the kitchen area, Vernon following her at a respectful distance. She opened a few of the drawers haphazardly, trying to find something that could help. When all she could find was an old tea towel, she handed it over. He accepted and found a seat on the counter that ran along the wall.

"What are you doing here so late?" Vernon draped the frilly scrap of fabric over his head and worked on unbuttoning his shirt.

Eulalie felt awkward watching, but there was nothing else she could pretend to be doing. "I was just closing up for the night. There was a lot of cleaning after the celebration."

"Why are you here alone? There ain't another soul in the city that can help you close up?"

"I wasn't alone for very long. Mama and Mother Edith just left." Her argument sounded feeble to her own ears. He was right. She'd been there all day. *Why did I have to be the last one?* Because she was an obedient daughter who would do anything asked of her—that was why.

"What are you doing walking out in the rain like a specter?" she asked.

"I need my horn," he answered.

"It can't wait until morning?"

"I can't lose my trumpet. It's all I got."

"Then why did you leave it?" Eulalie pursed her lips and leaned against the wall. "Why did you forget it here?"

Vernon stared at her, his wide eyes clouded over. If she hadn't been looking at him, she would have missed it. He pulled the wet shirt off, peeling it from his shoulders. His undershirt was soaked also, but he didn't bother with removing it.

"I must have been so distracted with your engagement that somehow, I walked off without it. Where's your ring? I didn't get to see it earlier."

Eulalie colored at his comment, unsure what his motive for mentioning it was. His eyes traveled down the length of her arm and focused on her bare left hand.

She had only two choices, either be bold and leave her hand out in the open or put her hand in her pocket and slip it back on. Eulalie had taken it off when the cleaning started, unused to the cold metal on her hand. It wouldn't do to lose the ring on the first day it had been given to her. She patted the front of her apron to make sure it was still in there, deciding against wearing it.

"I'll show it to you another time. Let's go ahead and find your horn so we can get you on your way." She turned to leave the kitchen, waiting for him to follow.

Vernon took his time jumping down from the counter. He folded the towel neatly and left it on the counter before grabbing his shirt. His shoes squeaked as he followed her down the long hallway toward the storage closet.

"Why haven't I seen you in a decade? Where have you been hiding?" His voice was light and easy, like he hadn't a care in the world.

"I've been here and the schoolhouse. Two places you haven't been in the last ten years." Now he was getting in her business.

"Yeah, and how's that working for you? Don't you get out and have fun? Don't you do anything interesting?"

Eulalie stopped walking and turned to face him. She'd thought she could handle him, that she could take his sly comments and toss them back into his face. Vernon was sharp and quick-witted. It had been one of the things she'd always liked about him. Now that admiration was coming back to bite her in the behind.

"Why do you always have to be an ass, Vernon?" The curse word reverberated off the empty walls of the church. She'd had to speak up so he could hear over the sound of the high wind and plinks of rain on the roof.

"How am I being an ass? Because I ask you what you do for fun?"

Vernon knew what he was doing. He was intentionally trying to vex her. *What is there for a woman, let alone the preacher's daughter, to go out and do?*

"You're right. Let's see. I've been spending late nights out, drinking, smoking, and whoring. I've also picked up gambling. It's one of my favorite things to do on a Saturday night. I'm surprised you haven't seen me around the town." She continued with a stomp of her feet, but the carpeted hall runner muted the sound. Reaching the closet, she stopped and fumbled in her apron for her set of keys. Her arms trembled as she unlocked the door and pulled the string hanging from the ceiling to turn on the light. The sooner she got his horn, the sooner they could leave.

"Hey. I apologize." He put his hand on her trembling arm.

The contact of his skin on hers sent a zap of electricity through her arm, a feeling she fought every time she saw him.

"I wasn't trying to upset you. I'm trying to be nice, Lalie."

For a second, she thought he might move closer to kiss her, but he didn't.

"You know how my life is. This is it." She gestured to indicate the church.

"What kind of life do you want? You know you can do any-thing."

He pulled his hand back, but she could still feel the sear of his fingertips on her skin. She'd felt it before and never thought she'd feel it again, especially not standing in the hallway of the church.

She started to speak, but a loud crack of thunder cut her off. The dim bulb of the closet light silently extinguished, as did all the other lights, plunging her and Vernon into darkness.

"Oh my Lord!" she exclaimed. "What's going on? Vernon, are you okay?" She didn't like the shakiness of her voice, but one moment, he was there, and the next, she could see nothing.

"Yeah, I'm here. Are you all right? Where are you?" The huski-ness of his voice sounded tender and calmer than hers.

She turned away from the open door and reached out her hand, waving it in the air. He'd been standing there a moment ago, but in the dark, it seemed like a canyon separated them.

She stumbled forward on a loose bit of the carpet runner, then Vernon's hand came out and touched her lightly on the soft part of her stomach. She jumped at the contact and the feel of his hand below her belly button, trying to ignore the elation she felt.

His fingers traced the contour of her body, moving from the front to the back. He slid his hand up until he found her arm then ran it down its length to find her hand. They clasped them to-gether, even though every fiber in her being told her not to.

"Are you all right?" he asked again.

The sensation of his hand on her body had her more unnerved than the darkness or the storm. She nodded, but realizing he couldn't see her, she spoke. "Yes, I'm fine. I think we should just lock up and go home. We can get your horn another time. Wait. Do you hear that?" A faint alarm sounded in the distance. The city's tornado sirens were alerting.

"You can't go home now. There's a twister nearby. We'll have to stay here until it passes. I know your fiancé won't be happy about that, but…"

Why did he have to bring up Samuel? She hadn't thought of him since they parted at the end of the picnic, and now there he was, at the forefront of her mind, standing between her and Vernon.

"I'll worry about him later. We should probably find someplace that doesn't have a window where we can wait." Eulalie racked her brain, trying to figure out where they could go. The sanctuary was filled with windows. So were the office and the hallway where they stood. "The nursery. We can wait there. I'll lead the way."

She walked, using the wall as a guide, until she reached the hall that opened to the right, just in front of her daddy's office. She passed his door then the small janitor-closet door before reaching their destination. Eulalie pushed open the nursery door and shuffled slowly, trying to make sure there were no knickknacks left on the floor. She found the stack of blankets they used to lay the children down and led him to a corner.

They tried to place the blankets on the floor in a way that would be comfortable.

"This is the best I can do," Vernon said from somewhere below her.

"It's fine. We shouldn't be here for very long."

They sat next to each other, listening only to the howl of the wind. Slats of wood rattled on the roof, making the situation more eerie. There was no safer place to be in a storm than in the house of the Lord. Surely he wouldn't allow his building to be ruined or either one of them be hurt.

Vernon started to hum softly, a light melody that contrasted with his deep voice. Eulalie relaxed, thankful that he was there. If he hadn't come to the door and distracted her, she might not have made it home, and perhaps she'd still be there alone, trying to decide what to do.

"You asked what I've been doing the last ten years, but what about you? Where have you been?"

Vernon cleared his throat and shifted next to her. He moved a bit closer so their shoulders touched but kept his hands to himself.

"I don't know. Working, I suppose. Playing my horn. Drinking, gambling, and whoring, the same as you." He had a playful lilt in his voice, so she could tell he was smiling.

"Are you satisfied, Vernon? With your life and the way things have turned out?"

"I suppose I'm as satisfied as I'll ever be. I don't think the people around here expected too much out of me, and that's what they've gotten. That's as good as anything. I don't have to work in the cotton fields anymore, so anything is better than that."

"May I tell you a secret?" For a moment, she was glad there were no lights. Something about the darkness enlivened her. The mixture of Vernon's presence and their being alone made her feel bold.

"You can tell me anything."

"You won't hold it against me?"

"Of course not. How could I?" He patted her softly on her thigh then retracted his hand.

"I wish I could be like you," she admitted.

"I don't know what you mean."

"I wish I could do what I want and live how I want." Eulalie fidgeted nervously, but now that she was speaking her mind, she couldn't stop. "I want to decide for myself. I want to choose where I go and have my own place to live. I want to determine whether I get married at all and not be pressured to make the decision." Her words hung heavily in the air.

Vernon let out a sigh before asking, "Do you not want to get married? Who's making you?"

"Who isn't? If I had said no to Samuel in front of everyone, what do you think would have happened? I'm not even sure I want to be married." She breathed a sigh of relief after admitting the truth. It finally felt good to say the words aloud.

"Then don't get married. You don't have to do what other people want you to do."

"It's not that simple. How do I change? How do you live, making your own decisions?"

"Change is not easy, Eulalie. When people have seen you a certain way, it's hard for them to accept you as something different. If I can tell you a secret, I want to be just like you."

She crossed her arms and huffed. "Why would you want to be like me?"

"Eulalie, you're a good person, and the community depends on you. Look at you. You were the last person to leave the church tonight after a full day. You even stayed to help me. People don't give me the same respect they give you." Vernon's voice was clear and sober over the sound of the blowing rain. "If I'm honest, I was a rascal. Womanizing. Boozing. Eulalie, I did it all. I'm trying to be an honest man, and now no one believes me. So which is better? The person everyone pushes to be great or the person they don't expect anything from?"

10

Vernon

Vernon knew it was wrong. It all felt wrong—the hand-holding, the touching, all of it. Eulalie didn't belong to him. She was engaged to someone else. But he couldn't help how he felt. He wanted to carry her to his home and protect her. He wanted to kiss her pouty mouth and let his hands wander freely on her body in the dark.

A year ago, he would have enjoyed the situation. Vernon would have whispered sweet nothings into her ear amid the dark cover of the storm. He would have been inside her already. He would have pleasured her until she begged him to stop. He would have taken advantage of her in the church, even with the threat of hell looming over his soul. But it wasn't a year ago. He was different.

"If I'm honest, Eulalie, I thought you were mad at me."

"If I'm honest, Vernon, I was mad at you. For a long time. We were good, then you disappeared on me. But I'm an adult now, and I understand that sometimes people don't feel the same way about each other. There's no reason to hold on to the past."

"I didn't disappear. It's a long story." Vernon sat silently, refusing to expound, regardless of the story's length. It didn't matter anymore. She was engaged, and he had his own life. They could sit quietly in the dark until it was safe to leave.

"Eulalie, are you awake?"

She'd been seated next to him so quietly that he wasn't sure if she was or not. Her light breaths and the occasional bump of her shoulder were his only indication that she was still there with him.

"I'm awake, but I think I might lie down for a bit. If you're okay with that."

That meant "I'm tired and please keep your hands to yourself," which was what he'd been planning to do anyhow, no matter how much he wanted to touch her.

"You're safe. I ain't gonna mess with you."

"I've just had a long day. It feels good to stretch out. What did you think of the celebration?"

"I think it's the nicest one I've been to."

"You haven't been to very many in the last few years," she said with a chuckle.

"Well, now that I know how nice they are, I'll have to start coming back."

"Will you tell me a story?" Her voice was slightly above a whisper, only a bit louder than the wind. She shifted next to him, their bodies bumping only slightly as she moved into a flat position. He thought she would take the time to scoot away from him, since she was adjusting, but she didn't. She remained close enough that he could feel the tickle of her hair on his arm. If he moved his leg an inch to the side, she was there.

Vernon racked his brain, trying to think of a story he could tell, and smiled at the first memory that came to mind.

"Do you remember the time when we were young'uns and snakes took over the tent revival?"

Eulalie laughed so hard he felt her body shake. "I remember, but I want to hear your version."

Vernon cleared his throat and retold the story as he knew it.

****

A few days before his fifteenth birthday, he was at church—again. The softness of spring melted into the harshness of July, the days when the sun lit the glowing Oklahoma plain until well after nine in the evening. For three days, there would be a circus—a spectacle of preachers, choirs, and elders with only one goal, the saving of as many mortal souls as they could. Reverend Hopewell would preach hellfire and brimstone, like they weren't sitting outside in the middle of summer. Evangelists would travel from towns across the state, following their pastor to the event. Mothers and grandmothers prepared food, as tables would be filled with people young and old. Every evening during the tent revival, the first pastor would preach, getting the crowd ready. The choir would sing a hymnal before Reverend Hopewell made his way to the front to dismiss everyone. The revival-goers would trek across the hard ground to the large fellowship hall, where dinner would be served. Once everyone had eaten their fill, they would return to the tents for another few hours of singing and preaching. It had happened the same way every year.

Vernon, Alfred, and Gerald were seated in the farthest set of chairs underneath a large white tent. Reverend Hopewell had preached, prayed, then looked out toward everyone.

"The ladies' assembly has so generously prepared a supper to be held in the gathering hall. I'm told there's roasted hen and fried chicken along with all the fixings. After we eat, we gon' reassemble here and let Reverend Jackson feed us the word of God. Can I get an amen?"

"Hallelujah," "Amen," and "Lord have mercy" were all shouted in unison, which made Hopewell smile. He dismissed everyone, leading the crowd toward the smells of fried food and fresh corn-bread.

The three boys had stood to head toward their evening meal when Gerald declared, "I got something to show y'all."

Al shook his head and jerked his finger toward the dissipating crowd. "I ain't interested. I'm hungry. I've been working all day, and we're going to be here for hours, so I ain't about to miss sup-per for no foolishness."

"It ain't gonna take long. Besides, it may be a way for us to get out of here early."

Vernon waited, torn between following his curiosity and get-ting supper. If they didn't eat when it was offered, there wasn't going to be anything else. He wasn't interested in going to bed hungry, but at the same time, he was all for getting out of church early. "What is it?" he asked.

"A ball of snakes," Gerald answered. "Come on. I'll show you." Gerald walked in the opposite direction of dinner, not bothering to look over his shoulder.

They walked for a few minutes away from the church, down the road, until they reached a cluster of trees.

"How did you even see this?" Al asked.

"I saw it when me and my granna walked up here for service. Though I heard it before I saw it." Gerald marched behind the trees then pointed his stubby finger.

Vernon rounded the trees to find the grass waving furiously. No fewer than fifteen snakes were all bunched up together in a large wad, slithering in and out of one another. A chill ran down Vernon's back as he watched the black-and-green wigglers move.

"Man, I can't take no more!" he finally yelled. "I ain't scared of snakes, but something about this don't feel natural."

"Don't be a chicken." Gerald reached down toward the wobbling mass and pulled one of the snakes up by his tail. He waved the snake at Al and threw it toward Vernon.

Al shook his head and started to walk back toward the church. Vernon began to follow, but Gerald called to them.

"Wait. Don't go. I need your help."

Vernon turned to face Gerald, who hadn't moved away from mass. "You need our help for what?"

"If we take all these snakes and move them to the tent, then the service will be over. All the ladies will be screaming, and no one will want to stay. We'll be able to go home." Gerald shrugged as if it were the simplest thing in the world.

Al had already started to walk away again, but Gerald's idea interested Vernon. His parents wouldn't be able to find out it was him. They were outside in nature, and snakes would go wherever they wanted to go. Vernon turned to ask Al his opinion, but his friend had disappeared, probably in search of his dinner.

Vernon took a few steps back toward Gerald, keeping his eyes on the high grass around his shoes. Every time the blades waved, it made him jumpy.

"I ain't picking them snakes up. How else can we do this?"

"They're just little snakes. They ain't gonna hurt you."

"I don't give a damn. I ain't touchin' no snake." Vernon's imagination felt the wiggle of a snake up his leg, and he jumped back.

"All right, go see if you can find me a box of some sort. I'll stay here and make sure none of the snakes get away. If you hurry, we can move them before everyone is done with supper." Gerald waved Vernon off with a flick of his hand.

Back at the church, Vernon looked around frantically. *I shouldn't even be doing this. I need to just go ahead and eat.* There was no reason they should be moving snakes. He mentally gave himself two minutes. *If I can't find something to carry them in, I'm going to go find Al.*

Completely avoiding the fellowship hall, Vernon walked into the church and made his way down the front hall. He wasn't even sure what he was looking for, just something that he could use quickly. He opened the front closet to find a few hanging coats and an empty milk crate sitting innocently on the ground.

"Where are you going with that?" Eulalie Hopewell stood just inside the front door of the church, watching him.

Vernon jumped at her presence. He'd been so focused on finding a crate for Gerald that he hadn't heard the door open. They were alone in the open entryway, suspicious of each other.

"What are you doing here?" If he turned the questions on her, maybe she would leave him alone. "Shouldn't you be at dinner?"

She held up a key attached to a long string. "My daddy sent me over here to get something from his office. Are you planning on bringing that crate back, or were you stealing it?"

"Come on, Lalie. I'm just borrowing it. I'll be right back." Vernon pushed past her out the front door and stumbled down the road. By the time he made it back to the trees, Gerald was gone, and so were the snakes. Vernon sent up a quick prayer of thanks and returned to the church, hoping he didn't see another snake for the rest of his life.

Once again, he met Eulalie in the hallway as he returned the crate to the closet. She was coming out of the reverend's office as he entered.

"I told you I was going to put it back," he announced to her down the hall. He threw the crate into the bottom of the closet and slammed the door.

Eulalie walked toward him, closing the space between the two of them. She wore a cream-colored dress, and her hair had been curled and pinned back neatly. When she got closer, the scent of her rose water curled around him and beckoned him closer. He looked down at his shoes, which were caked in dust, and wished he could brush off some of it. Had he known he was going to see her again, he would have taken the time to straighten his shirt.

"What did you need it for?"

"There were some flowers I was going to pick for my birthday. It's in a few days, and I thought I'd get myself something nice."

Eulalie leveled her gaze at him. Of course she didn't believe it, but he couldn't think of anything else.

"You wanted flowers for your birthday? Since when?"

"Since you won't get me the thing that I want most."

Eulalie's soft curls fluttered as she shook her head. "Vernon, I ain't got no money. What on earth can I get you for your birthday?"

"A kiss. Just one. That's the only thing I really want." His heart was beating out of his chest. He'd wanted to kiss her since Easter, when he saw her in her dress covered in light-pink roses and edged in white lace. She'd looked like an angel when she waved to him after church service, and he hadn't thought of anything since.

Eulalie stammered a few words and stomped her foot. "Vernon, this is the church. We can't be kissing in here." A nervous smile grew on her face.

"I don't mean anything big. You know, just a small one. It's only the two of us here." He stepped closer to her, until he was about a foot away. He wasn't going to press her, but he also wasn't going to miss an opportunity.

"I ain't never kissed nobody before. I don't know how to do it right."

Vernon could sense the hesitation in her voice, but she hadn't exactly said no.

"It ain't nothing to it. I can show you, real nice and easy-like." Even though thunder rumbled in his ears, Vernon licked his lips and wrapped Eulalie in his arms. She stood stiffly for a moment before relaxing in his embrace. He gathered all the daring he had in his chest and kissed her once softly on her upper cheek, next to her eye. Then he planted another soft one on her lower jaw, just a bit closer to her mouth. His manhood grew with the physical contact, and he pressed against the warmth of her. He'd stolen kisses from other girls before, but something about Eulalie being in his arms felt different. She was a good girl and hadn't been kissed before, so he wanted to make it special for her.

When she turned her face toward his, he pressed his lips gently against hers. She responded hesitantly at first before fully allowing herself to participate. She kissed back, finally parting her lips to allow him to explore the softness of her mouth. He almost imploded when their tongues touched.

"Ooh, Lalie, I'm gon' tell Mama," someone called loudly.

Vernon stepped away and let go of Eulalie's waist. Leona Hopewell stood in the door of the church, her eyes as wide as dinner plates. Then she walked out the front door with Eulalie chasing her.

Vernon stood in the empty entryway, unable to wipe the smile off his face. If he didn't get anything else for his birthday, he would still be satisfied.

****

"Anyhow, there were so many snakes your daddy sent everyone inside because it was starting to get dark and no one wanted to get bit. I don't know if you remember, but Gerald got caught with a snake in his pocket. He told everyone that I was supposed to be helping him, and I got a beating for that, you know. Not the kiss but the snakes."

Eulalie didn't answer with words but instead a heavy snore. He smiled.

In the distance, the siren stopped, and the rain slowed. The threat of a tornado had passed, and they'd made it to the other side intact. Eulalie's slow, deep breaths flowed in a steady rhythm. Though it was probably safe to go home, he didn't want to wake her. She needed the rest, and he wanted to be next to her if only for a few minutes longer.

Vernon shifted in his seat, pulling the lumpy cover from underneath his bottom. In the darkness, he did his best to spread it across her before sitting and relaxing against the wall. Then he crossed his arms and waited. He would give her a few more minutes of sleep before he woke her up.

11

Eulalie

"Eulalie Ann Hopewell! What is happening here?" Daddy's voice boomed across the expanse of the nursery.

She sat up, in a haze, trying to remember her surroundings. *The nursery. The storm. Vernon.*

"I thought I told you to stay away from my daughter. What are y'all doing in here? This is the house of the Lord."

"Daddy, it's not what it looks like. I was on my way home last night when the sirens started going off. We had to take shelter." Eulalie wished her voice was stronger, that she could convey the truth so he would understand. But it was early, and she'd been jolted awake. She couldn't even think straight, yet her father was interrogating her.

"Yo mama stayed up all night, worried about you. Do you know how concerned she is right now, and you're here? Hugged up with him?" He rushed across the room and stood over the two of them. Eulalie was used to her daddy's ire, but she didn't want Vernon to witness it.

"With all due respect, sir, we weren't hugged up. I didn't even touch her," Vernon said. He stood then reached out his hand to help Eulalie up.

"Young man, don't say another word to me. Get yo things and get out of here before I lose my trip to heaven. Lord, this is making my chest hurt." Daddy stretched his left arm out then pulled it back close to him.

"I only came here to get my horn. Then the siren started, and we couldn't leave."

"Don't y'all know better than to be inappropriate in the church?" Daddy was fussing like a steam engine. There was nothing they could say to stop him.

She and Vernon made eye contact, and she shook her head the slightest amount she could get away with.

"It's time to go on home now, young man."

"I'm not leaving without my horn," Vernon said firmly.

"It's in the front closet, Daddy." To Vernon, she waved her hand. "Come on. I'll get it for you."

The trio made their way down the hall. The closet door was still wide open where they'd left it, except the lone bulb on the ceiling let out a feeble bit of light. Eulalie grabbed the case she'd been reaching toward the night before. It was cold and awkward in her hand as she swung it around her body to give to Vernon. He opened it to make sure everything looked okay. When he was satisfied, the top fell shut with a click, and Vernon walked right out the front door.

Once Vernon disappeared, Daddy commanded, "Let's go home."

The early-morning sun streamed in over the horizon, barely visible. The sidewalk was covered in downed tree limbs and random trash that had blown in. If there had been a tornado, it must have gone somewhere else. On her side of town, the homes were still standing.

Eulalie followed her father down the sidewalk. He stomped hard, like he was trying to wake the devil. Once they arrived home, he threw open the door. Mama and Leona were sitting half-dressed in their Sunday clothes and curlers in their hair.

"Eulalie, I was so worried. Are you all right?" Mama jumped at the sight of her and pulled her into a tight hug.

"Yes, Mama. I'm fine. I was just at the church. Everything is okay there also. Are y'all all right?"

"I was up all night, worried whether you were alive. I didn't get a wink of sleep with the rain and siren going off. Thank God you're okay." Mama sat back down on the couch.

"She was there with that boy," Daddy jumped in. He didn't have to explain who "that boy" was, even though Vernon was a grown man.

"Why didn't you come home? You said you were right behind me."

"Mama, there was a storm, and the tornado sirens were going off. It was best to stay where I was."

"Why don't you girls go on upstairs and get ready for church while your daddy and I talk?" Mama pressed her lips together, done with speaking on the matter. Eulalie felt six years old again, dismissed by her mother. As much as she wanted to defend herself, it would only make things worse.

Eulalie tried to close herself in her room, but Leona was hot on her heels. She squeezed herself into the small crack Eulalie allowed and quietly shut the door behind her.

"You have to tell me everything." Leona, the third of the Hopewell daughters, was round like Daddy and bookish.

Each of the Hopewell daughters was different and special in her own way. Cassidra resembled Mama the most. They were svelte, with golden skin that shimmered in the sun. Everywhere the family went, a neighbor or friend commented on how much Mama and Cassidra looked like each other. They both had sharp, angular faces with high cheekbones and sensual eyes. Men loved looking at Mama, and Cassidra had followed in her footsteps.

It came as no surprise that Cassidra had been married first or that she married at all. She had suitors falling all over one another, not bothered that she was the preacher's daughter. She was beautiful enough to make a man promise his soul to the Lord just for a moment of her time.

Leona was the complete opposite of Mama and Cassidra and the spitting image of Daddy. She was round and soft with the perfect shade of mahogany skin. Daddy and Leona were the intellectual pair of the family, from their love of reading to the spectacles they both wore. They were happiest to be around the dinner table or curled up with a good book.

Somehow, Eulalie didn't resemble her mama or her daddy. She was rather plain in her face and dress and wasn't pretty like Cassidra. Even though she was the neighborhood teacher, she wasn't bookish or smart like Leona.

Cassidra was the pretty sister. Leona was the smart sister. Eulalie was there.

"Tell me who 'that boy' is," Leona demanded. She flopped onto the bed and propped her chin up with her fists.

"Leo, I'm tired, and it's very early. Can you leave me to sleep for another hour before we have to get up for church?"

"How can you sleep at a time like this? What were you and Samuel doing in the church? It must have been bad for Daddy to come in here yelling like that."

Eulalie paced for a moment, trying to decide whether she wanted to tell the truth. Leona would find out anyway. Besides, it wasn't as if there was something secret going on. They hadn't done anything.

"It wasn't Samuel." There. She'd said it.

Leona's mouth fell open so far that a family of birds could fly in and nest. "Who was it?" she whispered.

"Vernon Jackson." Eulalie sat on the bed next to Leona and gently used the tips of her fingers to close her sister's mouth.

"How in the world did the two of you end up in church together?"

"I was there, and he was looking for his trumpet." Eulalie stepped through all the events of the evening, straight up until Daddy had woken up the two of them.

Leona listened, enraptured, holding her breath.

"Did he kiss you?" Leona asked when she'd finished her story.

"No, of course he didn't kiss me."

"Well, don't get mad. I don't know. I wasn't there." Leona lay back again, giving Eulalie space to lie next to her.

Eulalie warmed at the thought of Leona finding her and Vernon kissing when they were teenagers. Leona had just been about to turn eight herself and knew exactly what was going on. She hadn't told Mama and Daddy right away, instead holding on to the secret until everyone was seated at family dinner.

That kiss had earned her a lecture from both Mama and Daddy. But in the end, it had been worth it. Vernon was the first boy she'd ever kissed, and it hadn't been short of anything magical, at least in her almost-fourteen-year-old mind.

"Did you want him to kiss you?"

"Leona, don't be silly. Just because you caught us once doesn't mean anything. Whether I wanted him to or not, it's not right. I'm seeing someone else. Vernon was the perfect gentleman."

"So then you wouldn't mind if I let him kiss me? Since he doesn't mean anything and you're seeing someone else?" Leona's smirk doubled in size at Eulalie's exasperation.

"Now, Leo, why would you say a thing like that? I can't stop you if you and Vernon Jackson want to go around kissing. It wouldn't make a bit of difference to me." A knot pulled in Eulalie's chest, but she didn't take back her words. She closed her eyes and wished Leona would just leave.

"Vernon's handsome and laughs a lot and says the funniest things. I wouldn't mind kissing him, but he only has eyes for you. Then again, you're probably right. Since you've kissed them both, you know Samuel's kisses are better. Since you said you'll marry him, you must like them." Leona finally got up from Eulalie's bed and sauntered over to the door.

Her sister was just trying to vex her, and she wasn't going to take the bait. It didn't matter how much she liked Vernon's kisses. That was if his kisses were still wonderful. She hadn't had one in ten years.

"For being twenty years old, you sure do talk like a child. Samuel's kisses are fine. Not that they're any of your concern."

****

"Everyone, turn with me to the book of Proverbs, Chapter 22, Verse 6. When you've found it in your Bible, say amen."

A hush fell over the congregation as everyone looked down at their Bibles to find the right page, then a chorus of amens went around the church. Eulalie fought the urge to roll her eyes. Instead, she kept her head down, like she was looking in her Bible, even though she knew the passage by heart.

"Y'all read it with me. 'Train up a child in the way he should go: and when he is old, he will not depart from it.'" Daddy cleared his throat so he could get into some good preaching.

She knew immediately the message was about her. It wasn't the first time he'd tailored a message after her behavior, and it certainly wouldn't be the last. Eulalie shifted in her seat. There was no way she was going to look up at the pulpit. She'd rather look at Jesus writhe in pain on the cross than face her father.

"Everyone, bow your heads. Heavenly Father, we are gathered here this morning to celebrate you and lift up your name." Daddy prayed hard but slowly, winding down the service after the sermon. He took a deep breath and paused for a moment before resuming a loud voice. "And, Father, we ask you to watch over our children. You said, Lord, that if we bring the children to you, you would take care of them. That you would be their shepherd, and they would be your flock. This morning, we ask a special blessing over our children. Please see to it that all who are lost be returned home. We ask that all who are sick be made well, and finally, Father, we ask you to give our children the ability to make good decisions when they walk out there in the world. In the precious name of Jesus, we pray."

The crowd answered with a resounding amen that rose all the way to the rafters of the church. Eulalie looked up at her father, and he stared directly at her.

****

"Eulalie, yo daddy sure preached a good sermon today."

On the front steps of the church, Eulalie stood with her mother, sister, and father. Every Sunday, they lined up together to greet all the congregants as they left the building for the week to venture back into their real lives. It lasted at least an hour after service was over, since her mama and daddy had to speak to each and every churchgoer, which meant she and Leona had to speak to each and every one also. They'd formed a line as a family of five for as long as she could remember, until Cassidra got married and could leave whenever her husband was ready. Daddy stood right inside the front door of the church, which was thrown open to allow everyone to leave. Mama waited proudly next to Daddy, wearing a pale-yellow dress with a matching hat that complemented her light coloring. That left Eulalie and Leona to stand on the steps to give one final goodbye.

"There's always a word in there for those who need it most," Eulalie answered the woman standing in front of her. Mrs. Jenkins was a serial church crier. She found meaning in every word Daddy spoke. Every Sunday, she could be found in the front row with a tear streaming down her face and her hand held up to glory.

"I tell you, the message touched my heart. I felt the spirit of God in that place."

Eulalie didn't have the heart to admit she was the reason for the message. If she hadn't been caught with Vernon, Daddy would have spoken about something completely different. Truth be told, her father impressed her. He'd probably been working on an entirely separate sermon but taken a last-minute turn when the opportunity arose.

"After everything that happened last night, a storm and a tornado, my daddy's message was about wayward children." Eulalie wanted her tone to come out light and jovial, but she could taste the bitterness in her words. The woman didn't seem to notice.

"You know these chirren will worry you to death. If it ain't one thing, it's another. His sermon was right on time."

Leona jabbed her in the side and leaned over to whisper, "Stop before you get us in trouble. Besides, here comes Mr. His Kisses Are Fine himself."

Eulalie pulled away from Leona to find Samuel slinking through the crowd. He'd been seated in the back of the church, uncomfortable with sitting in the front with her and the family. He was dressed in a pinstriped suit that had probably been tailored at Charlie's down on Greenwood Avenue.

He looked nice, but she thanked the Lord he wasn't sitting with them yet. Eulalie allowed herself to be pulled into a quick embrace before he turned his attention to the rest of her family.

"How you doing, Miss Leona?" Samuel asked then waved to Mama, but she jumped forward to hug him.

"Samuel, we're so happy to see you here. Please, you must come over to the house for Sunday dinner tonight. We're having fried pork chops, cabbage, and all the fixins." Mama's request was rhetorical. She wasn't going to take no for an answer.

"My brother, it's so good for Eulalie to have a man in her life who's present in church. That's all this old man wants." Daddy laughed and tapped his prodigious belly.

Samuel grabbed Eulalie's hand, and they stood together. She wondered if they looked like the picture of a happy couple. Though she tried to smile, she was too tired. It had been a long morning, and it appeared there was no end in sight.

"Reverend Hopewell, let's go allow these women make us some dinner," Samuel joked, and almost immediately, Eulalie pulled her hand away while he was distracted.

12

Vernon

Vernon cleared the brush in Mr. Winston's yard, helping his neighbor before the man hurt himself. The storm had not been as kind to his side of town as it had been to the west side, where the church sat. Although the tornado hadn't touched down, the storm had made enough of an impact to create work.

Vernon's back shed had been reduced to a large pile of firewood. The fence that stood between his and Mr. Winston's yard was missing every other stake. On the far side of his lot, the fence had been knocked completely down. His neighbors were missing windows, roof slats, and, in one case, an entire door. But they were safe. Everything else could be replaced.

"Mr. Winston, let me take care of that." Vernon rushed toward the older man, who was wrestling with a fence post that stuck out at an odd angle.

He was about half Vernon's size, three times his age, and four times as dark. His house had been the first one built on the block a few months before Vernon's mother and father built theirs next door. He'd been their neighbor for Vernon's entire life.

"Boy, you think just because you're young and strong, you can go around here manhandling everything? Let an experienced man

"

show you how to do things." He leaned his entire body weight on the already-slanted wooden slat. After a few persistent thrusts, the piece of wood broke at the base. Mr. Winston easily picked up the wood beam and added it to Vernon's growing pile.

"I suppose I'll just leave the rest of this to you. You don't even need my help," Vernon bantered.

"I'll have this all done before you even go to bed tonight."

The two of them walked around the yard, knocking down the barrier between their two properties. Mr. Winston told crude jokes, and Vernon laughed appreciatively. When they'd done all the work they could, Vernon brought out some glasses of lemonade.

"Son, after all this, I'm going to need something a bit stronger than sugar water."

"Mr. Winston, I got something that will knock your socks off, if that's what you want."

The older man laughed loudly but shook his head at Vernon's offer. He handed the glass back to Vernon and put his weathered hand on his arm.

"Your parents would be proud of you, especially your daddy. Your mama would be, too, but your daddy would be telling everyone how wonderful you are. You've turned into a fine young dandy. I know you're beating the women off."

"Thank you for the nice words, Mr. Winston. You don't know how much they warm my heart," Vernon said, and he meant it.

People didn't speak of his parents often. Four years ago, they'd passed away together in an automobile accident, which came as a shock to everyone in the community. Most people offered their condolences, but very few still spoke of either of his parents. Maybe they didn't want to bring up any bad memories, but Vernon relished the stories.

"I'm not fooling with any of these women. They don't bring nothing but trouble and heartbreak," Vernon said.

The men were falling over each other in laughter when Eulalie approached, her tentative footsteps tapping the sidewalk. Mr. Winston and Vernon eyed each other before the older man turned toward his house.

"As soon as you speak of the devil, he shows his face. You'd do well to remember that." The older man waved to Eulalie and disappeared into his home.

Eulalie's vibrant purple dress felt out of place in the wildness of Vernon's yard. She looked perfect and well put together, while he stood in front of her tired and sweaty, with a large mess to clean. She was the sun that came out after a week of rainy days.

"Good afternoon, Vernon. You doing all right?"

"I'm doing fine. How can I help you?"

"I wanted to talk to you about something if you have the time for it."

He had work to do. A large stack of fence posts needed to be hauled away or chopped up for firewood. He had planned to walk around Mr. Winston's house just to make sure that nothing was missing or broken, and he still hadn't gotten the chance to look at his trumpet to make sure it was working. Making time for the pretty brown-skinned woman standing in front of him hadn't been on his list at all. But she was there, and she smelled good.

"I got time for you. What do you need?"

"Do you mind if we sit down somewhere?" Eulalie looked toward the porch, waiting for an invitation.

Vernon waved her inside and told her to have a seat in the front room. He put up the dirty glasses and returned to her with a fresh one. She had settled into the flowered couch, which had seen better days, and looked around the small family room. A picture of the Jackson family sat on the mantel. It had been taken when Vernon was eight years old. There wasn't much else for her to look at. Vernon had moved everything out of the front and into Pearl's old room to make space for the band to practice.

"I, um. I…" Eulalie took a sip of lemonade before finally looking at him. "I'm here to apologize," she said finally. "I'm sorry for my father and the way he treated you. You left so fast that I didn't get the opportunity to say sorry and thank-you. Thank you for staying with me. If you hadn't been there, I don't know what I would have done in the dark. I would probably have tried to run home, and who knows where I would have blown off to."

She was rambling, but Vernon didn't try to stop her. Her exasperation was cute.

"You don't need to apologize, even for your father. He's been like that since the day he met me, so I'm used to it. I'm not sure why he doesn't like me."

"I guess I never really thought about it, but now that I'm going through our history, I can see why he may have some reservations." She ticked off the reasons on her fingers. "You punched Gerald Hayes when we were kids. You kissed me in the church. You pushed Alice Chambers down when she bit Pearl." Her tone was light and teasing, but she made good points. He had done all of those things. "You and I… We had that thing—"

"Yeah, but all of those things happened when I was a kid. I'm a full-grown man, and your daddy still doesn't like me. Which is fine."

The two sat quietly for a moment before Vernon stood abruptly. He collected her glass, which was still full of lemonade, his hands moving of their own accord.

"Well, if that's all, thank you for the apology, but I have things to do."

"What is so important that you have to do?"

"I have to bottle some of the devil's drink. I'm getting low on supplies and have a few orders that need to go out. You can add that to the list of why your father doesn't like me." He gave a tired smirk.

Eulalie stood and looked around. "Can I help?"

Vernon leveled his gaze at her. *She showed up unannounced, and now she wanted to help bottle liquor?* She'd probably gotten an earful from her father about the previous night, and now she was in his house and didn't want to leave. Even if he didn't want to admit it, he was happy to see her.

"Why are you here, Eulalie? What do you want?"

"I already told you I wanted to apologize. And I needed to get out. If I'm truthful, I'm bored. I need some other things to do, and... I have fun with you."

"All right, come on." Vernon waved her toward the kitchen, where he rummaged around, opening drawers, until he found what he was looking for. He unrolled one of Pearl's aprons and handed it to Eulalie. It was old and wrinkled, but it would do the job. "Put this on. I don't want you to mess up your pretty dress. Besides, I can't have you going home smelling like alcohol. That will get added to the list."

Eulalie unrolled the brown apron and pulled it over her head. He led the way to a back room, where he'd set everything earlier. Thirty glass bottles lined the side of the room, waiting to be filled. Vernon had hand-washed and dried them already. He'd spent money at the printer to have a label made and bought glue to set it.

His little alcohol business had grown immensely from the first batch of hooch he and Al had created. It was better now—fuller. The venture was keeping his head above water. He was able to put food on the table, which was something he'd struggled with the last few years.

Vernon siphoned a bit of the liquor from a large pot into a handheld pitcher. He inhaled to make sure he couldn't smell the sharp tang of alcohol before handing it toward Eulalie.

"Do you wanna try it?" He pulled it back toward himself and took a small sip then swished the clear liquid in his mouth. "You don't have to have much." The sip of alcohol felt good in his throat, calming his nerves.

Eulalie proudly took the pitcher and smiled before turning it upright and taking a gulp. Immediately, she coughed and sputtered, spitting most of her mouthful onto the floor. Vernon took the pitcher back so she wouldn't spill any of it as she bent over and coughed hard.

"Are you all right? I told you not to drink too much." He gave her a few gentle pats before letting his hand rest on her lower back. He'd meant it to be soothing but found his manhood hardening. Electricity zapped through the fingers resting on the purple fabric. He could grip her waist and pick her up easily if she would allow him to kiss her.

Vernon shook his head to let go of the thought. Eulalie wasn't his. She hadn't been his when they were teenagers, and she was someone else's girl now. Still, the feeling of her body underneath his hand had his mind twisted in knots.

Eulalie stood up and wiped her mouth with the back of her hand. "I only took a sip, but it went down the wrong pipe." She smiled and flattened the front of the apron. "It's good. But don't tell my daddy."

He promised he wouldn't. As a matter of fact, he wanted to stay as far away from Reverend Hopewell as he could. Even though he hadn't invited Eulalie to come over or bottle hooch, he would be blamed for being a bad influence. It was better to keep his hands—and thoughts—to himself.

After cleaning up the spill, he said, "Well, if you're okay, then let's start with the labels. It will go faster with the two of us here." He gave her the labels and the glue. "You'll probably be better at fixing the labels on there than I am. Just add a bit of adhesive and get the paper as straight as you can." He picked up one of the clean bottles and did one as an example.

Eulalie nodded and sat on the floor in front of the thirty bottles.

They worked silently, outfitting each of the clear bottles with a midnight-blue label. When he felt himself getting frustrated, he stole a glance at Eulalie. Her tongue stuck out in the corner as she focused on the bottle she was working on. She must have felt his stare and smiled without looking at him.

"Tell me why you aren't having fun. Every time I've seen you out and about, you're doing something." He wanted to focus on the work that needed to be done, but he couldn't take his eyes off her profile.

She shrugged. "When have you seen me enjoying myself?"

"At Al's Club."

"Other than that. Name one other time."

"I was at the church picnic."

"Yes, and you saw me running around, helping everyone. I didn't even get to sit down and eat." She spread the glue on another bottle and kept working. Even when she was lamenting about doing things for others, she kept working. The fact wasn't lost on Vernon. She was there, helping him.

"I just want to do something new and exciting for a change." She winked at him before turning back to the last few bottles they had.

"So you think this is exciting? This is work," Vernon said.

"At least it's something different. Something a little naughty. I got to help bottle hooch today." She held up the bottle toward the light streaming in from the window.

Vernon had been right. All of his labels were a bit off-kilter, but hers had been placed perfectly straight.

They spent the next few hours filling and capping the decorated bottles. Vernon showed her how to pour the exact amount using a funnel and how he stuffed the neck with a small piece of cork. They made the perfect team, working until the sun started to set. Eulalie was standing on the porch, ready to depart, when she turned to him one last time.

"Before I go, I need your help with something." Eulalie moved her hand up to conceal her growing smile.

"I knew there was a reason you were stalking around here. Gal, if you don't tell me what you want..."

"I wanted to get someone in to speak to the kids about music, and I was hoping you or the band could come in. Perhaps to give them a music lesson or even just show them your horn. Lord knows they need a break. And it would be something fun for them."

"Yeah, I'll see if Ronnie or Mike can come by. They're better with that kind of stuff."

"It would be nice if you can show up."

"I'm not real good with kids. I'll have to think about it." Vernon had spent a peaceful evening with her, one of the best he'd had in awhile. She could ask for the moon, and he'd try to move the world to get it to her. Now he had to figure out what he would tell a class full of children about music. He wasn't a teacher.

"I thank you anyway."

Vernon crossed his arms. "Why is it you want to spend time with me now when you didn't fight for us before?"

Eulalie let out a long sigh, expelling all the breath from her lungs.

"Vern, we were young then. I–I don't know what happened." She turned away from him and started down the front porch, her shoulders rounded on the edges.

If he was expecting her to explain what had occurred, that wasn't going to happen. *At least not today.*

13

Eulalie

Eulalie hadn't expected him to show up, but somehow, he'd made it. It had been a lark, a crazy idea she'd had and asked for on a whim.

She was up at the board with her back to the class, trying to go over sentence structure. One second, everyone was listening and repeating what she'd said. The next second, there was murmuring and conversation. She turned to find Vernon standing in the doorway of the classroom. His shoulder rested on the frame, and his arms were crossed. He hadn't announced himself, instead choosing to watch her work. She warmed at his presence, hyperaware of her body and backside. Vernon looked handsome in his brown hat and matching suit. He waved at the children cautiously, like they would all somehow turn on him and eat him.

Eulalie walked to the door, welcoming him in with a wave. She needed a break from being up at the board. The chalk was all over her dress, and her hands were dry.

"Everyone, please settle down, as we have a visitor. This is Mr. Jackson, and he's going to teach us a bit about music today."

A loud round of applause went around the room. Dorothy bounced in her seat, thrilled at the lesson's interruption. Next to her, another girl jumped to her feet and shook her body in excitement.

"Good afternoon, everyone. I don't mean to interrupt, but is it all right if we play a little?" A sly grin grew across Vernon's face when the class cheered louder. He held his hands up, waiting for everyone to quiet before he started again. "I'm going to need some help unloading the instruments. Do I have anyone strong here?"

Boys and girls alike jumped up, wanting to be the ones to help their new visitor. A gangly kid named Thurgood jumped from his chair and met Vernon at the front of the room. The rest of the children followed suit, quickly crowding around. Eulalie waded into the fray, sending most of the students back to their seats with a wave of her hand.

"Thurgood, Ernest, the two of you go help Mr. Jackson with whatever he needs."

With a large jump, Thurgood pumped his fist in the air, and Ernest pulled Vernon's hand toward the door. They disappeared as Eulalie worked to calm the rest of the class. Whatever she had planned before was going to have to wait. Vernon's appearance had already distracted the students, and she wasn't going to be able to pull them back into a boring lesson.

The other fifteen students wiggled in their seats, watching Vernon, Ernest, and Thurgood enter the room, each carrying a cardboard box. Vernon left the classroom one more time before returning with his trumpet's carrying case.

He moved to the front of the classroom, standing before the neat rows of desks. Each of the students sat on the edge of their chairs, waiting for him to speak. Eulalie pulled her stool to the back corner, where she could watch Vernon and the students simultaneously.

"Is there anyone here who knows how to play an instrument?"

A few hands shot in the air and waved frantically. Eulalie was fairly certain some of the students were fibbing, but it wasn't her presentation. Vernon pointed at a large girl seated in the middle of the pack named Cora. She put her hand down and claimed that she knew how to play the harmonica.

Vernon turned toward one of the boxes he'd brought in and said, "Lucky for you, young lady, I have a harmonica." He rummaged around for a moment until he found what he was looking for. "Would you be so kind as to come up here and play a little for me?" Vernon held up the shiny rectangle so the class could see.

Cora eased from her desk and stood next to him with the harmonica positioned by her mouth. She pulled a large breath into her round belly and blew hard, easily letting out a few bluesy notes. She cupped her left hand over the front, which made a *wah-wah* sound as she played up and down the scale.

The hairs on Eulalie's arm stood up, and the class burst into appreciative applause. Cora had been in Eulalie's class for months, and she'd had no idea Cora had such a talent.

Cora handed the harmonica back to Vernon with a shrug.

"Young lady, how'd you learn to play the harmonica like that?"

"My pa taught me. He said he'd rather hear my wailing than listen to my talkin'."

Vernon laughed loudly as Cora made her way back to her seat. He held up his hands, waiting for the class to settle down, before he began again. "The beauty of music is that it can be made by anyone. You look at someone and think they're too young or too old. They may even be somebody you think is wild or someone who isn't good at school." He raised his hand to indicate he was that person. "Music is the great equalizer. It brings us together in good times and bad. Can anyone give me examples of the times when we listen to music?"

Hands shot up all over the classroom. He pointed at Dorothy, who answered, "At church."

Ernest called out, "During funerals."

When Vernon called on Cora, she smiled and said, "With my family."

A tingle went straight to Eulalie's heart as she watched him speak to the students. Seeing Vernon at the front of the class, knowing the children made him nervous, sent her heart aflutter.

"Would you all like to hear about when I played some music for Miss Hopewell?" Vernon waggled his eyebrows before finally meeting her eyes for the first time since he'd arrived.

Eulalie started to protest, but she waited to see what he was going to say. If he told the children she'd been out at night, drinking at Al's, she was going to pitch a fit.

"Now, Vernon, these are children," she said, her nervousness getting the best of her.

He ignored her warning and continued with his story. "The last time I played for Miss Hopewell was at the church celebration. How many of you were there?" Vernon winked in her direction.

Eulalie relaxed in her seat as the children waved their hands in the air at yet another one of his questions.

Vernon opened the carrying case and pulled out his trumpet. He fiddled with the finger buttons before holding it up to his mouth. "Do y'all want to hear what I played for Miss Hopewell?"

A hush fell over the class when Vernon let out a few test notes. When the room was absolutely still, he played a flirty song. Next, he played music showing every emotion, from happiness to sadness and even anger, pulling the students in. Then he pulled the horn from his mouth to a boisterous round of applause.

Over the next thirty minutes, he showed everyone the differences in sounds between the trumpet and a trombone. He played the harmonica only slightly better than Cora had, if Eulalie was being honest. He showed the children how notes in the same key sounded on all the different instruments. When he was done, Eulalie—and the class, she was sure—were fully convinced they could stand at the front and give a full concert. That was how much conviction Vernon spoke with.

"How about another volunteer? Is anyone willing to come up to the front and try?"

Most of the students squirmed in their seats until Dorothy tentatively raised her hand. Vernon waved her forward. She stood cross-legged and looked over all his instruments.

"Which one would you like to play?" he asked.

She pointed at the saxophone, to which she wasn't significantly superior in size. Vernon handed it to her and stood over to the side, placing her small fingers on the separated keys. Dorothy brought the saxophone to her mouth, filled her belly with air, then blew hard. A forceful *bleeert* came from the curved end and stopped abruptly. Everyone laughed a little until Vernon held his hands up.

"Wait, now. Don't laugh. She was brave enough to come up here and try."

Dorothy's face flushed at Vernon's comment.

"Take a little bow. You just played for your first audience."

When Dorothy bowed at the waist, Vernon gestured to the seated students.

"Give her a clap. She did good."

Rousing applause went out across the room. Dorothy waved her hands to the adoring crowd and returned to her seat.

"Why don't we have Miss Hopewell come up here and try to play something for us?"

Eulalie shook her head when all the children turned toward the back of the room to face her. "No, this is for the children. I can't play an instrument."

"Who wants to see her play?" Vernon asked.

Dorothy jumped up from her seat and waved her hand. Every fiber in Eulalie's body told her to remain seated, but her feet moved of their own volition to the front of her class. She stood next to Vernon and looked over the group of instruments.

"Will you choose something for me? Pick something easy, please."

"Why don't you try out my trumpet?" Vernon held out his baby, the horn he'd gone looking for during an impending tornado—the one he didn't want to be separated from.

"I can't play that," she said tentatively. She knew how special it was to him. At that point, it wasn't about embarrassing herself in front of the children. She didn't want to break anything.

"Of course you can play it. Hold it up to your mouth, and I will help you."

She took the trumpet and held it up to her mouth before turning to face the class. It was surprisingly cold and heavier than she'd thought it would be.

"How about I show you where to put your fingers?" Vernon walked up behind her, wrapped his long arms around her, and placed his fingers over hers. She was completely enveloped in his embrace, and there was nothing she could do about it. She willed herself to relax, to look at peace in front of the children. If she didn't make a big deal, they wouldn't.

"Go ahead and blow, and I'll help you push the buttons," he whispered into her ear.

Eulalie's heart was pounding, but she took a deep breath and pressed her lips into the circular opening of the trumpet. Vernon's fingers pressed hers lightly, which in turn pressed down the buttons in a methodical rhythm. Vernon stepped a little closer, until he was completely pressed against her backside. Eulalie's heart pounded faster than the notes she and Vernon played together. When she couldn't take it anymore, Eulalie pulled the horn away from her face and stepped forward away from Vernon to a rousing round of applause.

"Everyone, please say thank you to Mr. Jackson for coming to talk to us today." Eulalie turned to look at Vernon and locked eyes with him, wondering if he could read the pleasure flaring in her.

"Does anyone have any other questions for him before we let him go?" she asked the group, and a hand shot up.

"Mr. Jackson, why come we don't never see you in church?" Henry asked.

Eulalie held up her hand to stop Vernon from answering. "Now, Henry, first we need to correct that sentence. Repeat after me. 'How come we don't see you in church?'"

Henry put his hand back down and repeated her sentence.

She nodded and continued, "Most importantly, it's none of our concern what Mr. Jackson does on the weekends. You know some people have to work. Does anyone else have any questions?"

Eulalie called on Dorothy, whose grin grew wilder. "Are you married, Mr. Jackson? Last time we had a visitor, it was Miss Hopewell's man, but he isn't as handsome as you are. Maybe you two can get married instead."

Vernon hooted with glee, but Eulalie waved her hands wildly. Everything about the day had gone off the rails, and it was almost time to dismiss the class anyway.

"All right, that's enough. Does anyone have any questions about music for Mr. Jackson? About music," she repeated.

They all talked over one another, no longer interested in class.

"When will you come back? Please say you'll come back," Ernest said.

A buzz of agreement went up over the class. Eulalie tried to holler over the noise but gave up instead, freeing them all to leave. It would be easier to go over anything they needed another day.

The children gathered their items and ran to the front to say their goodbyes. Eulalie stood back as Vernon patiently showed off the instruments to the ones who hadn't gotten a chance. He patted the boys on their shoulders and smiled at each of the girls before they all walked out.

"Maybe I'll see you next week in church." Dorothy held her hands up for a hug.

Vernon stood awkwardly for a moment before bending at the waist and pulling the girl into a tender hug. "I'll see what I can do, sweetheart."

After a few minutes of chaos, Eulalie and Vernon stood alone in her classroom. Vernon busied himself with gathering the instruments while she washed the blackboard and tidied up. When she couldn't avoid him anymore, she faced Vernon.

"I really appreciate what you did here today. You may not know it, but you may have changed someone's life today."

"Come on, Eulalie. All I did was show them my instruments. I ain't nobody important like a doctor or lawyer."

"You may not be, but you are very special. One of those children is going to go home and tell their parents how much fun they had today and how much they want to play the horn. Just like you."

"I don't know why you're saying all these nice words to me. I really ain't done nothing." He waved off her compliments before turning to tap his temple with his pointer finger. "You know, I know what you're doing. You're trying to butter me up so you can ask me to do you another favor."

Eulalie grinned, and she held her hands up in protest. "I swear it, Vernon. I'm not. I don't have anything else to bother you with. You've done enough for me and the children."

"Tell me what it is so I can get it out of the way." He gave his familiar grin, the one that she'd always loved.

"There is nothing else. Truly. What can I help you with? Can I carry some of these instruments out?"

Vernon shook his head and grabbed the first box. "Don't you carry nothing. I'll take it all out."

As Vernon moved the instruments out to the car, Eulalie gathered her own items so she, too, could leave. Once he'd gotten everything, she pulled her bag onto her shoulder, shutting the lights off. They walked out together, him heading toward the car, her walking in the opposite direction.

"Thank you again, Vernon. Your presentation meant the world to the children." She gave him a small wave before turning to walk away.

"Eulalie, wait. Why don't you let me give you a ride home?"

"You don't have to do that. I can walk. I don't live too far."

"It ain't no trouble. Besides, it's too hot to be walking anywhere. We might as well take the ride while we got the ride." He carefully took the bag from her shoulder and gestured toward the cab of the car. Then he walked her around to the passenger side and opened the door, waiting for her to settle in before giving her bag back.

After he got in, she asked, "Vern, where'd you get this car? I was wondering how you got all this stuff here." Eulalie indicated everything lying neatly in the back.

"I borrowed this from Big Mike. He said he'd let me use it so long as he didn't have to come talk to the kids." Vernon shrugged then pulled onto the street.

"That's wonderful. I'll have to ask Big Mike if I can borrow the car when I need something for the children."

Vernon narrowed his lips. "Doesn't your intended have a vehicle? Surely he wouldn't mind driving you around for the children."

Eulalie couldn't tell if he was fooling with her or not. *Is he intentionally trying to take a dig at me, or is he genuinely curious?* "Yes, Samuel does have one, but he also works most days and needs it."

"Wouldn't he just let you borrow it?"

"I don't know how to drive. Besides, I don't even want to ask. All he'll want to talk about is how I should give up teaching when I get married."

"Do you not want that?" Vernon stared at her, his attention off the road. She could feel the warmth of his gaze on her face, but she refused to meet his eyes.

"I don't know what I want."

"Well, I think you're a wonderful teacher. You should do it as long as you like." Vernon pulled the car to a stop in front of her house and turned off the engine.

She waited for him to say something else, but he didn't, so she climbed out. "Thank you for everything. For the ride, the instruments, and speaking to my students. They will be talking about it for weeks. And thank you for the nice words." She walked into the house, wondering how she would get him out of her mind.

14

Vernon

As long as Vernon had Big Mike's car, he was going to use it. It was the weekend, and as far as he was concerned, Mike could wait a few days. Vernon had some deliveries to make and was going to take full advantage. Friday evening and all day Saturday, he zipped the open-air car all over Tulsa. He made six stops, delivering bottles of freshly brewed alcohol to all his business partners. He met Alice while delivering to the juke joint and promised her a date sometime. Then he moved furniture for Al and spent all afternoon rearranging said furniture at the supper club. Two days later, at sunrise Sunday morning, Big Mike was at his front door, cussing, and Vernon finally turned the keys back over. He pulled two dollars from his pocket and handed them over as well so Mike could fill the gas tank back up.

Vernon went to lie back down but found he couldn't sleep. He'd spent the weekend taking care of everything that needed to be done so he could rest on Sunday. Now that Sunday was here, he didn't know what to do with himself. He paced the house, ignoring his horn, before finally deciding it was just as good as any Sunday to go to church. Vernon hadn't been in years, and the little girl from Lalie's class was looking for him. He didn't have anywhere else to be, and his mother would be proud of him for going. After washing and pressing his clothes, he made his way to the church at the appointed hour. He was certainly going to hear the word of the Lord, but if he did see Eulalie, well, he wouldn't be mad about it.

By the time Vernon was ushered to a seat, the service was in full swing. The choir was a breathtaking mix of sopranos and altos with a few tenors mixed in to create a rich harmony. The choir sang like the good Lord had let a few of his angels come down to earth to sing his praises for the mortals. If there was one thing the Greenwood Baptist church was known for, it was their choir. Vernon studied each of the brown faces in the crowd until he found Eulalie. Her hair was braided on each side, and she wore the same blue robe as everyone else standing before the congregation. He watched her sing, but she didn't meet his eye. Whether she didn't know he was there or she was avoiding him, he couldn't tell. She was beautiful, nevertheless, and he would look at her as long as he could see her.

They finished their rendition of "At the Cross" and sat before Reverend Hopewell made his way to the pulpit.

"Let the church say amen." He mopped his already-sweating brow then raised his voice to the congregation again. "I can't hear y'all this morning. Let the church say amen!"

The congregation answered with a resounding amen.

Vernon settled into the hard pew when Reverend Hopewell picked up his Bible.

"Our word today comes from the book of Ephesians. Today, we're going to talk about what it means to live as a new person." The reverend looked over the crowd, locked eyes with Vernon, then turned his attention back to his Bible.

****

After the firestorm of a service, Vernon tried unsuccessfully to exit the sanctuary but was held up with every step. Each elder woman came over to kiss him and thanked him for showing up. Mother Edith hemmed him up for ten minutes over how much he "looked like his daddy" and how good of a friend she'd been to his mother.

"I can't believe you're here, Mr. Jackson," Dorothy squealed. She ran up and gave him a hug and pulled her mother by the hand.

"This is Mr. Jackson. I told you he came to our school and showed us the instruments."

Vernon nodded at Dorothy's mother, a heavyset woman wearing a plain dress and sensible flat leather shoes. She had a kind face with round cheeks and brightened at the introduction.

"So you're Mr. Jackson? All Dorothy's been talking about is how you let Cora play the harmonica and let her play the horn. She's determined to learn to play something. Lord, I don't know what I'm gon' do with this girl."

"She's one of the smartest students in the class. I'll tell you that. Eulalie... I mean Miss Hopewell will agree with me. She's way smarter than I was at her age. She can do anything she wants, and that includes playing an instrument. I hope I live to see the day."

"Well, it's a pleasure to meet you all the same. If you start giving music classes, let me know. Dorothy will want to be the first to sign up. I hope to see you again at another service."

"The pleasure was all mine, Mrs. Stephens. I won't be a stranger." Vernon hadn't stepped foot in church in years, but magically, nothing had changed. Some of the matrons he knew from back in his time had passed on, but their daughters had stepped in to become responsible for saving souls. The men he drank with on Saturday night were there in their three-piece suits, clear-eyed and fresh faced like their previous evening's discretions had never even happened. They sat next to their wives and across from their mistresses, waving their hands about how good the Lord was. As difficult as it felt to come back into the building, Vernon felt like he was coming home.

By the time he was able to get outside, the sanctuary was mostly empty, save for a few ladies working to clean the pews. Almost everyone had stepped out front to do their socializing. Vernon walked around the line in the vestibule, passing those who wanted to speak to the pastor. He'd already outstretched himself by coming to church and wasn't quite ready to see Reverend Hopewell face-to-face. Though he'd hoped to speak to Eulalie, she disappeared in the crush of churchgoers, through a side door, before he could get close to her. He'd thought he'd have to do with the memory of her face, but she called his name from the bottom of the church steps. He made his way to her, smiling.

"I can't believe you made it. Dorothy will be so happy to see you," she said. She took a couple of steps away from the crowd, moving closer to him.

"Well, I told y'all I would try. I saw Dorothy, and she *was* happy to see me. Told her Mama that she wants to play an instrument, so now I'm gon' find one for her."

Eulalie's face brightened. "I told you that you made a difference. Before you know it, you'll have a stage full of band members. Vernon's Bandstand—what do you think of that?"

Vernon started to make a joke about Eulalie being their lead singer when a man walked up and joined the two of them. Instead of speaking, Vernon cleared his throat and nodded, the moment lost. He was a head and a half shorter and thicker in the chest than Vernon was, but it didn't matter. Vernon could look in his eyes and tell the man didn't have a lick of fight in him. He was soft, a peace-keeper. Vernon stood a little taller, knowing he could knock him across the block if it ever came to it.

Vernon lifted his hat at the new arrival and stuck out his hand in greeting. "How do you do? The name's Vernon Jackson."

"Samuel. Samuel Wright." He gave Vernon a firm handshake, but when he pulled back his hand, he wiped his palm on the side of his pants.

A zip of irritation raced through Vernon's chest, but he kept his face pleasant.

"I haven't had the opportunity to meet you yet," Samuel said. "I'm Eulalie's intended. How do you know my future bride?"

"I've known Eulalie my entire life. We went to school together. We have attended this church since the day she moved to Green-wood and her daddy started the ministry. I've been around for years and years. How long have you known Eulalie?"

Vernon looked Samuel up and down. His suit looked like one of the expensive ones that hung in the front window at a depart-ment store. Samuel's collar was stiff and new, without the dark ring of wear. The buttons shone and didn't hang loose, like he'd just bought it.

"Not as long as you, but it didn't take Eulalie long to decide what she wanted, did it, Eul?" Samuel laughed at his own joke and bumped Eulalie in the side with his elbow.

Did he really call her Eul? Her nickname was Lalie. Eul sounded like "mule," and Eulalie was far too pretty to sound like an old farm animal. Meanwhile, Eulalie stood unmoving next to him, rendered mute.

"Go ahead and show him your ring, Eul. That band is one hun-dred percent gold all the way through, and the sapphire, I bought from my very own jeweler in Chicago. How could she say no to a ring like that?"

When Eulalie didn't move to put her hand up, Samuel turned to face her with a questioning look.

"I was in a rush this morning and didn't get the chance to put it on. You know Momma doesn't like being late for church. I'll show it to him another time," she said softly.

Samuel turned to Vernon and waved him off before pulling Eulalie by the crook of her arm.

"We got to get out of here. We got big plans for tonight, but it truly was nice to meet you, Virgil."

"My name is Vernon."

"All right, Vernon. I ain't gon' forget again. Listen, if you have any accounting needs, you come and see me. I'll have your bottom line looking perfect like Eulalie's." Samuel guffawed again and led Eulalie away, leaving Vernon where he stood.

Eulalie gave a small wave and followed Samuel toward the rest of her waiting family. Vernon turned his back to walk home, reaffirming what he'd already known. Eulalie belonged to someone else.

****

Vernon held open the door for Alice Chambers and allowed her to walk in front of him. When he had seen her on Saturday, she'd been walking home. Even though it was only a few blocks to her house, when Vernon offered her a ride, she couldn't say no. When he left church, he stopped by her house to see if she wanted to spend the afternoon out. He promised a picture show at the theater and a bite to eat after. She said she didn't have any plans, and they were off.

They spent an hour in the darkness of the theater before making their way to Ray's Cafe for an early dinner. If Vernon was lucky, maybe she would consider spending the night to help him forget all that nonsense with Eulalie Hopewell. He followed Alice to a table on the far side of the room. Instead of sitting in the seat across from her, he slid into the booth on the same side, with their backs against the wall. He wanted to be able to watch the door while simultaneously keeping his hand on Alice's thigh. Alice loved physical contact and was always receptive to his advances, although lately, she had been asking for more of his time.

"What are you going to order?" she asked, snuggling a bit closer.

"I always get the steak sandwich, but you can order anything you want. You know I got you covered."

Vernon had moved to rest his hand on her thigh when the small bell of the diner rang as the front door swung open. In walked Eulalie, followed very closely by Samuel.

Eulalie made eye contact with him for a split second before she turned to whisper something to Samuel. She headed toward the front of the restaurant, away from where Vernon was sitting, but Samuel grabbed her hand and marched straight toward them.

"Well, if it isn't our friend Vernon. How do you do, young lady?" Samuel said to Alice. "I'm Samuel, and this is my fiancée, Eulalie. Do you mind if we sit with y'all for dinner?"

Alice let out a loud sigh and straightened in her seat.

"I know Eulalie Hopewell. Everyone knows the Hopewell girls," Alice said with a bit of sarcasm dripping from her tongue. If Samuel had grown up in Greenwood like everyone else, he would have known that Alice Chambers and Cassidra Hopewell were mortal enemies.

In the summer when the two girls turned twelve, there had been a variety show planned in which everyone in the community could put together an act or showcase their talent. The Hopewell girls had practiced a song for weeks. Mrs. Hopewell had sewn the girls matching dresses with a small bit of blue silk stitched along the collar. They were the sweet daughters of the pastor who were sure to steal the show.

Alice Chambers had been planning to sing as well, but she didn't have anything like the Hopewells. She didn't have a new dress or sisters to stand up there with her, and to be quite honest, she wasn't as pretty, even though she sang like a bird.

During the final rehearsal, on the night before the variety show, Alice sat behind the Hopewell sisters, waiting for their time to practice. She took a pair of scissors she'd found somewhere in the church and cut one of Cassidra's pigtails off. The left side of Cassidra's hair hung past her shoulders, and the right side, which had been silently hacked, looked like a fraying piece of cut rope.

The result had obviously been devastating. Cassidra wailed like there was no tomorrow, and Alice got beaten so badly she didn't come out of the house for weeks. That was only the start of their contentious relationship, which had only gotten worse over the years.

But there was no way for Samuel to have known any of that. It didn't seem to matter to Samuel whether they wanted him there or not, because he sat in the chair across from Vernon without an answer from anyone. Vernon hoped Eulalie would fill him in later. For the moment, it appeared Eulalie was stuck with her sister's worst nightmare.

"Actually, do you mind if I sit on this side? You're left-handed, and I don't want us to bump arms as we eat." Eulalie batted her eyelashes at Samuel and pointed toward his chair. He shrugged and scooted over to the chair in front of Alice, leaving her to sit in front of Vernon. Samuel reached his hand out and introduced himself to Alice.

"What are y'all doing out and about on a Sunday? I thought that was the Lord's day," Vernon said. He laughed, fully meaning to be as nasty as it sounded.

Ray's newest waitress, Henrietta, carried four glasses of water to the table and hurried away to get the silverware.

Samuel turned his attention back to the table. "We wanted one last meal together before I leave." He put his hand over the top of Eulalie's and patted it softly.

"Oh, you're leaving?" Alice asked.

"I gotta get up to Chicago and check on a few things. I have business everywhere, you know. Have you ever been to Chicago, Vern?"

"With all due respect, call me Vernon. Only the people I know well call me Vern. And yes, I've been all over the Midwest, from Saint Louis to Kansas City. My band's been to more cities than you'd believe."

Henrietta interrupted Vernon when she appeared at the table to ask what they wanted to eat, then she left with their requests.

Samuel took a sip of water. "That's wonderful. I asked Eulalie to come with me so she can get used to Chicago, but she said she can't go. She's too busy worrying about what her daddy will think. If we just go ahead and get married, she ain't got to be up under the good reverend."

Eulalie interrupted, "My father doesn't have anything to do with it. I have a classroom full of students who expect me to show up every day. I can't just run off to Chicago whenever I want."

She didn't seem amused. Vernon wondered what she even saw in him. Samuel wasn't funny or witty.

"It don't matter if you take a few days off. It ain't gonna make a difference to some of those kids. I saw a few of the knuckleheads running around. Most of 'em will quit school before it's time anyways."

Alice shifted heavily in her seat and cut her eyes at Vernon. She was clearly ready to go, but Vernon ignored her. They hadn't even gotten their food yet.

When Henrietta finally served their food, Vernon looked up, catching Eulalie looking at him. As soon as their eyes met, she looked away, but in that split second, Vernon felt like they were the only two in the room.

After that, Vernon couldn't taste his food. It didn't matter who else was in the restaurant or how badly Samuel was getting on his nerves. It didn't matter how well Alice's dress fit or if she was having a good time. The only thing he could think about was Eulalie's lips and how he ached to kiss them.

****

"Vernon, I thought we were going out on a date with just the two of us. I didn't want to sit through an entire dinner with Eulalie Hopewell and her fiancé. I wanted to spend some time with you."

They ambled along the sidewalk in front of Alice's apartment after getting through the meal unscathed. It had taken everything in Vernon to be nice to Samuel while paying attention to Alice and at the same time not trying to be too nice to Eulalie. It had been a delicate balancing act of trying to keep everyone's needs at bay. For the most part, the women had been cordial with one another, and Samuel carried the conversation.

Vernon stopped in front of the three-story brick building so he and Alice could talk.

"Yeah, me, too, Eulalie. That's what I wanted too. I just wanted to spend time with you."

"My name is Alice."

"Alice, that's what I said. I know your name." Vernon wiped his brow with the back of his hand. The evening was still early, but he was eager to get home. Ever since Mike had woken him up, every move he made seemed to be a misstep.

"You called me Eulalie," Alice said.

"No, I didn't. I know what I said."

"Anyhow, you want to come up for a nightcap?" Alice pulled the strap of her pocketbook up on her shoulder, looking longingly at him then at the front door.

"Actually, Lalie, I'm tired. I'm just going to go on home."

"Oh my Lord, you just called me Eulalie again. Good night, Vernon. Come find me when you don't have her on your mind." Alice stormed off as Vernon called after her. She didn't bother turning around to look at him, instead walking into Miss James's boarding house and letting the door shut behind her.

Honestly, it was what he deserved. It wasn't that he wasn't interested in Alice. She'd been a lady he'd spent plenty of evenings with. But for some reason, he couldn't get Eulalie out of his head.

15

Eulalie

Eulalie couldn't stop thinking of Vernon either. Later that evening, she stomped along the sidewalk, pushed the wobbling gate open, and let it slam on itself. A head full of steam pushed her up the few stairs to Vernon's front door. It was a little after sunset, dark enough to create long shadows but still light enough to recognize a friend. She would only be there a few minutes, once she'd given Vernon a piece of her mind.

Eulalie banged on the front door, half hoping he wasn't home, but when the door opened, she found her courage again. She'd wanted to speak first, but Vernon stepped onto the porch bare chested, and she lost her nerve.

"Are you here to apologize for your husband? You've been over here apologizing a lot lately." He rubbed the back of his head.

"Me apologize? Absolutely not. I want you to explain to me why you were out with Alice Chambers. And he's not my husband." Surely that wasn't what he thought she was there for.

"Why do you care about what me and Alice are doing? I thought you were engaged to Amazing Samuel. Samuel the Bookkeeper, who doesn't even know that you and Alice don't get along."

"Why can't you be a little nicer, Vernon?" She put her hands on her hips and rolled her neck.

"Because I don't need to be nice, Eulalie."

"I just wanted to warn you about being seen out with her. That's all," she said in an effort to change the subject.

"Is that why you came all the way over here? To tell me who I can go out and about with? Why are you here, Eulalie?" He growled her name, and the floor almost crumbled beneath her feet. She'd needed to see him one more time without Samuel or Alice or anyone else there to distract her.

"I don't—because I... because I can't stop thinking about you. I want you to tell me why you disappeared so I can move on with my life." She choked out the words, like her throat didn't want to admit the truth.

Vernon closed the distance between the two of them and wrapped his arms around her waist. They cuddled under the darkness of the porch, Eulalie relishing in his strength. He moved his hand from the middle of her back to the curve of her neck and brought his lips to meet hers.

Eulalie thought she'd expire from the feel of his embrace. Vernon's kiss was like the cool drops of rain that fell on your face during one of those quick summer storms. Her body was burning, but her face felt bright and alive. Eulalie answered his kiss with all the passion she wanted to express but wouldn't allow herself to voice. She pulled back, but Vernon moved slowly, placing small kisses on the curve of her top lip.

"I shouldn't be here. I don't know why I came. I couldn't stay away."

"Wait. Don't rush. Just let me just hold you for a moment."

The old wood creaked under their feet as they stood together in the perfect summer's evening. Eulalie looked into the sky and wished on a star at random. If Samuel's embrace could feel like the one Vernon currently had her in, she would marry him the next day. If Samuel's kisses gave her butterflies like Vernon's, there wouldn't be any hesitation in her mind. But they didn't.

"Do you remember when we were young and I used to hold you like this?"

Vernon's voice was husky, and his breath was soothing on the back of her neck. Surely he could feel her heart pounding out of her chest.

"Tell me you remember. Did you forget?"

As if she could ever forget. "No, I remember."

****

It had been a few hours before midnight, and eighteen-year-old Vernon Jackson could only talk about one thing, the 1910s. As far as Eulalie was concerned, the year 1910 would certainly bring new-decade blessings. Vernon was only interested in one thing—getting out of the New Year's Eve church service. Eulalie didn't want to be there, either, but she didn't have a choice. Where else would the reverend's daughter be other than at the church, celebrating the coming of the Lord?

Vernon, Alfred, and Gerald were milling around the front entrance of the church along with the group of other teenage boys and girls. The young people had been separated from the rest of the congregation in an effort to make them feel special, like they were spending the evening with a bunch of friends. The children had been escorted to the nursery, where they could play games.

"Come on, Eulalie. You can sneak away." Vernon stood on Eulalie's left and hissed at her without his lips moving.

Eulalie focused on the floor and leaned against the wall next to the hall closet.

Cassidra was old enough to help with the children, including Leona, who was despondent about not being old enough to be included with the teenagers. At sixteen, Eulalie could have her choice but wanted to stay with the young people.

"Vernon, you know good and well I can't sneak off. My pa would turn the hounds loose looking for me."

"The reverend's too busy to be looking for you. Besides, we ain't gonna be gone long. Gerald says he got some poppers he's planning to set off. It's gon' be a real light show, and I know you'd hate to miss it." Vernon shrugged like he'd sold her the deal of a lifetime and she'd be silly to say no.

"How? I can't just walk out of the church into the evening. Even if it is for a few minutes." Eulalie turned her back to him and looked around for a few of the girls she usually spent time with. Sarah Jane and Beulah were in the corner, chittering to themselves, unconcerned with everything else going on around them.

"Just tell your mama you're going to the nursery with the rest of your sisters. She'll tell you to go sit down somewhere, then she won't be looking for you," Vernon said. "We're going to be in the field around the corner. The one right behind Gerald's grandma's house." Vernon walked away to join the other boys, who jostled each other. She followed his stride with her eyes as he walked away, and when he turned to look at her, he winked.

Just then, one of the youth leaders, Mrs. Canady, came to gather the group. "No noise in this hallway unless you're praising the Lord. We're going to meet for an hour, then y'all are big enough to go to the sanctuary for the rest of the service. I expect the best behavior out of y'all."

The twelve teenagers who had been milling in the entryway cobbled together and started to follow Mrs. Canady down the hallway. Eulalie brought up the rear of the line, following everyone else slowly. They passed the reverend's office and turned down the other hall, passing the nursery to get to one of the Bible-study classrooms. There, they would go over some lessons and have a small bite to eat before they were handed back to their parents.

Eulalie reached the doorway of the classroom and leaned on the dark-wood frame.

"Eulalie, baby, are you feeling all right?" Mrs. Canady asked.

"My stomach hurts really, really bad." Eulalie pouted and motioned for the older woman to come closer. Once she was an appropriate distance away, Eulalie whispered, "It's lady troubles. The cramping is so bad in my back."

"Oh no, sugar. Well, go find yo mama, and she'll know what to do." Mrs. Canady patted Eulalie softly on the shoulder and rushed into the room to corral the other wild teenagers.

Eulalie locked eyes with Vernon before she turned to walk off.

****

As it turned out, Eulalie didn't even have to try that hard. When she found her mother, instead of using her menstrual cycle as an excuse, because there was a chance Mama was tracking it, she said her stomach hurt and her head was throbbing. All Mama wanted to do was get back to the service. She didn't have time to be suspicious.

"Let's go home and lie down. If you wait a few minutes, I'll get my purse and go home with you," Mama said.

"I'll find Cassidra. Don't worry about me. We'll go straight home." Eulalie limped toward the nursery until her mama was out of sight then pushed open the front door and headed straight home.

She'd been there for ten minutes and was headed upstairs when a hesitant knock on the door sounded. If she'd been up in her room, she would have missed it. Eulalie padded to the door, all of her confidence lost now that it was nine thirty at night and she was home alone. She cautiously opened the door to find Vernon standing by himself on her front porch.

"How did you know I was here?" she asked.

"I asked your mom where you'd gone. She said you were home, so here I am. Wanna go to Gerald's?"

"I'm too scared to leave. I don't want to get caught."

"You've done all the hard stuff. And it won't be but for a few minutes."

"I think I'll be able to see the light show from here. I'd rather just stay here if you want to come in for a minute." Eulalie stepped back to allow Vernon inside.

Vernon stepped in and looked around the family room. The Hopewells were blessed enough to have a two-story home. Just inside the door was a long hall leading to the back. On the left was an open parlor, where the reverend received their guests, and a steep set of wooden steps lined the right wall. In the dark parlor, a grandfather clock ticked, counting down the seconds until midnight.

Ever since their first kiss, Vernon had been sneaking kisses every chance he could, but that evening, he stood seriously.

"Eulalie, there was something I wanted to talk to you about, since we're here by ourselves."

"Why don't you come sit in the parlor? That way, we can see anyone coming up the walk. Just in case my mama or daddy shows up." She pointed at a small door next to the bookcase at the far end of the room. "That leads to the kitchen and the back door. You can go around the back."

Vernon sat on the small love seat as Eulalie pulled the heavy drapes open. She wanted to be able to watch the front. It was one thing to leave church service early, but it was an entirely another bold display to be caught at home with a young man.

"Do you mind if I leave the lights off? I want to be able to see outside." The lone light came from a small lamp that sat burning low on a side table in the entry hallway.

"Yeah, that's all right with me."

"So, what is it you wanted to talk about?" Eulalie perched next to the window and looked at Vernon's shadowed face.

"Why don't you come over here and sit next to me so I can see you better?"

Eulalie's heart pounded faster the closer she got to Vernon. He was there in her home, on a cold winter evening, and she wanted nothing more than to sit closer to him. Her mind pulsed like an alarm, like she shouldn't be there, but she couldn't stop herself. Vernon was brave and handsome, the only boy who'd dared to talk to her. All the others were scared of her daddy and scared of their own parents. Vernon only cared about her, and she liked it. He wasn't afraid of anyone.

Eulalie sat next to him, and Vernon immediately put his arm around her shoulders. She eased into the comfort of his embrace, resting her head in the curve of his arm.

"You know how I feel about you, right?" Vernon's heart was thumping so hard Eulalie could feel it sitting next to him.

"No, I don't know. Why don't you tell me."

"I like you. I like you a lot. I want you to be my woman."

"Why do you like me better than any other girl?"

Vernon gave her an easy smile and ran his hands through the curls at the nape of her neck. A shiver ran down her back when the tips of his fingers touched the sensitive skin.

"You know how beautiful you are. I don't have to tell you that. But I like you for more than that. You make me laugh with the silly stuff you say. You're smart, and you try so hard. Everyone likes you." He bent over and kissed her softly on the ear. "If I'm being honest, you're the only girl to be nice to me."

"Oh, stop it, Vern. You don't mean that. I know for a fact that I'm not the only girl nice to you."

"Yes, ma'am. Yes, you are. Most girls think I'm stupid or treat me like I'm trouble. They look and laugh and don't speak. You have always smiled and asked how I was, no matter how much trouble I got into." Vernon took her hand. "Do you like me like I like you? I think you do, but I want to hear you say it."

A rush of wind outside rendered them mute for a moment as they tried to hear if someone was coming. Neither one of them moved.

When she was sure no one was there, Eulalie faced Vernon. "I like you because you show me your soft side. You may be rough and wild, but I know better. You've always been sweet, and you make me feel special."

"You are, Eulalie. You are special. You're special to me. What do you think? Will you be mine?"

Eulalie inched her face closer to him, and Vernon pressed an unhurried kiss to her mouth. She responded enthusiastically, wanting to show him just how much he meant to her. He wrapped his arms around her waist and shifted her until she straddled his lap. Sitting on top of him, she pulled him closer. From her vantage point, she could feel his full manhood growing the more she circled her hips. Her dress and slip had been pulled up to her waist so she could stretch her legs across him, leaving the thin layer of her panties between her warming center and him.

"Yes, I'm your girl. Today and forever." She punctuated her words with kisses, pulling her tongue in and out of his mouth, teasing.

His caresses started playful then turned serious. He massaged his hands up and down her back, sending zips of excitement throughout her. When he'd gotten his fill of her mouth, he brushed his lips across the base of her neck, where her bare skin was exposed.

"I want to marry you and make you my wife. I'm going to ask your daddy. What do you think about that?" Vernon pressed needy kisses along her jawline.

"I want to be yours, Vernon. You make me feel so good, like I can fly." She returned his kiss with the fury of a spring wind. When Vernon started to pull her shirt from the band of her skirt, untucking it, she didn't stop him. He reached under the edge of her clothing and tickled the points of her nipples, awakening a passion in her. Eulalie had never felt such heat from the touch of another. She helped by unbuttoning the top, starting from her neck and working her way down.

"I need to make love to you. Let me show you how much I care. Let me show you how good you make me feel." Vernon buried his face between her breasts, leaving a trail of wet kisses on each of the mounds.

Eulalie wanted nothing else more. She stood to unbutton her skirt and let it fall to the floor. Vernon jumped to his feet and pulled his clothes off faster than she could blink. She still wore her undergarments, but Vernon stood nude in front of her with the exception of his socks.

Eulalie had never seen a fully naked man and took her time staring at Vernon's body. His velvety brown skin stretched tautly over his muscular frame. He didn't have an ounce of fat on his body. Instead, his muscles had been honed from hours of outdoor work and exercise. Eulalie let her eyes linger over his privates and the area covered in dark hair. She took his jutting manhood lightly in her fingertips, making Vernon pant. The more she touched, the deeper his breaths became.

"Do you like it when I touch you here?" she asked. She closed her fingers over his shaft and stroked gently.

Vernon pulled her close and engulfed her in a flurry of kisses before pulling her slip up from the bottom. He unhooked her brassiere and pulled down her panties so she, too, was standing before him in only her stockings.

He guided her to lie on the floor, stretching out next to her, and had his way with her mouth and breasts before he looked her deeply in the eyes.

"Are you sure you want to do this? We don't have to. I don't want to rush you." Vernon stroked his shaft longingly.

She was too far gone and wasn't about to say no. "I want this, Vernon. I want you. I want to be your wife."

He eased himself between her legs, going slowly. Eulalie winced at the initial pain but spread her legs wider to welcome him in. The pinches turned to pleasure as she lost herself in the friction. A spark started between them at Vernon's furious pumping. Just as she was starting to enjoy herself, he withdrew, leaving her wanting more.

****

"Well, how was it?" Vernon's face was hopeful, right on the edge between excitement and despair. Eulalie searched for words, ones somewhere between the truth she told herself and the truth she was going to tell him. She hadn't expected it to be over so quickly, but it had been enjoyable nonetheless.

"Did you like it?" he asked.

"I liked it, and I love being with you." She rushed to get dressed under the sober light of what they'd done.

Vernon dressed himself then helped her button the front of her shirt back up.

"Eulalie, I want to stay, but I can't. I don't want us to get in trouble. Will you see me again?"

He kissed her sloppily, like a puppy, and she lapped up all the juicy kisses he placed on her face.

"Can I tell you something now that we've—you know?" Vernon took her face gently in his hands and forced her gaze to meet his. "I love you. I always have. One day, you will be mine, and we will have our own house. We'll have our own life where we can do whatever we want. I promise you that." He kissed her softly on the lips.

"I love you, too, Vern," Eulalie said.

"Will you marry me?"

"Yes, of course I will."

"I'll make you proud, Eulalie. You'll see. I'll be the best husband." He kissed her deeply one last time before she showed him to the front door.

From that day forward, they were inseparable.

16

Vernon

Vernon couldn't take it anymore. He eased his hand from around Eulalie's waist and cupped her yielding breast. She was here, and she wanted him. She'd come to him voluntarily. He hadn't done anything to deserve her attention.

"Does he make you feel like this?" He found her nipple beneath the fabric of her clothes and massaged it to a hard point.

Eulalie whimpered, making him grow harder.

"Why don't you come in for a moment?" He stepped away from her to pull open the door, and she followed him inside. Vernon didn't bother to light a lamp and instead left the front door partially open to allow the rising moon to light the living room.

Eulalie moved close, and he covered her chin and neck with a flurry of kisses. They inched to the couch, unwilling to part. Reluctantly, he sat down first and opened his arms wide, welcoming her into his embrace. She hesitated for a second, standing before him.

Eulalie's presence felt so good, like the comfort of a warm quilt.

"Come closer." He threaded his fingers in hers and gently pulled her down.

She straddled his waist, and he willed himself to relax, but the more he thought of his crotch, the stronger the yearning got.

She wasn't supposed to be there, and he wasn't that type of man anymore. He'd slept with married women, women who knew he was up for a good time, but that wasn't what he wanted with Eulalie. He didn't want to be that type of man anymore. Fighting his thoughts, he forced himself to keep his lips away from her neck.

As if reading his mind, Eulalie said, "Vernon, I can't. I want to, but I just can't."

Something about the two of them sitting in the dark room alone forced them to decide what they really wanted and who they really were.

Suddenly, she jumped from his lap, and he got to his feet.

"Why can't you, Eulalie? Tell me why. Tell me why I'm not good enough. I've never been good enough for you or your family. Why not?"

The air in the room seemed to change. One moment, he'd been having a great time and had Eulalie's breast in his hand. Now he felt like screaming. He'd thought Eulalie had come to his house because she wanted him. He was the shoulder she could cry on, the one who would make her feel better. But he wasn't sure what she wanted.

"Why am I not good enough for you?" he repeated.

"Stop, Vernon. Whether or not you're good enough is not the issue."

"So what is the issue?"

"The issue... The issue is I'm... My family is pressuring me. I have to be the woman they want me to be," she finally spit out. "You wouldn't understand. I can't disappoint my father."

She looked as if she was going to cry, but Vernon steeled his resolve. He wouldn't be fooled by her tears.

"I thought you said you wanted to live your own life. Wanted to do what makes you happy. Ain't that what we talked about?"

"It's not that simple."

"I'm trying to be a good man. I don't want to be a man no one can trust."

"You *are* a good man."

"Don't say things you don't mean, Eulalie."

"I wouldn't be here if you weren't."

"What about Samuel? Is he a good man?" Vernon didn't care that it was twisting a knife in her stomach to bring up Samuel. He wanted to see what she had to say about him.

"Why do you always have to bring him up?"

"Because that's the man you're going to marry."

"I don't know that to be true. If everyone would just listen to me..."

"Then stop coming over here until you know. You can't have both of us. If you pick him, then pick him and leave me alone." Vernon pulled her face to his. He wanted to see the sparkle of her eyes in the moonlight but also needed to know that she was listening. "I love you, Eulalie Hopewell, but don't come over here again. The next time you come to my home, I'm making love to you all night long, and I don't care who you're married to." He pulled Eulalie through the front door and led her down the stairs. He needed the walk to get his penis to go down and wasn't about to let her walk home in the dark alone.

****

"Vernon, focus. We have to go over this stuff." Pearl sat in front of him with her arms crossed, tapping her foot impatiently.

As much as he loved his sister, he couldn't concentrate on anything she was saying.

They sat at the dining room table, trying to go over his financial obligations. Ever since their fallout the previous year, they'd come to a gentleman's agreement, in which Pearl would help him with keeping everything on track. Each month, they sat together over pieces of pie. Pearl told him what was due, and Vernon came up with the money. Or in the instances when he didn't have the money, Pearl worked the figures into what needed to be paid first and what he could go without.

"I'm listening. Just keep going."

"How am I supposed to keep going when I asked you a question? Did you pay the mortgage for the warehouse or not?"

"Yes, Birdie, I paid the mortgage. I went to see Mr. Blankenship, and everything is on track."

"Good. Now, there are a few other things I'd like to discuss with you." Pearl's voice drifted to the background again as Vernon gazed longingly over to where he and Eulalie had been seated the night before. He didn't want to think about kissing her or bedding her, but his mind wouldn't stop.

"If something happens to me, Eulalie, I know everything is in good hands. You have always taken care of everything, and I appreciate your help now." He'd interrupted her in the middle of her sentence.

"Vern, that's wonderful, but I'm your sister, Pearl." She smirked but didn't bother looking up from the paper in front of her.

"Jesus Christ. I'm sorry, Birdie. I know your name. It's just..." He had a lot on his mind, and Eulalie Hopewell was at the forefront of it.

He looked up to find Pearl staring at him with a smile growing across her face.

"What in the world is going on, and why are you confusing me with Eulalie Hopewell?"

"There ain't nothing going on. I'm just thinking."

"Is that why you're so distracted? What are you thinking about?"

Vernon paused, unsure of what to tell his sister. She was the only family he had and also one of his few true friends. He could tell her anything, and she would understand, but there wasn't much to tell about Eulalie. He wanted her—in his bed, in his house, and in his life. Eulalie, however, was engaged to someone else. It didn't really matter what Vernon wanted. He needed to focus on what was going on in his life and worry about those things.

Vernon was thinking of something to tell his sister when the front door of the house opened widely. Alfred Harris lumbered in, like he'd done for many years, straight to Vernon's side of the table, and they shook hands. He made his way to the opposite side and planted a chaste kiss on Pearl's forehead before joining the two of them at the table.

"Everything going all right? She ain't giving you no trouble today, is she?" Al boomed across the table, forcing Vernon from his thoughts.

"He's not paying attention today, but I suppose that ain't no different from any other day. We got through everything we needed to. Now that Al's here, we wanted to talk to you about something."

"Oh Lord, are y'all expecting?"

Pearl blanched, and Al laughed loudly, but they shook their heads at the same time.

"Naw, we ain't having a baby. Not yet anyway. We were hoping to talk about the wedding," Pearl said. She shifted slightly to look at Al, who nodded in encouragement.

"We'd like to go ahead and plan on the fifteenth of July and are wondering if you'll stand up there with us. That's two weeks from now. I was hoping—" Pearl had a slight hitch in her voice. "I hoped you would walk me down the aisle and stand up next to Alfred."

Vernon cleared his throat, pinching back some of the emotions that threatened to spill.

"Pearl, nothing would mean more to me in the world than to walk you down the aisle."

For the moment, Vernon's problems didn't exist. He had his sister, and that was all that mattered.

17

Eulalie

"Leave me alone, Daddy. I'm not in a good mood."

The next evening, Eulalie had wanted to stay in her room, but the smell of Mama's roast wafted up the stairs. She didn't want to be bothered with anyone else, but there was no way she could take any food to her room, so she had to join everyone at the table. Besides, she had company coming.

"I didn't even say anything to you. I'm sitting here ready to enjoy my food." Reverend Hopewell had a confused look on his face. He'd been seated at the dinner table, reading his Bible quietly.

Usually, though, he always had something to say about one of the girls and what they were wearing or how they'd styled their hair. Eulalie had just been trying to head off the inevitable comment.

"Now, Eulalie, don't come down here with a bad attitude," Mama said. She brought a large bowl filled with stewed meat, carrots, and potatoes to the table. "Your sister and her husband should be here shortly. Your fiancé too. Are you planning on wearing that old dress?"

Eulalie looked down at her plain gray dress. She had no intention of changing. The dress was fine. She didn't need to look fancy.

They weren't expecting anyone important, and she didn't want to dirty another dress to have to wash it later.

"Why does he have to come to our family dinner anyway? Wouldn't it be nice if, for once, we could eat as a family? Why does someone always have to join us?"

"Because Daddy is a preacher, and everyone wants to be closer to God," Mama answered. "We have to host our flock. What kind of shepherd would he be if he didn't? Besides, Samuel will be a part of our family soon."

A heavy knock came at the front door, making Eulalie groan.

"That's probably him now, and Eulalie, please try to smile. Men don't like a woman with a frowny face. It makes you look old." Mama waved Eulalie toward the door with a flick of her cotton tea towel.

Eulalie wanted to run upstairs, but she dragged her feet toward the door because there was no sense in delaying the inevitable. She turned the cold brass knob and pulled the door open, trying to cobble her facial features together into a pleasant smile.

But standing on the porch were Cassidra and Dr. George. Cassidra's belly led the way as she stepped over the threshold and pulled Eulalie into a deep hug.

"My goodness, Mama's got it smelling like heaven in here. I hope it's almost ready, because Little Bit is ready to eat." Cassidra ran her hand over her expanded stomach.

Eulalie pushed her sister's hand away, replacing it with hers.

Cassidra exhaled before stepping out of the doorway to let George in. "Can you let us in first, Lalie? George can't even get in the door good."

"Aww, leave her alone, Cassidra. She's just excited to see you." Dr. George was the color of soft sand. He stood taller than Cassidra and everyone else in the house, his long legs and wavy hair making him look like a tree. His hazel eyes shone with good nature when he winked at Eulalie. He stepped past the ladies and closed the door behind him.

"I'm going to see if I can help with anything," he said and turned left toward the family room.

"George, you'll do nothing of the sort. Go sit down and keep Daddy entertained. I'm sure he'll be looking for you anyhow," Cassidra called. "Come on, Eulalie. We're gonna go help Mama."

They turned away, but another knock sounded.

"That's Samuel. You go help Mama, and I'll let him in." Eulalie let out a small sigh then straightened her skirt.

"You gon' be all right?" Cassidra asked, raising a questioning eyebrow.

Eulalie shrugged and nodded at the same time then turned to answer the door.

Samuel was dressed in a white Oxford shirt and a blue tie with no jacket. George had worn a full suit, including the jacket, and the first thing that crossed Eulalie's mind was that Samuel would be vexed that he hadn't done the same. But he looked nice, with a fresh haircut and shave. She welcomed him in, and the smell of his aftershave followed him.

He carried a bouquet of flowers wrapped in brown paper and waved them in her face. "You look beautiful today, Eulalie. What do you think of the flowers?"

"Samuel, you shouldn't have. They're wonderful."

"Oh, darling, these ain't for you. I got these for your mama. She's the one who's done all the cooking." Samuel laughed.

"She'll be very appreciative."

"Eulalie, I hope you've been paying attention in the kitchen. Once we get married, are you sure you'll be able to cook like your mama? If not, we'll have to come over here for dinner." He laughed again, and her throat tightened.

"Samuel, she's been in this kitchen every night since she was a little girl. If she can't cook, I've done something wrong." Mama met them in the entryway, took the flowers Samuel offered to her, and enveloped him in a strong hug. Her sweet perfume mixed with the flowers' scent made Eulalie slightly sick to her stomach. The sooner dinner was over, the faster she could go lie down.

****

As always, Mama's dinner had been perfect. The roasted meat had been slow cooked all day. It fell apart with only the smallest nudge of a fork. She'd baked rolls served with a peach jam homemade by one of the bible study members. As if that wasn't enough, Mama had put together a pound cake with a dollop of whipped cream that resembled a cloud fallen from heaven.

When they'd all finished, everyone sat around the large table with sated bellies and happy hearts. That was, everyone except Eulalie, who kept her eyes focused on the ornate gold clock sitting atop the mantel at the end of the room. The minutes moved slowly, punctuated with the light ticking.

"Girls, help your mama clean up. Someone bring me something to drink. My chest is hurting from all that food," Daddy said.

The table was long, and the reverend had always sat at the far end in front of the fireplace. On his right sat Dr. George, and to his left sat Mama. Growing up, Cassidra had always sat in the seat next to Daddy, with Mama sitting across from her, but once she got married, she had to move a seat down so her father could talk to George. It was better than Daddy hollering across the table to the beloved doctor. Leona, as the youngest, had always sat next to

Mama. That all changed when Samuel had started showing up for dinner. Whether he'd been offered the chair next to Mama or he'd somehow found his way there, it didn't matter. Samuel sat next to Mama and across from Cassidra, leaving Eulalie and Leona to fend for themselves together at the end. At least Eulalie had someone to look over at.

Cassidra stood obediently and grabbed the serving bowl of stew from in front of her father. Once she did, Eulalie and Leona inevitably rose from their seats also. Samuel stood at the same time as the women but pushed his chair in and moved to sit in Mama's chair to be closer to Daddy. The men started a deep philosophical conversation as the women cleared the table and took everything to the kitchen.

"Thank goodness that's over," Eulalie said under her breath. She stood in the kitchen over the refuse bucket, scraping all the uneaten bits from the china.

"Are you too good to have dinner with us anymore?" Cassidra asked from the edge of the sink. "You've been in a bad mood all evening."

"I have not. Besides, I'm always happy to see you. I'll be even happier when that baby gets here."

"Then what are you grumbling about?" Leona asked.

Eulalie lowered her voice to a whisper. "I just don't understand why Samuel has to be here. He's not family yet." Eulalie tapped her foot and looked toward the door that led to the dining room.

Cassidra rushed across the room and stood next to Eulalie. "I thought you were happy to finally be married. What's wrong with Samuel?"

Eulalie shrugged. "There's nothing wrong with him."

"Then why don't you like him?"

"He thinks he knows everything. His jokes aren't funny, and I... I just don't think I want to marry him."

Leona joined the two girls in the corner, clearly wanting to be included in the conversation after eavesdropping.

"Does Vernon Jackson have something to do with this? Why were you in his car?" Cassidra asked.

Leona's eyes grew wider than the lenses of her glasses.

"How do you know I was in Vernon's car? Besides, it wasn't even his car."

"Girl, the neighborhood is only this big." Cassidra snapped her fingers in Eulalie's face. "Just because I didn't see you with my own eyes doesn't mean someone didn't see you. You're just lucky they said something to me and not Daddy and Mama."

"Sidra, I don't care what these nosy neighbors saw or what they said. And I don't care what they tell Mama and Daddy. I'm a grown woman."

"Sweetheart, you ain't grown until you move out and get married with a place of your own. Until then, you gotta answer to Mama and Daddy for everything."

"Maybe I'll start working on moving out, then." Eulalie twisted her face, but she knew it was all a facade. She didn't have the money or the resources to be able to get a place of her own. It would take her months to save and buy items to even be able to live on her own. That was if her parents let her leave.

Cassidra opened her mouth to retort, but something behind Eulalie's back made her sister's mouth form into a wide smile. Eulalie turned to find Samuel standing in the doorway of the kitchen. He held his hat in his hand and grinned sheepishly, like he'd caught them in the middle of a family discussion—which he had.

"Ladies, it's been wonderful to see you, but it's time for me to take my leave," he said.

"I'll walk you out," Eulalie said.

****

Eulalie leaned against the wood slats of the front porch and crossed her arms. The uneven surface felt uncomfortable on her back, but she hoped she wouldn't be there long. Samuel had been so nice during dinner. She didn't want to have to break up with him, but the notion was at the forefront of her mind.

"Samuel, thank you for having dinner with my family. It was nice, but I need to talk to you about something."

He smiled easily and placed his hat on his head. "I already know what you're going to say." He stayed a respectable distance from her, next to the big picture window just off to the left, in front of the living room. Even though they had privacy standing there on the porch, any of her family members could sit and watch their interaction. She had to be appropriate—not that she was interested in anything inappropriate and especially not with Samuel.

"You know what I'm going to say?" she asked.

"Yes. You're going to go off on me about what I said."

Eulalie's head swirled with confusion. "About what you said? What did you say?"

Samuel kept his eyes cast down to the floor. "I said after we get married, I wanted you to be a housewife. Ain't no sense of you toiling out there with them kids when I can take care of you. You can take care of our children."

At least he had the decency to look sheepish. Eulalie was flabbergasted but not because of his words. She had missed that conversation completely, but there was no doubt in her head that he'd said it and no doubt that her father agreed. *How had I been sitting at the table and missed it all?*

"Samuel, don't worry about that right now. There's something that I need to talk to you about."

"So you're not mad at me?"

"No, I'm not mad, but I think you're going to be upset at me."

"What would I be upset at you about?"

Eulalie swallowed hard and looked out over the yard, trying to figure out how to say the words. She knew how she felt, but saying the words out loud was so much harder.

"Samuel, I don't think I want to be married. We should probably hold off. I'm not... I'm not ready to be married." *To you,* she thought, but she couldn't give a voice to those last two words.

"What do you mean? Is it something I did?"

All Eulalie could do was shake her head. Samuel had been the picture of respectfulness. He hadn't done anything wrong. He just wasn't right. He wasn't what she wanted.

"Eulalie, now, don't make any rash decisions. I'll be gone for a week or so, and we can talk about it when I get back from Chicago. We'll see how you feel then."

Eulalie knew exactly how she would feel in a week but didn't want to argue. She'd had a taste of Vernon's luscious lips and had dreamed of his kisses. No way could she go back to Samuel's dry, perfunctory ones. If she had to break things off with Samuel in a week, she would do so. For the moment, all she could do was nod.

18

Vernon

A sharp wind blew through the open windows as Vernon cruised along, enjoying the warm summer air. The end of the week rolled around and he'd borrowed Big Mike's car, promising everything short of his firstborn before Mike relented. That time, Vernon agreed to return it in a timely manner. He wasn't planning on using it for long, just for a few deliveries. He couldn't tote bottles of liquor through the streets. Though he didn't mind walking, there was only so much he could carry.

He'd just turned to head back toward the city to pick up his delivery items when he saw her. Eulalie walked alone, down the tree-lined street, with a brown cotton satchel over her shoulder. He stopped at the far end of the street, hesitating. From forty paces away, he could tell it was her. The switch of her full hips and thighs caught his attention, even though he could only see the back of her. Her hair was pinned up like it always was. Vernon wasn't sure what to do. Maybe he should turn the vehicle around and go the other way.

Blood left his head and rushed to his crotch. The memories of having Eulalie in his arms and on his lap were making him feel invincible. Though he knew he should stay away from her, he couldn't make sense of his feelings. He shouldn't even be think-ing about her, let alone talking to her, but it was harmless, he rea-soned. She was alone, and there was no excuse for her to be when he was there.

He pulled the car back onto the road and drove her way. He was only going to say hello and see if she needed his help. She could be lost, for all he knew, and Samuel was nowhere in sight.

"Where are you headed, Eulalie?" he called.

She turned and hesitated, like she needed to decide whether she wanted to fool with him. After the last evening they'd spent together, Vernon couldn't blame her. He thought about how he'd kissed her, asked about her fiancé, then kicked her out of his house. The visit hadn't gone how he'd planned, but then again, he hadn't planned on her arrival that night, just like how he hadn't been expecting to see her on the street.

Eulalie shrugged and pointed toward where the paved road ended and a gravel road began. "I'm only going to sit by the water and read."

"Are you going alone?"

"Why? Is there something wrong with being alone?"

"What if something happens?"

"Vernon, what in the world is going to happen? There ain't no-body out here but me and you."

Vernon hadn't passed a soul, and in the few minutes they'd been talking, no one else had appeared. Still, he had to think of some-thing.

"It's gon' be dark soon."

Eulalie let out a breathy sigh and looked over toward the west, where the sun was well above the horizon.

"The sun's not going down for another couple of hours. I'll be home before it gets dark if you let me go about my business." She gave him a small wave and turned away from him to continue on her way.

"Why don't you let me give you a ride so you don't have to walk?"

"I don't mind walking. Besides, the last time I got in that car with you, it got the entire neighborhood talking."

"Is that a good thing or a bad thing?"

Eulalie huffed then continued her walk, ignoring his question. Vernon parked the car at the end of the pavement then got out and followed her on foot down the path toward the water's edge.

The lake wasn't large but rather a decent-size fishing pond. If he hadn't caught Eulalie out there, he would have forgotten its existence. About fifty feet across, it was filled with murky-brown water. Reedy grass grew high along the edge, waving in the breeze. Farther back from the water, the grass grew sparse in a flat area covered by a large green tree whose branches reached out to provide a shady area.

Eulalie pulled a thin, ratty blanket from her bag and laid it out under the tree's branches. Then she sat and pulled a small book from her bag, ignoring him. Vernon looked around and found a clear patch of grass. He sat about ten feet away from her and gazed out over the quiet water, letting his mind wander. He wasn't in a rush. If she wanted to sit for an hour, so could he.

Eulalie sighed quietly, and he glanced over his shoulder to sneak a peek at her.

Their eyes met for a second before she turned back to her book. When she couldn't ignore his stare, a smile peeked at the corner of her lips.

"What's wrong, Eulalie?"

"I can't read with you sitting there watching me."

"Do you mind if I come sit next to you?"

"I suppose not. What were you planning on doing before you decided to bother me?"

"Bother you?" He laughed. "How can I be bothering you when I'm just sitting here watching the water?"

"What were you doing before you decided to watch the water?" She wrinkled her nose, and his heart melted.

"I have a few deliveries to make."

"What exactly are you delivering?"

"Alcohol. I brew it, bottle it, then deliver it," he said.

Eulalie closed the book she'd been pretending to read and set it down on her lap. "How did you even get involved in all that?"

Vernon lay back across the blanket, rested his head on his arms, thought back, and told her the story of how he and Alfred had gotten everything they needed. He'd taken a trip on the train one weekend and learned how to brew everything from an old head down in the country. He told her that he'd had to borrow the money to pay for everything and how he'd started the first batch. After that, he and Al had worked together, and for the last few months, he'd perfected the process. He wanted to tell her how much money he was making and that he didn't have to work for anyone else anymore, but he stopped just short.

They sat together, her reading and him relaxing, until the crickets started their evening call. The haze of the evening cast longer shadows over the ground. Vernon had relaxed himself nearly into a stupor when Eulalie put her book down.

"I'm ready to go now," she said, shaking him awake on the arm.

Vernon sat up quickly. He raised his arms high in the air and stretched to his full length. He would have given anything to reach over and kiss her but restrained himself.

"I'll take you home. That is, if you don't mind riding in the car with me."

"Well, I'm not quite ready to go home yet. Can I go with you on your deliveries?"

"I would love your company. Are you sure you don't need to get home?" Vernon brightened at the thought of Eulalie riding with him. He had only two stops to make. They would go quickly, then he'd get her home.

They walked to the car, Vernon rushing ahead of her to open the passenger door for her. Eulalie slid into the seat and settled the blanket-stuffed bag on her lap. The sun settled low in the horizon as Vernon started the ignition and headed for his first destination.

****

They stopped in front of Lucky's Juke Joint and pulled up at the last bit of light. Since it was still too early for the usual revelers, there was no crowd to speak of. Only a couple of men milled about outside.

Vernon turned to Eulalie. "I think it's best if you stay here in the car. We don't need anyone talking about Reverend Hopewell's daughter being seen in Lucky's. It's bad enough you're here with me."

Eulalie pouted but nodded. Vernon thought she had probably never been in a juke joint, but as much as he wanted to invite her in, he would also be inviting a storm of trouble to his door. He pulled a cardboard box filled with six bottles from the back and ambled to the delivery door.

The back door led to a small office where all the business was conducted. The room, only about ten feet in diameter, held a small writing desk in the corner and a couple of chairs for visitors. The wood-paneled wall had recently been replaced and gleamed under a fresh coat of oil.

"Well, well, if it isn't the man of the hour. We've been looking forward to your brew all week," Jarvis called out as Vernon walked in. Jarvis was one hell of a piano player, and Vernon would love to have him in his band. Jarvis was standing around with Henry Stuart, who owned Lucky's, and Alice Chambers.

Alice smiled when Vernon looked at her, seeming shocked at his sudden appearance. He hadn't seen her since she left him standing alone at her doorstep. She looked good in a drop-waisted red dress cut low on her chest and wrapped around the curve of her hips. For a moment, Vernon forgot where he was and what he was there to do. She strolled closer to him in a pair of black heels, swaying to a beat it seemed only the two of them could hear. As she neared, he could smell the notes of her perfume, and she pulled one of the bottles out of his box.

"Now, Vernon, why haven't I had the opportunity to taste your drink? I'm sure my throat would love it." She returned the bottle to its place and gave Vernon a heated look.

"Your throat would like a lot of things I make," he answered.

Henry and Jarvis's mouths fell open simultaneously. Vernon gave a nervous laugh as the room closed in on him. Once upon a time, Alice had had him in a chokehold. He would have traded the entire box of alcohol to spend the evening with her. But he had Eulalie in the car waiting for him. He didn't have the time or the inclination to fool with Alice.

"I'll be here working all evening, if you want to come in and have a drink with me." She winked and walked away, leaving the three men standing there flabbergasted.

"She ain't never invited me to have a drink with her," Jarvis said once she'd left the room.

"I ain't studying Alice. I'm trying to be a good man, but she's pulling me back to the dark side," Vernon said, handing the box over to Henry.

In Henry Stuart's fifty years of life, he had amassed several of Greenwood's most popular businesses. He shook his head and trailed his eyes out the door Alice had left through. "Son, I don't know how you say no to that. I've been trying to get her attention for months now, and she won't even sniff my way."

Henry was hale and hearty for his age, his salt-and-pepper hair cropped close. Vernon thought that even though he was an old dude, women would be falling over themselves for Henry's attention, even though he was married. He was wealthy and keeping himself fit and could buy a woman anything she wanted.

Vernon shook his head, trying to forget the feel of Alice's bottom in his hand. "I don't need those kinds of problems. Alice is a good woman, and I hope she finds what she's looking for. But I don't think I'm that man." He accepted payment from Henry and gave him a handshake before he returned to the car, excited that Eulalie was waiting for him.

****

"Are you sure you feel like waiting for me at another stop? I can take you home." Vernon parked and looked at Eulalie.

She nodded with a sweet smile, warming him from the inside out.

They sat on a dark block in a neighborhood full of row houses. Vernon had only a couple of bottles to give Lloyd. One quick stop, then they could be on their way.

"Are you hungry? Do you want to go over to Al's and get a sandwich?"

"Vernon, I'm not dressed for the supper club."

"We'll sneak in the back and stay in the kitchen. What do you think? I'm not dressed, either, but he and Pearl won't kick us out without giving us something to eat."

Eulalie let out a big sigh. "Vern, before we go anywhere else, there's something I need to tell you."

Vernon's heart dropped into his stomach. He'd been nice to her all evening. He hadn't tried to kiss her or even so much as hold her hand, even though it was all he could think about. Alice's perfume had been overpowering, almost choking the lust out of him. He'd been side by side with Eulalie all evening. She smelled simply of fresh soap and oiled skin, which pleased him.

"What do you want to talk about?"

Eulalie opened her mouth to speak, but a bloodcurdling scream rang out in the dark neighborhood. They turned away from each other to look out the window. A hushed silence fell over them. Vernon sat back, looking for a hint of movement.

The door to Lloyd's house flew open, spilling light out onto the shadowed block. Lloyd's one-story brick house sat on the end of the quiet street. A heavyset woman stepped onto the porch, which had room for only two slim people or the large-chested woman.

Vernon snuck a peek at Eulalie, whose mouth dropped open in confusion. He wasn't sure if he should start the car and leave or stay quiet until all the hubbub died down.

"I'll set this motherfucker on fire before I let you lie up in here with another woman!" the woman yelled back toward the house. Leaving the front door wide open, she trudged back inside.

"Who was that?" Eulalie whispered.

"That's my friend Lloyd's wife, Marion. I came here to drop off a few bottles he ordered, but it doesn't look like now is a good time."

"What do you think we should do?"

Vernon shrugged, keeping his eyes fixed on the yellow light that trailed into the yard. There was a good chance Lloyd might need a ride somewhere.

Eulalie started to whisper again but sealed her lips when she saw movement. Marion stomped back through the front door, carrying an armful of clothes. She raised her arms past her head then sent everything flying into the yard.

"Get the hell out of my house!" she yelled on the way back in. From around the corner, a silhouette creeped in the shadows. A slim nude figure tiptoed into the yard and pawed through the clothes.

"Oh my God, is that a woman?" Eulalie gasped.

Vernon focused his eyes, catching a glimpse of rounded breasts and skinny legs.

The doorway darkened, except that time, Marion wasn't alone. Lloyd followed, clad in a white cotton shirt and a pair of underpants.

"Come on, Marion. Don't do this. I don't know what you think you saw, but it don't call for all this."

Marion didn't seem to hear Lloyd and instead threw another load of clothing over the railing. Vernon looked for the naked woman, but she seemed to have slipped back into shadow.

"I know what I saw, Lloyd. I'm not blind. Nor am I stupid!"

"Don't throw my stuff out here. Can we talk about it?"

"There ain't nothing to talk about. You can come back for the rest of it in the morning. Get the hell out of here before I get my shotgun." Marion pushed Lloyd hard on the shoulder then lumbered back into the house.

Lloyd stood motionless on the porch as she closed the door hard, cutting off their only access to the light.

"Eulalie, wait here. I'm going to see if he needs my help."

"Vern, no. She said she was going to get her shotgun," Eulalie hissed.

Vernon didn't really have a choice. He couldn't leave Lloyd standing outside.

He stepped out of the car and slammed the door, which made Lloyd jump.

"Hey, man, it's just me—Vernon. What the hell is going on?"

"Vern?" Lloyd squinted to see in the dark. "Vernon, what the hell are you doing out here?" Lloyd stood tall, like it was normal to see a grown man out on a dark porch in his underclothes.

"I came to drop off the hooch you ordered. What the hell are you doing?"

"Marion says she saw some woman up in here. She was supposed to be visiting her sister over in Sapulpa but came home tonight." Lloyd shrugged, as if that explained everything.

Vernon didn't bother asking any more questions. He knew Lloyd wasn't going to tell him the whole truth.

"Help me pick up the clothes and put them in the back of the car. You can come to my house tonight until you get all this figured out."

The two men had started to pick up the loose garments when a hiss came from the side of the house.

"Lloyd, do you see a skirt out there?" A woman emerged from the shadows again, clad in only a button-down shirt.

"Just go get in the car, and we'll pick all the clothes up. We'll find something for you to wear," Vernon whispered. He kept one eye on the door of the house and one on the car, hoping Eulalie wouldn't be surprised when the woman walked up.

Once they'd picked up everything they could, Vernon and Lloyd made their way to the car. The two women huddled in the cab, and Lloyd got comfortable in the back bed with the pile of clothes. Vernon started the ignition and drove straight to his house.

19

Eulalie

The ride back to Vernon's place had been deafeningly silent, punctuated only by the loud chugging of the car's motor. When the half-clothed woman had walked up to the car, Eulalie lost the ability to speak because she couldn't close her mouth. Never in her life had she ever seen an affair up close.

She pulled herself together just as the woman neared and moved to jump into action and throw open the passenger door. The woman scooted in, keeping her eyes downcast and mumbling her thanks. Eulalie kept her voice bright, as if it were completely normal to welcome a half-dressed stranger into a car that wasn't hers after witnessing a domestic altercation. The woman didn't offer her name, and Eulalie didn't ask for it. Instead, she reached into her bag, pulled out the fraying blanket, and placed it over the young woman's legs. Another soft thanks was all she got.

When they reached Vernon's, everyone tumbled out and silently made their way to the front door. Vernon stopped to grab one pile of clothing, and Lloyd took the other.

Once inside, Eulalie tried not to watch as the young woman riffled through the clothes to find her items. In the light of Vernon's home, Eulalie could finally get a look at the couple. Lloyd, wearing a pair of wrinkled pants, had to be the same age as her daddy. His hair was balding on the top and in the back, and the hair he did have was graying around the temples. The hair that was missing from his head was all over his chest, arms, and back, like it was trying to escape from the confines of his undershirt. He reminded her of a grown teddy bear, brown skin and dark hair all over, with a round belly that matched his round face.

The lady, on the other hand, looked younger than Eulalie's twenty-six years. Her high-pitched voice lacked the maturity of a woman who'd seen life firsthand. Eulalie didn't recognize her face, which held bright-brown eyes set in hazel skin. If she had seen the two together, she would have thought them father and daughter.

Eulalie found a seat at the dining room table, back from the other three in the living room, and watched quietly.

Once the woman pulled her skirt from the pile, she looked straight at Lloyd, speaking for the first time since they'd left the house. "Why didn't you tell me your wife was coming home?" she demanded.

Lloyd pursed his lips tightly. "Had I known she was coming home, we wouldn't have been there, now, would we?"

"You had me outside. In the dark. Naked!" she wailed. "I should have known better than to start fooling with you. You told me y'all had separated."

"We did separate. Velma, it's complicated."

Eulalie shifted uncomfortably in her seat and tried to get Vernon's attention. He, however, was focused on Lloyd and Velma, his eyes snapping between the two of them.

"Vernon," she hissed through clenched teeth. "Vernon…" she called, finally getting his attention.

Everyone stopped talking and turned to see what she wanted. With everyone's eyes turned to her, she warmed under their attention.

"Do you mind if I have a glass of water?" she asked.

Vernon's glazed eyes cleared as if he'd just realized she was there too. He nodded and told Lloyd he could stay the night if he needed to. Eulalie noticed Vernon only said "he" instead of "they." She wondered if the omission was intentional.

He led her through the rectangular dining room to the kitchen and reached for a glass to get her water. Once they'd left the room, Velma and Lloyd restarted their argument.

"You're going to let them stay here?" she asked.

"What other choice do I have? I can't just put him out. You saw what he's been through."

Eulalie's eyes almost bugged out of her head. "You mean what he's put himself through. Not to mention what he's put his poor wife through. He brought all of this on himself," Eulalie whispered. She hoped the words were making sense to Vernon, but he didn't seem bothered.

"He made a mistake, Eulalie."

"A mistake?"

Vernon rubbed the top of his head and flailed his arms hopelessly. "I'm not saying I agree with him. I would never cheat on my wife. What he did was wrong. But it's done. It's done, Eulalie, and it has nothing to do with us. The only thing I can offer him is a clean bed and a place to rest his head so he can think about everything that's going on." By that point, Vernon was talking at full volume.

"I think it's time for me to go home. I've had enough excitement for one night."

Vernon nodded and put the glass back, forgetting the water request. They left the kitchen and walked through the dining room to find the sitting room vacant. The pile of clothes remained in the middle of the floor, but the front door was cracked open, with Velma and Lloyd nowhere to be found. Vernon opened a bedroom door, which sat on the wall next to the front door, but the house was empty.

"What the hell is going on around here?" he asked. "It's almost ten o'clock. Let's get you home before your parents come looking for me."

****

Once they were safely parked a few houses down from Eulalie's, she let out a deep sigh. "This has been the most exciting night I've had in years. Thank you for letting me ride with you."

"Gal, I ain't never taking you with me again when I go out for deliveries," Vernon said with a laugh. Even though his tone was light, she still wanted to talk about what had happened.

"I'm sorry for the mishap in the kitchen. I was so shocked that you were going to let him stay there."

"You know, sometimes we all make mist—" He started over. "Sometimes we make bad decisions. It's nice to have someone there that don't judge us for the wrong decisions we make. I feel like if anyone could understand that, you should."

Eulalie's face burned. She'd been showing up to his house and kissing him, all the while engaged to someone else. Even though she hadn't married Samuel, maybe she wasn't any different from Lloyd, running around with who he wanted and following his heart, no matter his commitments.

"I feel like there was something you wanted to talk about before all of this started. Are you good?" Vernon rubbed his face.

He'd interrupted her train of thought, and now she wasn't sure what to say.

"Yes, I'm fine. We can talk later. When we're not so tired. Can I come see you tomorrow?" She didn't have the energy to tell him that she'd broken her engagement. It would have to wait.

"If you want to come see me tomorrow, I would like that."

****

"You came in awfully late last night." Mama looked up from the bowl she'd been stirring. "We were about to send someone out looking for you."

The familiar smell of cinnamon and nutmeg filled the warm, small kitchen, beckoning Eulalie forward. A sugary sweet treat was exactly what she needed to get her morning started before she made her way to the school. Unfortunately, she didn't have time to wait for what Mama was making. A few pieces of cold meat would have to hold her stomach.

"I went out to read then got caught up with some friends. They were having some problems, so I stayed to help. Then I came straight home." Eulalie felt bad about not telling her mother the entire truth, but there was no need for her to worry. Nothing had happened to her, and she was there, ready to start another day of work.

"Nothing good happens after dark when you're out alone."

"Mama, I'm twenty-six years old. I can go out in the evening."

"I'm not saying you can't. I'm only saying it's not a good idea." Mama turned back around to face the bowl.

The wooden spoon beat furiously against the side of the bowl as Eulalie moved quickly to make her breakfast before Mama launched into a tirade. If Mama started up, Eulalie might be late for school. Quickly, she wrapped a few pieces of cold chicken in a piece of bread and tied it up in a square of butcher paper. She'd moved to leave the kitchen when Mama spoke again.

"Eulalie, have a seat. I know you aren't planning to sneak out of here without eating something."

"I don't have a lot of time, and I don't want to be late."

"You won't be late. Just sit down." Mama left her spot at the counter and moved toward the stove. She pulled the top off one of the bubbling pots and spooned a healthy serving of grits into a white bowl. Then she returned to the counter and added a pat of butter and a dash of salt. Mama lovingly mixed the ingredients, grabbed a peach, then brought both the bowl and the peach to the small table, where Eulalie waited.

The antique wooden table had been handmade by her grandfather, Mama's daddy. Only two people could sit around it, maybe three if they squeezed together. After Eulalie was born, the table had been relegated to the corner of the kitchen, unusable for most meals. When one of the girls had to help Mama or when they'd been in trouble as children, they were bidden to sit at the table to "collect the minds they'd lost."

Eulalie sat there, her legs stretched underneath, and luxuriated in her mother's nourishment.

"Do you want me to fry you some meat?" Mama asked.

"No, thank you. I'm okay."

Eulalie ate her grits first, filling her belly, before appreciating the sweet peach. She finished and watched her mother work in the kitchen. If Mama knew what time she'd come in the previous night, it meant she'd been awake. Her mother had probably gotten up early to make sure that everyone had something to eat before they rushed off. She would be there waiting for everyone to come home. If she wasn't, she could be found at the church. Eulalie watched her mother moving about the kitchen in her house dress, wondering if that was what she could expect in the next few years.

Not if I stick with Vernon, she thought. Being married to Vernon would mean a new adventure for them every day. He would take her to see new things and make her laugh. Samuel would have her stuck in the kitchen, barefoot and pregnant, before she knew it.

Eulalie shook herself out of her daydream. She put her bowl on the counter to be washed then kissed her mother on the cheek.

"Thank you for breakfast. It was wonderful."

Eulalie was walking to the door when Mama called her back.

"Don't forget your lunch." Gone were the hastily wrapped meat and bread. They had been replaced with an entire sack full of treats her mother had put together while she'd been eating.

Eulalie gave her mother another quick kiss and headed for the door.

"I hope you're making good decisions," Mama called without turning around.

"I am, Ma. I'm doing the best I can," she said and started out the front door.

****

Eulalie was standing outside the school when a car parked next to her. For a moment, her heart leaped when she thought it was Vernon, pulling up to offer a ride somewhere. She would have said no, but the thought of seeing his grin made her smile.

Instead, it was Marva Vance. Marva was a teacher at the secondary school in a building across the street from Eulalie's. They'd met many times over the years, trading stories and tips for keeping the children in line. She hopped from the car, giving her husband a wave, and headed straight to Eulalie.

"Oh my heavens, you'll never guess what I heard." Marva was an energetic woman who loved nothing more than being a teacher. She matched the energy of the kids around her and was constantly called their favorite.

"Tell me. What did you hear?" Eulalie asked.

"Marion Parrish's husband left her. Said she was cheating on him with Vernon Jackson." Marva smiled sweetly.

Eulalie's mouth fell open. "I'm sorry. Say that again for me?"

Marva nodded knowingly. She fiddled with her necklace before stepping closer to Eulalie.

"You heard me. Vernon Jackson has been having an affair with Marion Parrish. Poor Lloyd came home and found the two of them in bed together. Somebody said the poor man was so distraught he was walking around last night with no pants on. He didn't have time to get anything."

Eulalie opened her mouth and let out the heaviest belly laugh she'd ever let go. If she hadn't been there in person, she would have found it hard to believe, but she would have considered it possible. But she had been there with him and seen how Vernon tried to help the lying, cheating Lloyd.

"That's not true. Don't go around telling anyone else that. It doesn't even sound logical. Besides, Vernon's not that kind of man."

Marva didn't even seem to hear her. "I don't know if it's true or not, but that's what they're saying. Girl, that's not even the best part. Someone told me that Vernon got picked up for vagrancy, and he's sitting in the county jail. It serves him right for sleeping with a married woman." Marva waved to another woman she saw across the street. She said goodbye to Eulalie before moving to walk away.

Eulalie reached out to grab her by the arm. "Do me a favor and don't tell anyone else that. Until we know exactly what's going on, it isn't Christian to be spreading those types of rumors."

Marva nodded but narrowed her eyes. Eulalie didn't care. It was one thing to gossip about true things, but it was another to spread completely unfounded stories.

All day, she was distracted. She couldn't think of anything other than Vernon. *Is he okay? Has he been hurt? What's happened since the last time I saw him?*

Surely the rumor of him being in jail wasn't true. None of the other things Marva had said were, so that shouldn't be either. *How could someone even make that up?*

She'd rushed the kids through their lessons and snapped when someone spoke out of turn. Sensing her foul mood, most of the class had been quiet. There was only one thing on her mind. She needed to get through the day and find out what was going on with Vernon.

20

Vernon

Vernon rested his head against the cold stone wall. He sat on a wooden bench that ran along it. The seat wasn't very sturdy, and at some point, it would yield under the wrong amount of weight. Vernon just hoped he wasn't still there when it happened.

An older white man shuffled over and sat on the opposite side. "What'd they get you for?" He smelled of piss and alcohol, like he hadn't washed in weeks.

Vernon wanted to go to the other side of the room, but that would mean vacating his seat. Only the two of them were in there, so he wasn't worried, but he didn't feel like standing. He didn't feel like talking either. He swung his legs away, turning his back to the man, trying to avoid talking.

"They pulled me in here on public drunkenness and vagrancy. Hell, I may have been drunk, but I ain't no vagrant. I got a home and everything." The man rattled on as if Vernon were asking him questions. He stretched out down the length of the bench, laying his head too close to Vernon's backside.

"I wasn't even doing anything. Had a couple of drinks because my old lady was riding my ass. Rather be in here than listen to her mouth."

Even Vernon couldn't help laughing at that. The man was still lying too close to him, but Vernon couldn't help but relax a little. He couldn't do anything about his situation. At some point, they would let him notify someone, but he wasn't sure who he would try to notify. Al and Pearl didn't have a phone line set up in their home. Either of them would come running and pay whatever it took to get him out, no matter the time of day. More than likely, he was going to have to send a message to Legal Clyde. Clyde would post his bond and take care of all the paperwork, but he was a busy man. Everyone in the neighborhood called Clyde when they needed something. Hell, Vernon would be stuck for three days before Clyde showed up. He would stop and talk to every man, woman, and child he met before he got to Vernon. But he didn't really have much of a choice. Vernon would be there until someone came to release him.

"Young man, are you married?" the man asked, pulling Vernon from his thoughts.

Vernon shook his head. "Naw, I ain't married."

"Let me tell you something. The best decision I ever made was to get married. I know it doesn't look like it right now." The man let out a gruff laugh. He rubbed his eyes and nose then crossed his arms. "Even right now, Betty is at home, ironing my clothes and cooking my food. When I get out of here, she's gon' give me an earful. It's what I deserve. I can't argue with that. One thing I can say, though, is that she will take care of me until the day I die." The old man sat up and placed his feet on the floor before turning toward Vernon. "Do you have a sweetheart?"

"Yeah. Yeah, I got a sweetheart," Vernon answered. Eulalie's face flooded his brain, irritating him. He willed himself to think of something else, but as he sat there, all he could think of was the curve of her lips.

"Marry her. Especially if she loves you and is willing to take care of you."

"I don't know if I'm ready to get married yet. There are so many beautiful women out there. I don't know how I will choose just one." Vernon shrugged, wondering why he was being honest with the man. In no other situation would he be talking to him, yet there was a sort of strange kinship between the two of them stuck in that jail cell.

"I understand how you feel, but the right woman will change your life. Once you find her, you won't need all the rest of them."

"How will I know when it's her?" Vernon asked.

"You'll know when you'd rather spend time with her than you do anyone else."

"Sir, with all due respect, you just said you'd rather stay here than hear her mouth."

Vernon smiled widely, and the man gave a dry laugh that turned into a harsh cough. He sat quietly for a while as the man worked to clear the phlegm from his throat.

"Young man, you're not wrong. I did say that. That doesn't mean she's not the best thing that ever happened to me."

The man went silent for a moment, and Vernon thanked God. The last thing he needed was advice from a drunk man who was in the same predicament as he was. Besides, Vernon didn't have energy to get his heart broken anymore. He was too grown for that. He was better off by himself. He closed his eyes and let his thoughts drift off.

✳✳✳✳

Ten years prior, Vernon straightened his tie one last time before he knocked on the door. He wanted everything to go perfectly. All he needed to do was speak to Reverend Hopewell. Best-case scenario, the reverend would be happy for him. He wasn't the reverend's favorite person, but he wasn't that bad of a man. Eulalie loved him, and that was all that mattered to him. They would make their way in the world the same way his parents had. Ida and Joseph Jackson had worked their fingers to the bone to make sure he and Pearl had everything they needed. His parents didn't play about their kids or their marriage. They took care of each other, always harping on the importance of "family first." His daddy worked long hours at two different jobs but always made sure to come home and have dinner with his family every night. His mother worked as a domestic on the other side of town, but she made every meal for his daddy and took care of the entire household. Ida loved her some Joseph and told everyone she knew. Not that she needed to tell anyone anything. Everywhere they went, they held hands and stayed within each other's proximity. If love didn't feel like his parents' marriage, Vernon didn't want it. Eulalie was the first girl who'd made him believe a love like his parents' could be real.

Vernon knocked on the door then waited until he heard the "Come in" before he turned the knob. His heart raced, but he swallowed it down.

He stepped into the small office to face Reverend Hopewell. The reverend sat behind a large oak desk and stood when Vernon came in. His glasses had been resting on the top of his bald head, but he pulled them down to his nose.

"Hello, sir. I was hoping you had a few free minutes to talk."

Reverend Hopewell held out his hand, indicating the empty seat in front of his desk. Vernon settled in to think about what he was going to say. His foot tapped uncontrollably, but there was nothing he could do to stop it. He hoped it was hidden from view.

"What is it you wanted to talk about, son?"

"I wanted to speak to you about Eulalie."

"Eulalie?" The reverend said his daughter's name with an air of confusion. Whatever Reverend Hopewell had been expecting Vernon to speak about, it certainly wasn't her.

"Yes, your daughter Eulalie."

"She isn't giving you any trouble, is she?"

Vernon smiled and shook his head. She wasn't giving him the kind of trouble Reverend Hopewell was thinking about. He didn't think he should tell the man about the passion burning in his pants for Eulalie. That was the only trouble she was giving him. He'd had a sweet taste of her nectar, and he couldn't think of anything else.

"No, she isn't giving me any trouble. I was hoping… I was hoping to ask for your blessing."

"My blessing?" The lines etched even deeper in the reverend's face.

"I want to marry your daughter." There. He'd said it. He'd told the truth about his feelings to the scariest man in the neighborhood other than his father. He'd put what he wanted out there, hoping for the best.

The two men sat in silence for longer than Vernon liked. At least a minute passed as the older man sat contemplating what Vernon had requested.

"That's interesting, young man, because as I understand it, Eulalie is already seeing someone else." The pastor folded his hands neatly, resting them on the desktop easily, and sat unmoved.

Vernon studied the older man's face for the slightest hint of jest. There wasn't one.

"What do you mean, Eulalie is 'seeing someone else'? Who is she seeing?"

"I'm sorry, son. I'm not really at liberty to speak with you about her life. Surely you can understand that." The reverend's voice was calm, but Vernon could hear the words that weren't being spoken. The pastor didn't approve of him, plain and simple. He didn't want someone like Vernon marrying his daughter.

"I understand very much, sir. I just didn't know Eulalie was dating someone else. We've been spending so much time together that I can't see how she would have time for anyone else to be courting her."

He knew he shouldn't have said it. He shouldn't have told the reverend, who was also his intended's father, that they had already been spending time together. Vernon and Eulalie hadn't behaved properly at all.

Vernon should have called on Eulalie at her house. He should have asked if he could court Eulalie properly. They should have been chaperoned. They shouldn't have been kissing or touching the way they had. Vernon shouldn't know her the way a man knew a woman. She should have been saved for her wedding night. But they hadn't chosen that way.

"When? When and where have you been spending time together?"

"I see her at church and talk to her a lot. And I walk her home from school every day." As much as he wanted to, Vernon couldn't tell the reverend all the real time they'd been spending together. It wouldn't do to get Eulalie in trouble more than she was already going to be.

Reverend Hopewell inhaled, seeming to suck all the air out of the room. For a moment, Vernon couldn't breathe. He'd stepped over a line, gone too far. Silence descended, covering them like a blanket, and for a few moments, neither man moved.

"Can I walk you home, son? I need to talk to your mama."

Vernon nodded. They didn't have anything else to talk about, and he was ready to be gone.

****

The walk home was just as tense and awkward as Vernon had been expecting.

When they pushed open the fence gate at his house, Vernon's mother, Ida, was outside, hanging the laundry. She smiled when she saw the two walking toward her, but the smile fell from her face when she realized neither of them was joyous.

"Mrs. Ida, we need to talk."

"What's wrong, Reverend? Is everything okay?" Mama's tone made Vernon stop a few feet away from her. She cut her eyes at him. Surely he wasn't about to get in trouble. For once, he hadn't even done anything wrong. He was eighteen now and was trying to be an honorable man. He wanted to do right by Eulalie, and he wanted to be with her. *What's the trouble in that?*

Reverend Hopewell cleared his throat and moved closer to Ma.

"I can't have your son asking around for Eulalie."

"What do you mean, 'asking around for her'?"

"Vernon says he's been courting Eulalie and wants to marry her. I can't have that, Ida."

"I see." Ma hummed under her breath before speaking again. "Please remind me—what exactly is the matter with Vernon trying to court your daughter?"

Reverend Hopewell removed his glasses to wipe a line of sweat from his brow, hemming and hawing, trying to find the words. "She is going to marry someone else. That's all there is to it. Vernon will have to find another girl."

Vernon had always questioned God's existence, but in that moment, he prayed the earth would open up and swallow him. He'd put his heart on the line with the man everyone believed in, the one who everyone confided in. That man had walked him home and told his mama all his business. It should have stayed between the two of them. If he didn't want Vernon to marry Eulalie, he could have just said that. He didn't have to embarrass him in front of his mother.

"Our families have been through a lot, Ida. We don't need this. We need to stay away from each other and let bygones be bygones," Reverend Hopewell continued.

"I had nothing to do with our families going through a lot, William. The things that happened in the past have nothing to do with these children." Ma rested her hands on her hips.

Vernon's eyes almost fell out of his head. Vernon had never, ever, under any circumstances, heard anyone call the reverend by his given name.

"Please, just keep your son away from my daughters. I've already promised her hand in marriage to someone else." Reverend Hopewell dropped his hands as if he'd run out of words.

It felt like something else was going on that didn't have anything to do with Vernon.

Reverend Hopewell moved to walk away, but Vernon finally spoke up. "I'll stay away from Eulalie. I won't speak to her again."

The older man nodded then left the Jackson home without another word.

21

Eulalie

Eulalie paced the floor of her bedroom manically. Something about the feel of her feet hitting the floor brought her a small bit of comfort.

"Is there anything you want to talk about?" Leona lay across Eulalie's bed with her chin resting on her hands.

Eulalie had forgotten her sister was even in the room with her, which showed how fast her mind was spinning. Surely Vernon hadn't been locked up. Marva had to be mistaken. Eulalie had been there. She'd seen everything. *What could have gone wrong?*

Eulalie stopped her pacing for a moment to answer her sister. "No, there's nothing I want to talk about. Why would you think that?"

"Well, you've worn a hole in that rug. Not to mention the fact that you've been talking to yourself for an hour."

"That doesn't mean I have something on my mind."

"Lalie, you're only wearing one shoe. You have so much on your mind you stopped to take one off, then you started pacing again." Leona smirked and gave Eulalie a once-over.

Realizing Leona was right, Eulalie kicked off her shoe toward the corner of the room. It hit the wall with a crack and fell down hard.

"Daddy's going to be mad if you left a mark on the wall," Leona said.

"Is there a reason you're in here?"

"I was trying to help. You're obviously thinking about something. Do you want to talk about it?"

Eulalie looked at her sweet sister's face. Leona was earnestly trying to help. Eulalie wanted to spill everything that was going on, but Leona was so young. She'd never even had a beau or been kissed. She would never understand. But Eulalie tried to find the words, ones that wouldn't get her in trouble.

"Have you ever been somewhere you shouldn't have been and seen something you probably shouldn't have?"

Leona's eyes grew wide, and her mouth bobbed up and down like a fish's. She jumped from the bed and pulled Eulalie to sit down.

"I don't think… No, I can't think of a time when I have. You have to tell me everything."

So she did. She told her sister about going out to read and meeting Vernon. She talked about how he'd been the perfect gentleman, only offering to give her a ride home. Eulalie had been the one who'd said she wanted to ride with him. She'd wanted to go on the deliveries. Eulalie told her about stopping in front of the Parrishes' house and the scene that had played out in front of her.

"Leona, you cannot tell anyone that I told you this," Eulalie said. "I mean no one. This is their real life."

"I won't. I promise. Keep going."

"The woman walked to the car because Vernon told her to, and I think she has to be about your age. Do you know someone named Velma? She's a bit lighter than you and has chicken legs."

"Nooo. I mean yes, of course I know Velma. Wow!" Leona fell back onto the bed and pressed her hands over her face. "Velma is Mother Edith's granddaughter. Every time Mother Edith goes to visit someone, she has to take one of her grandchildren. I wouldn't be surprised if she'd been to the Parrishes' house before."

Eulalie lay back on the bed next to her sister in surprise. "Oh my Lord, I would never have remembered that. That's probably where she met Mr. Parrish. Because where would they even meet each other? He's probably twenty years older than her."

"You're right. What else happened?" Leona asked.

Eulalie closed her eyes and recounted the rest of the story, about Velma and Lloyd coming back to the house and starting to argue, her and Vernon's disagreement, and how the visitors had disappeared before Vernon brought her home.

When she couldn't sit still any longer, Eulalie hopped back to her feet and started the pacing again. She spilled everything she'd heard from Marva and told Leona that since she'd last seen Vernon, he had somehow been arrested and was being held in the county jail.

"And now I don't know what to do. I was there, Leona. I saw it all. Vernon wasn't having an affair. He had nothing to do with it. As a matter of fact, he was trying to help Lloyd, and I told him not to." Eulalie paced to one side of her room, turned around, and walked to the other.

"Lalie, I hate to tell you this, but you know what you have to do."

"Tell me. Tell me what I have to do."

"You have to tell Mama. Or Cassidra. If you tell one of them, they can help you."

Eulalie shook her head. She stopped in front of the bed to think about what Leona was trying to tell her. No way was she going to tell Mama, and Cassidra didn't seem like a good option either.

"Now you see what my problem is. Do I try to find out what's going on or leave everything be? I would hate to tell Mama everything while Vernon's sitting at home. I would get an earful from Mama for no reason," Eulalie said.

Leona nodded. "That's exactly what we can do. We can go to Vernon's house and see if he's there. If he is, then everything is fine. If not, then we'll figure out something else."

She rolled out of the bed, seeming excited to be a part of the adventure, but Eulalie was hesitant. It was one thing to tell Leona everything that was going on, but it was another thing to have her involved.

"Leona, you can't come with me to Vernon's. I can't have you get in trouble."

"If we go together, then you can't get in trouble. We were out and about together, not sneaking around. Besides, we're only going to knock on the door anyways. If he doesn't answer, then we'll figure it out."

That sounded simple enough. They could go to his house and see if he was there. If he wasn't, well, she would worry about that later. It could all be a rumor.

****

It had taken an hour. Eulalie and Leona walked to Vernon's house and knocked on the door. There had been no answer. They knocked on his next-door neighbor's house, and the older man who answered said he hadn't seen Vernon all day. They walked past Al's Supper Club to see if they could talk to Pearl, but the shop was locked and dark.

On the walk home, she and Leona had argued about whether or not they should have just gone to downtown Tulsa. When Leona finally convinced Eulalie they had no idea what they were doing, she realized she was standing on their porch. Another hour wasted, and she was no closer to finding out what had happened to Vernon.

"Eulalie, please," Leona said. "If you want to help him, we have to tell Mama or Daddy. We don't have any other choice."

Eulalie nodded and headed inside. The smell of hot oil filled the air as the girls moved closer to the kitchen, where Mama was preparing dinner.

"Mama, are you busy?" Leona asked tentatively.

She looked up from peeling her potatoes and twisted her head to the side. Of course she was busy. Daddy would be looking for his dinner soon, and Mama didn't have a minute to waste.

"What do you girls need? Eulalie, why do you look like the cat that caught the canary?" Mama dropped the fully peeled potato into a bowl of cool water and looked between the two girls. "What is it?"

"Eulalie needs to talk to you." Leona stepped back and took a seat at the table, leaving Eulalie standing alone.

Eulalie wasn't sure whether she should move closer to her mother to be able to keep her voice down or sit back where Leona was. She didn't want to be in striking range when she told her story. Instead of moving, she decided to just come right out with it.

"Mama, we heard Vernon Jackson is being detained by the sheriff."

"Wow, I'm so sorry to hear that. That doesn't surprise me. That boy's always been kind of wild." Mama turned her attention back to another potato and started to peel it.

Eulalie turned to look at Leona, who waved her back toward Mama.

Eulalie started again. "No, Mama. Actually, he's a very nice man. I was out with him last night, and I believe he's been wrongly accused." Eulalie pursed her lips tightly.

Mama dropped the half-peeled potato in the water and turned her full attention to Eulalie. "What do you mean, you were 'out with him last night'? Do you not care for your reputation at all? What will Samuel think? What will your father think?"

"Mama, we can talk about all that later. Please. I need your help to get him out."

"No, we need to talk about it right now. Doesn't he have any family or someone else who can take care of it? Why is it your responsibility to get him out of jail?"

"Because I love him, Mama. I'm not going to marry Samuel. Even if I can't be with him, I can't stand by and watch him be mistreated. We have to do something, Mama. We are the pastor's family." Hot, thick tears filled Eulalie's eyes. She wiped the first one away, but that seemed to welcome the others. When her nose started to run, she knew there was no use. She'd laid bare all the things she'd wanted to say for weeks. It felt good to let go of all the expectations that had been weighing her shoulders down.

Mama let out a loud sigh, expending all the air from her belly. She pulled Eulalie into the comfort of her bosom and held her until she stopped crying.

"I will go talk to your daddy under one condition."

Eulalie nodded, unable to speak.

"I need you to sit and listen to my story."

"Okay, Mama. I'm listening."

"No, not right now. We'll talk later." Mama dropped the potato peeler in the front pocket of her apron then wiped her hands on the tea towel draped over her shoulder. She started to walk to the door before she remembered what she'd been doing.

"Leona, finish peeling the potatoes and season that fish."

Leona pouted. "Now, why do I gotta do it? Eulalie's standing right there."

"Naw, Eulalie's going to go to her room and lie down. Get over there and finish dinner."

Leona crossed her arms, and Mama did the same.

"I need the peeler. Can I at least listen to your story when you tell her?" Leona asked, dropping her arms.

"I'll think about it. Don't make that fish too salty." Mama handed Leona the peeler then flounced from the room, and Eulalie followed. At least she didn't have to cook dinner.

****

"I will go and take care of everything. Please, go on home. This isn't a place for ladies." Daddy's voice was tired. He exhaled sharply, like he couldn't breathe from frustration.

Eulalie realized the longer she distracted her father, the longer it would take for Vernon to be freed, but she was adamant. She wanted to be there. Eulalie didn't know what her mama had said to her daddy. She had gone to the bedroom and closed the door to talk to him. Eulalie had stood by the door to listen, but she couldn't make out anything from the muffled conversation. All she knew was that even though he was irritated, he'd put on his shoes and headed downtown.

When Mama and Leona had turned their backs, Eulalie snuck out the front door and followed him all the way. She'd gone mostly unseen until he stopped to talk to someone and saw her from the corner of his eyes. She had no choice but to walk up and talk to him.

"Daddy, I just want to make sure he's okay. He didn't do anything."

"Eulalie, what are you going to do if he's not okay? How are you going to help?"

She was stumped. Daddy was right. There wasn't anything she *could* do. Eulalie had never been down to the Tulsa County jail. Her hands shook, but as long as she kept them locked together, no one would notice. The stoic government building looked ominous when she and Daddy walked up. Traffic swirled around her, jumbling her thoughts. All she wanted was to make sure Vernon was alive.

"Okay, but, Daddy, please tell me everything when you get home."

"I promise I will. Please go home. I'm not going in until I see you walk down the street. Please, Eulalie."

"Fine. Thank you for your help." She kissed her daddy on the cheek and turned to walk home.

He stood stock-still in the middle of the sidewalk, watching her. She made it to the end of the block and turned to see if he was still watching. He was. He removed his hat from his head and waved it at her as if waving her home. She waved back and continued walking down the street until she couldn't see her father anymore.

Leaning against the brick wall of a building, she let pedestrian traffic pass her by. After she'd counted to one hundred, she turned away from home and retraced her steps back toward the county building. She wasn't going home until she saw Vernon's face.

22

Vernon

The population in the small cell where Vernon was being held had grown from two to four. He'd been there all day and hadn't heard a word from anyone. It was almost dark, and he hadn't had anything to eat all day either. At some point, the old man had fallen asleep, leaving Vernon in peace until the other two men showed up.

When the door opened again, Reverend Hopewell stood there, his hat in his hand, next to the sheriff. He kept his face impassive, neither smiling nor frowning. Vernon didn't know if he was happy or not about seeing the pastor.

"Come on out, Jackson. You're being released." The sheriff was a broad-chested man with a thick mustache that wiggled when he spoke.

Vernon didn't bother to look at him or anyone. He stood up and walked with the reverend toward freedom. He shouldn't have been there anyway.

The sun was starting its descent into the western sky, pulling back the hotness that had baked the entire day. The clock on the tower in front of him declared it a quarter after seven.

"Well, young man, here we are again," Reverend Hopewell said once they'd stepped from the building.

"What do you mean? When have we done this before?"

"We haven't. I mean, here we are, the two of us. This reminds me of when you were a teenager and we walked home to speak to your mama."

"With all due respect sir, I didn't walk home to talk to my mother. You did. I came to you to speak to you as a man, and you ran to my mother." Vernon was too tired to argue and wasn't interested in walking down memory lane, especially when it came to that memory in particular. All he wanted to do was find something to eat and get home to bathe. He'd been in the same clothes since the day before and hadn't eaten since the previous night's supper.

"I suppose that's fair," Reverend Hopewell said. He seemed to be thinking of the right words to say because his eyes danced behind his wire-rimmed glasses. "I wanted to talk to you. Do you want to stop at Ray's for a quick meal? I'm sure you're hungry."

Vernon paused, unsure of what he'd heard. For the last twenty-eight years of his life, Reverend Hopewell had given him nothing but the cold shoulder. Now the man wanted to go have a meal together. Vernon's stomach roared at the thought of one of Ray's steak sandwiches, but he tamped down the thought.

"I know I'm not your favorite person. Why did you come, sir?"

"It was actually Eulalie. She insisted, saying she was with you and you hadn't done any of the things you'd been charged with." Reverend Hopewell pressed his lips in a thin line, like he hadn't wanted to speak the truth. "I told her I would see to it that you get home safely."

"I appreciate you and Eulalie, then. She's right. I didn't do anything. I was only trying to help someone else who'd made a mess." Vernon sighed. "If you don't mind, sir, I'm going to pass on Ray's.

I just want to get home. Was there something you wanted to talk about?"

Reverend Hopewell's eyes shifted from side to side. He looked around the streets before finally meeting Vernon's eyes. "What kind of relationship do you have with my daughter?"

The thought crossed Vernon's mind to ask, "Which daughter?" but he sensed Reverend Hopewell wasn't in the mood. He wasn't, either, if he was being honest.

"So that's what you meant about us being here again," Vernon said when the realization hit him. "You're expecting me to say that I want to court your daughter, then you're going to tell me to stay away from her. Is that what you wanted to talk about?"

"Well, I… Not… See, now…"

Vernon knew that was exactly what the older man wanted to talk about. They'd been in the same situation ten years earlier. He wasn't going to give the man the satisfaction of besting him twice.

"Reverend Hopewell, I have no relationship with your daughter other than the innocent neighborly kind. She is safe with her Samuel. I hope they are very happy together." He'd shaken the pastor's hand before the man even knew what was happening. "Thank you to you and Eulalie for being there for me in my time of need. Like I said, I was in the wrong place at the wrong time. If you will excuse me, I'm going to take my leave now." Vernon dropped the pastor's hand and gestured toward the county jail.

Reverend Hopewell nodded. There was really nothing else to say.

Vernon turned on his heel and started on his journey home. He walked to the end of the block and was about to cross the street when he made eye contact with a brown-skinned woman standing on the opposite side. Eulalie was hiding around the corner of the brick building. Her face brightened when she saw him, her eyes sparkling in the way he loved. She raised her hand only slightly, giving him a small wave. If he hadn't been looking at her, he would never have seen it. He winked at her then continued home.

****

Vernon knew he was risking jail again, but he couldn't stop himself. When he found himself under the light of the moon in the Hopewells' side yard, he prayed it would all go well. It was ten o'clock at night, and the house was as dark as a cellar. But he only needed a few minutes.

He looked around until he found a stick that'd fallen from a nearby tree and threw it so it would hit Eulalie's window, hoping she hadn't decided to switch rooms in the last few years. Her room sat on the north side of the house, above the dining room, with no other bedroom windows next to hers. Her parents were on the back side of the house and her younger sister on the south side. If he was lucky, he could talk to her for a few moments and thank her for her help.

The stick tapped the side of the window gently and fell back to the ground. He would try only a few more times. If Eulalie didn't wake up, he would have to see her another time. He picked the stick up again and hurled it toward the window. After a few more times, the curtains moved. He stood flat against the house until he could clearly make out who it was.

The window opened slowly, squeaking along the frame. Vernon risked a look up, praying it was Eulalie. No one stuck their head out, but from where he stood, he could tell the window was still open.

"Eulalie? Are you there?" he asked in a loud whisper. His feet were pointed toward the road, ready to run off at any moment.

"Vernon, is that you?" came Eulalie's quiet reply. She stuck her head out the small window, and he stepped forward.

"What are you doing here?" she asked with a smile. Her head was wrapped up. She pulled her robe closed over her chest and rested her forearms on the windowsill. The moon shone on her face as Vernon moved to where she could see him.

"Can you come outside? I just want to talk."

Eulalie shook her head and looked back toward the inside of the house.

"If I come out, I'm going to get caught. I don't think everyone is sleeping yet, and they're going to want to know what I'm going outside for."

"I ain't gonna keep you. I know you gotta get to bed. But I know you had something to do with me getting out. So I wanted to thank you. I shouldn't have even been in there in the first place." Vernon stopped talking to look around him. He didn't see any movement, but he felt like he was being too loud. He just wanted to see her face and get out of there.

"Yeah, how did you even get picked up? When I heard you were in jail over Lloyd and Velma, I could hardly believe it. I saw everything with my own eyes."

"I should have just listened to you and left Lloyd alone. I was headed home after I dropped you off, and Lloyd and the girl were arguing in the middle of Fourth Street, in front of the pool hall. A crowd gathered, and Lloyd was getting real angry because every-body was starting to be all in his business. The more they talked, the angrier he got. Before I knew it, he was swinging on everyone and acting crazy. They called the sheriff, and I swear I was only trying to calm Lloyd down. They took me, and somehow, Lloyd disappeared into the dark. The sheriff charged me with disturb-ing the peace and loitering. I shouldn't have even been there." Vernon paced under the window. He wished he could hug Eulalie. He wished he could lay his head on her lap and let some of the pressure he felt melt away. Instead, he had to be content with hearing the silk of her voice.

"Anyhow, thank you for being there when no one else was. I'm sure it took a lot to ask your father, so thank you. Get some sleep, and I'll see you around." Vernon waved for Eulalie to step back from the window, but she held up her hands.

"Vernon, I have something to tell you."

"Tell it to Samuel, Eulalie. He's your fiancé. I'm sure he will want to hear it. I only wanted to say thanks."

"I broke it off with Samuel. I told him I couldn't marry him." She pinched her lips together.

Two minutes ago, Vernon had been ready to run, but suddenly, he was rooted in his spot. His mind raced as he thought of what Eulalie was trying to tell him. *Does her separation from Samuel have anything to do with me? Now that she isn't seeing anyone else, would she be interested in seeing me?* Vernon felt like a teenager all over again.

"Why did you do that?" Vernon asked.

"I want to be with someone else," she said.

Even under the cover of night, Vernon could see Eulalie smile widely.

"Do I know this lucky fellow?"

"You know him very well. The only issue is I don't know how he feels about me."

"Eulalie Hopewell, I'll climb up there right now and show you how I feel about you." Vernon moved to the side of the house, as if to scale the wall.

She squealed loudly in delight, and they both stopped moving for a second. Only when nothing but the sounds of evening-time animals rustling in the leaves could be heard did Vernon move again. He'd spend another night in jail if only to hear the sounds of her pleasure again.

"When can you meet me?" he asked.

"Tomorrow night. I'll meet you at ten."

"I'll be right here waiting for you. I love you, Eulalie." He waited for a moment, unable to hear over the roar of blood rushing in his ears. He couldn't believe he'd told her he loved her, but he meant it. There was no use being ashamed.

"I love you, too, Vernon." She blew him a kiss then closed the window with a squeak.

Vernon walked away, counting down the minutes until ten o'clock. Finally, Eulalie was his again.

23

Eulalie

Eulalie's pulse thumped hard when a knock on her door sounded. Vernon had just left. Had he stayed three minutes later, she would have gotten caught. But he was gone, and she was alone.

"Eulalie, are you still awake? Is everything all right in here?" Mama pushed open the door to her bedroom and looked around.

Eulalie had moved away from the window but stood in the middle of the room guiltily. She didn't have a lamp lit, nor did she have any reason to be standing there in her robe and night-gown. She probably looked like a ghost to her mother, but there was nothing she could do except smile. "Mama, I'm fine. Thank you. You can go back to bed."

"Did I hear you scream a few minutes ago? What are you doing out of bed?"

"I heard something outside. A bird knocked into the window. When I got up to look, it scared me. That's all you heard."

Mama peered around the room, like she was looking for some-thing. Eulalie didn't move, waiting. Her face was burning at her planned secret meeting. Eulalie felt like her skin was glowing. She pulled her robe tighter across her chest, trying to hide how good she felt. Her mother would never understand.

"Do you mind if I come in? I wanted to speak with you."

"Do we have to talk right now? I thought you were going to let Leona listen to the discussion."

"I did say that, but I think it's better if you and I talk alone." Mama walked in without waiting for an invitation and shut the door behind her. She shuffled into the room, her nightgown flowing, then sat on the bed and looked Eulalie up and down.

"I know you won't believe this, but I used to be young and beautiful like you." Mama gestured, inviting Eulalie to sit next to her.

"You're still beautiful. The most beautiful woman in town other than Cassidra and Leona."

Mama smiled. "You count yourself in that number also. I'm proud of all three of you girls. You're all as beautiful as you are smart." She patted Eulalie on the hand gently.

"That's not what I came here to talk to you about. I know you won't believe this, either, but... I had options when I was younger."

Eulalie was trying to follow what her mother was saying, but she wasn't sure she grasped her meaning.

Seeing the confusion on Eulalie's face, Mama took a deep breath and started again. "I was a little bit younger than you, about seventeen or eighteen, when we moved to Oklahoma Territory. Greenwood wasn't even a thing yet. The men talked about it, but back then, it was a dream. A fully colored town?" Mama let out a little laugh. "I didn't know if it could be done. Anyhow, when I was young, there were several young men who asked to court me. I talked to all of them, and they were all different and special in their own ways."

Eulalie's ears burned at Mama's speech. She was finally talking about something interesting. It had never really occurred to her that her mama had had a life before she and her sisters were born. Mama had a sister, who Eulalie hadn't seen since she was a child. She'd gotten married and moved out west with her husband to get land and start a family of their own. It gave Eulalie chills to think of her mother and aunt at the same age as her and her sisters.

"Tell me about when you met Daddy. I love hearing about it."

"I want to tell you about Joe first," Mama said.

Eulalie froze. "Joe? Who in the world is Joe?" Her eyebrows were nearly at her hairline. The conversation was getting better by the minute.

"Joe was the first man I ever loved." A small smile grew across Mama's face.

Eulalie, on the other hand, felt like she couldn't breathe. In one sentence, Mama had turned her world upside down. Eulalie had never heard her mama speak about a man named Joe. She tried to think of men in the neighborhood named Joe who were about her mama's age. She could think of a few, but none of them seemed to fit a man that Mama would have fallen in love with.

"Don't act so surprised. You think Daddy was the only person I've loved?"

"Yes, that is exactly what I thought. When did you even have time to fall in love with someone else? You got married so young. Were you even twenty?" Eulalie asked.

"I was nineteen, and Daddy was twenty-one," Mama answered with a laugh. She shifted on the bed before continuing her story. "Anyhow, yes, Joe was the handsomest man I'd ever laid eyes on. He had the most beautiful black skin that gleamed in the sunlight and a smile that would rival any angel's. His arms were so big and strong, and I loved to watch him work outside. Sometimes, when it got hot, he would take his shirt off, and…" Mama mimicked fanning herself, and the two women fell back, letting out loud peals of laughter.

Eulalie closed her eyes for a moment and let herself imagine Vernon. She thought of his well-formed shoulders and the deep veins that ran down his arms, along the round muscles. She imagined watching Vernon, wearing only a pair of short pants, jump into the lake, but then Mama's voice called her back.

"Not only was he handsome, but he was smart and kind too. Everything you could want in a man."

"Joe sounds wonderful, Mama. How come you didn't marry him?"

"You know, your daddy was a great man also. He was handsome and smart and still is. Back in the day, your daddy was very serious and cared about his studies like no other man I've ever seen. I had a serious decision to make."

"What happened?" Eulalie asked.

"When I was eighteen, Daddy asked about me first. He would come around with his very serious demeanor. Daddy did everything proper. He asked my parents for their blessing, as he should. Joe showed up one day, all brass and brawn. He was so funny and, if I'm being honest, a bit of a troublemaker, but he was so wonderful. Your daddy hadn't done so much as hold my hand, but Joe… Joe took me behind the McInnis farm and kissed me until my lips swole. At one point, I wanted to leave Daddy alone and be with Joe."

"Then what?"

"My mother pulled me aside and asked me what I wanted from my life. I told her I wanted a family. I wanted to be a wife and have a bushelful of children. You and your sisters were one of the things

I wanted most for my life." Mama ran the back of her hand sweetly along Eulalie's cheek.

"Then your grandmother asked the simple question that changed my life. She told me to look at Daddy and Joe and to decide who would be the best man to give me everything I wanted." Mama let out a small sigh then took Eulalie's hand.

"I don't deny that you may think you're in love, and there are some men that are very fun. They are a good time, no doubt about that. But what do you want for your life, Eulalie? Do you want a responsible man who will always take care of you? Or do you want a man you will have to bail out of jail? A man you will have to take care of for the rest of his life? It's something to think about, darling." Mama stood and gave Eulalie a kiss on the forehead.

"Get some sleep, and we can talk in the morning." She walked to the door, bidding Eulalie a good night, and closed it tightly behind her.

Eulalie dropped her robe on the floor by the bed. She didn't have the energy to get up and hang it up properly. All she wanted to do was lie down and think. A few minutes before, she'd wanted to sneak out of the house to meet Vernon, but her mother's story made her rethink everything. *What kind of woman do I want to be? What do I want for the rest of my life?* Eulalie pulled up the covers, knowing she probably wouldn't get much sleep.

✳✳✳✳

"Did Mama already talk to you?" Leona sat across the breakfast table from Eulalie. Her glasses slid down her nose, and she pushed them up with a huff.

Eulalie almost laughed at her sister's curious eyes. She was dying to know what they'd talked about.

Nodding, she looked over at her parents. Mama stood over Daddy, fussing. He'd asked her to fix the hem of the pants he'd been planning to wear, and Mama wanted to know why he'd waited until the last minute to ask her.

That morning at breakfast, Eulalie looked at her father a little differently. Even throughout all the hardships, trials, and life lessons, her family had been extremely happy. It had been difficult growing up as a preacher's daughter, being held to a higher standard than some of the other girls in the neighborhood, but she'd survived. Her parents had always loved and supported each other and all of their girls. She took in her daddy's creamy black skin and chubby cheeks, awed that he could have been her mother's second choice. She wouldn't have existed as the same person, perhaps not existed at all, had Mama chosen differently.

"We talked last night," Eulalie whispered over the table to Leona.

"What did she say?"

"I can't really talk about it right now. I'll have to tell you later."

Leona shook her head, unwilling to accept Eulalie's answer. "Mama, I have a baby blanket to take to Cassidra. Is it all right if Eulalie walks with me?"

Mama looked at the girls with a puzzled expression, seeming to wonder why Leona had interrupted her rant. When she shrugged, the girls excused themselves from the table and disappeared to Leona's room.

Leona's room was across the hall from Eulalie's, about the same shape and size, but it looked completely different. They both had a bed with a floral bedspread and vanity, but that was where the similarities stopped. Where Eulalie's room was neat and tidy, Leona had items lying about everywhere. Her vanity was covered in random bits of fabric where Leona had been practicing her sewing. Stacks of books sat in each corner of the room, and a pile of skirts lay on the bed. Leona snatched a bag filled with cloth, and the two ladies rushed outside before Mama could stop them.

"Girl, you'd better clean that room before Mama sees. She's already mad at Daddy. You'll be next on the list," Eulalie said.

"Don't worry about that right now. Tell me what Mama said." Leona huffed from the exertion and handed the bag to Eulalie.

"Mama wanted to talk about a man named Joe and how much she loved him until Daddy came around."

Leona's mouth fell open in the same manner as Eulalie's had when her mother first mentioned it.

Eulalie couldn't help the little laugh that escaped her mouth. She nodded and continued the story. "Yes, she said that Joe was kind of wild, but he was so handsome, and he used to kiss Mama behind a barn when she was your age."

"I wish I had a handsome beau," Leona said.

As they walked the mile to Cassidra's home, Eulalie recounted Mama's story to Leona. Leona listened intently, offering an excited gasp or raised eyebrow when necessary. Before they knew it, they were climbing the front stairs of their sister's stately home.

Cassidra lived on the other side of town, in one of the larger, newer homes. Her house had a full two stories with four bedrooms on the second floor. The home had been painted white and had a large, well-manicured lawn that surrounded the house. Ever since she'd married Dr. George, Cassidra had all the latest advancements and more than enough space to start a family. Eulalie and Leona loved to visit, touching all of Cassidra's nice things and playing in her cosmetics.

When Cassidra opened the front door, Eulalie and Leona ambushed her with a flurry of hugs and kisses. Reunited, the girls fell into a familiar rhythm of sisterly consternation and affection. Cassidra welcomed her sisters into the drawing room, where Eulalie had to recount Mama's story all over.

"She never told me any of that. Why did she tell you?" Cassidra took a sip of tea and balanced the cup momentarily on her motherly belly.

Eulalie shrugged, wanting to avoid the question, but Leona piped up. "She's been seeing Vernon Jackson. That's why Mama told her."

Eulalie flicked Leona hard in the arm, making her sister grimace. Cassidra's eyes turned to slits as she watched the girls engage in horseplay on her expensive seating.

"I swear I will put you two out if you spill anything. I have to keep this room nice for all the visitors we keep having." She moved her own teacup to a side table. "Go back and tell me. What does she mean, you've 'been seeing Vernon Jackson'?"

"Well... I'm not really seeing Vernon. It's just... I called off the engagement... with Samuel."

Eulalie didn't know where to start. She took a moment to clear her thoughts before starting again. "Samuel is a very nice man. We all can see that. But he's not the man for me. I just don't see myself being married to him for the rest of my life. He doesn't even make me laugh."

"I suppose Vernon makes you laugh," Cassidra said sarcastically.

How am I supposed to tell my sister, who sits and mocks me, that yes, Vernon makes her laugh? He made her smile. He made her feel beautiful and wanted and wonderful.

"This is not about Vernon," Eulalie said.

"Then what is it about?" Cassidra asked.

"It's about me and what I want from my life. Mama asked me to think of what was important for me. What did I want for my life? So, Cassidra, I'm asking you. What do you want for your life?"

Cassidra waved her hands around to indicate her surroundings. "This is what I want. I wanted a nice house and a comfortable life. I want a man who takes care of me and makes me happy. I want children, and I want to be a good mom, like our mother was to us."

Eulalie was happy for her sister that she'd gotten everything she wanted. But she had to think about herself. For the next hour, Eulalie spoke about her feelings for Vernon and how she'd promised to meet him later. They talked about how he'd spent time at the school with the children and how he made her feel.

"So Vernon is your Joe, and Samuel is Daddy. Who are you going to choose? What do you want for your life?" Leona had finished her tea and sat looking at Eulalie.

Cassidra had her arms crossed, but so far, she'd been listening.

"At some point, I want children. And I do want to be married." Eulalie bit her lip and thought through what she wanted to say. "I want to have a happy home. I want a man I'm happy to see when I wake up, one who loves me."

"Oh my Lord, gal, you're going to ruin your life," Cassidra said with a huff. "You're worried about the wrong things. That's what Mama was trying to tell you. There's so much more to life than laughing. Vernon's going to have you living out on the street. Then we'll see how funny life is."

"Well, I think it's romantic. True love always wins," Leona said.

Cassidra stood to gather their tea service, and Leona and Eulalie jumped to help her clean.

As they were walking to the kitchen, Eulalie asked, "Sidra, do you mind if I tell Mama I'm spending the night over here tonight?"

Leona clapped happily, but Cassidra crossed her arms.

"I will do this for you this one time, but you need to figure your life out and soon." Cassidra's lips were tight, but Eulalie knew her sister would always have her back.

"Are you sure Vernon is what you want?" Leona asked.

"I don't know for certain, but I feel like tonight will make it very clear if we're supposed to be together."

Cassidra rolled her eyes but pulled her sisters into a hug. "We will figure it out together."

24

Vernon

Vernon waited at the end of Eulalie's street and tried to see his watch in the dark. It was five minutes past ten, and the block was eerily silent. All the homes, including Eulalie's, were completely dark. No one walked outside, and no traffic could be heard from any of the nearby streets. The wind wasn't blowing. Even the summertime grasshoppers had taken the evening off. Nature seemed to be conspiring to get Vernon caught, standing in the darkness, but he wouldn't be deterred. Eulalie had said she would meet him at ten o'clock. Therefore, he would wait for her.

What if she doesn't show up? The small voice in the back of his mind nagged him. *Would she not show up because she didn't want to or because she couldn't?*

A whisper shot through the shadows, jolting him. "Vernon, over here." Eulalie walked up from behind him with a bag slung over her shoulder.

"What are you doing here? I was waiting for you to come out."

"I told Mama I was spending the night at Cassidra's. You know there's no way for me to sneak out of the house. Mama can hear everything, and she never sleeps." She stopped in front of him and held her arms open wide.

Vernon stepped forward, accepting her invitation, and wrapped his arms around her, enjoying the feel of her body pressed against his. He brought his face down to meet hers and placed a gentle kiss on her lips. He'd been thinking of her tender touch and sweet mouth since the moment he'd left her house the night before. Now that she was in his arms, he felt a genuine sense of peace surrounding him.

"You said you wanted to see me, and here I am," Eulalie cooed. "What are you going to do with me?"

Vernon's blood heated. Her sultry teasing danced into his ears and sent currents of excitement coursing through him. He ran his hands over the small of her back. Before he could stop himself, he palmed the round curve of her bottom and pulled her closer.

Eulalie let out a contented gasp and brought her lips to meet his again.

They stood in the darkness of the street, relishing the sweet taste of each other. It felt sordid, like they were doing something where they shouldn't. They could be caught at any time, be seen by any of the church members and neighbors, but still, she insisted on being there with him. In all the times he'd been with women, it had never felt so sensual as when he was with Eulalie.

"You do something to my good senses. I can't explain it," Eulalic said when their lips parted.

"Do you want to go back to my house?" Vernon asked. "At first, I only wanted a small taste, but now, I don't want to let you go."

Eulalie nodded and joined her hand with his. He closed his fingers around her delicate ones, and they walked toward his house.

Vernon had never walked with a woman and held her hand. It had never even occurred to him to do something like that, but in that ten-minute trip to his house, with Eulalie's hand in his, he felt like a different man.

****

Vernon opened the door to his home and let Eulalie step in ahead of him. She waited off to the side as he went around the house, lighting a few of the lamps. Now that he had her there alone, Vernon found himself a bit nervous. He'd hosted other women before, but Eulalie was special. She was the girl he'd wanted for his entire life, and he had to impress her.

"Can I get you something to drink?" he asked.

Eulalie shook her head and walked around. She stared at his family picture on the mantel and walked around the room like she was seeing it for the first time. "You have a nice home. You're very lucky. Do you plan to always stay here?"

Vernon shrugged. He hadn't really thought about it. "It doesn't make much sense to move to another house when I have a perfectly good one."

"Do you mind if I have a look around?"

"Be my guest."

Eulalie walked through the sparsely furnished living room. When Pearl lived there, she'd had it decorated with fancy lamps, rugs, and wall hangings. Now that he lived alone, the room seemed underdressed.

She walked to the closed door that sat between the couch and front door and pushed it open. It had been his sister's room. Save for the bed that was still pushed up against the wall, it was mostly empty. She had taken her dresser and vanity with her.

Eulalie's shoes clicked along the wooden floor as she walked around. When she was finished, she pushed open a door on the other wall to the small washroom. She ran her fingers along the tiled wall and looked into the bathtub as if inspecting it. Continuing straight, Vernon followed her through the other door in the bathroom that led to the kitchen. From the kitchen, she explored the extra bedroom, which had been his as a child and had become the room where he took care of all the liquor he produced. She meandered into the dining room, having made the full circle of the home.

"What do you think?" he asked.

"It certainly needs a woman's touch. You need new curtains and something pretty to please the eye. There's nothing in here to look at."

Vernon nodded at her assessment. The place was functional, a place to lay his head. He didn't need to have anything exciting to look at. *What's the purpose of rushing home to look at a nicely decorated home when no one else is there?*

"I didn't see your room. Will you show it to me?" She turned sweetly on her heel toward him.

Vernon took her hand and led her to the back of the house, down a short dark hallway.

Vernon thanked God he'd cleaned everything that morning. He hadn't expected her presence that evening, but the potential existed, so he wasn't taking any chances. He'd mopped all the floors until they shone. His bed linen was clean and pulled up neatly. He might not have much to look at in his home, but by God, it was clean.

Vernon let Eulalie walk around the room to look at everything, and he lay on the bed, watching her. She pulled open the door of his closet to sneak a peek inside.

"Did you find what you were looking for?" he asked.

Eulalie smiled. "I wasn't looking for anything in particular."

"Then what were you doing?"

"Just seeing where I would fit into your life." She moved over to the bed and pushed him lightly. "Scoot over. Let's see if you have room."

Vernon's crotch hardened at her touch.

Eulalie pulled off her shoes then lay on the bed next to him. "Do you mind if I sleep with you tonight? I want you to show me what it would be like to be your wife." She rolled closer to him and put her arm around his waist.

He met her hand, entwining his fingers with hers. "I didn't bring you here to take advantage of you. I only wanted to spend time with you." He twisted his body to press a kiss to her mouth.

She answered with warmth and passion. He licked her lips teasingly, nibbling and sucking, making her moan. She let her hand travel down his stomach to rest on his growing manhood. Even through his trousers, he felt the heat of her hand.

In the span of moments, they'd gone from respect to full-fledged intimacy. He wanted nothing more than to take her, but trying to move slowly was like trying to stop an advancing train.

"You're not taking advantage of me," she whispered between kisses. "I wanted to be here with you. I'm not interested in anyone else."

"You've always been mine. I don't care what anyone says." He moved his kisses down to her neck. "I don't care who thinks they're going to marry you."

"I'm yours right now. Show me what you'll do for me."

Eulalie's breathy words almost sent him over the edge, but he focused on her writhing body next to him. He carefully unbuttoned her shirt and skirt, trailing kisses over her bare skin. She eased up just enough to allow him to remove her clothing.

"I brought a nightgown. Should I put it on?"

"Baby, you won't need it. Not tonight." He breathed slow, measured caresses down the length of her body before loosening the rest of her garments, her body quivering in the cool air.

"Wait, Vernon. Please don't finish inside me."

He kissed her fingertips and laced his fingers with hers. "I will always be careful to not spill my seed in you. We can go as far as you want."

Once Eulalie lay on the bed completely nude, Vernon stood to remove his clothing. Her nipples shone like dark gems, making his mouth water. The curve of her hips and the apex of her heat called to him, making him harder. He moved on top of her gently, settling his shoulders between her legs. He trailed kisses along the plane of her stomach, enjoying the rise and fall. When he reached her tangle of curls, he kept going, letting his tongue take over. Eulalie almost levitated off the bed when he swiped his tongue in the manna of her love.

"Lie back and let me taste you." He licked and sucked her until she screamed for salvation.

"Vernon, where in the world did you learn that?" Her chest heaved.

He crawled up to suck her nipple, which tasted like sugar. After separating her thighs, he pushed himself between them and positioned his manhood at her entrance. He moved slowly, inch by inch, savoring the soaking-wet folds of her love.

"Eulalie, I love you. Please know that you feel so good."

She moaned unabashedly at his slow stroking. It was going to be his undoing. He'd never thought the day would come, and he was going to enjoy every moment.

****

Basking in the warmth of Eulalie's nearness, Vernon closed his arms around her and pulled the covers over them. He felt like he'd died and gone to heaven. Eulalie was in his bed, naked. He couldn't remember feeling so on top of the world before.

"What do you want for your life?" Eulalie asked, interrupting his musings.

"This is exactly what I want."

He ran a finger over her nipple, and her body responded to his touch. She let out a soft whine, making his manhood stand at attention again.

"No, I'm serious." She took his hand from her breast, brought it to her mouth, and kissed it softly. "Are you going to brew alcohol forever, or will you work somewhere else?"

"I'm sure I'll figure out something else," he said.

"Are you going to live in this house forever?"

"What's wrong with this house?"

"Nothing. I just wanted to know if you planned on raising children here."

"I guess I never thought about it."

"You never thought about having children? If we keep carrying on like this, I'm sure it's inevitable."

"You're right. Maybe we shouldn't do it again. I would like to be a papa one day, though." Vernon smiled and traced his fingers over the outline of her lush lips. "Why do you have so many questions tonight?"

She shrugged. Turning to face him, she said, "You are the only man I've given myself to, and I just wonder... I wonder if you've considered our future or if you really like me like I like you."

"I love you, Eulalie. I like you, and I love you. I don't know what the future holds, but I do know that I want you here with me."

"Do you want to marry me?" she asked.

"Of course I want to marry you someday. I love you, but I want to court you properly. I've been given a second chance, and I want to make sure I do this right. Can you give me some time to get my life together? I can't have you living in this house with nothing."

He pulled her closer and pressed kisses into the crook of her neck. She turned her back to him, and he pulled their bodies together. Vernon closed his eyes and thought about all the things he was going to do to make her his wife.

****

Eulalie jumped from the bed with a start and looked frantically for her clothing. Vernon sat up, watching her with sleepy eyes.

"I slept too long. I didn't mean to. The sun is all the way out, and I can't be seen here. Lord, I'm going to get in trouble." She slid into her stockings and fumbled with her skirt.

Although he was having fun watching her, he ambled out of bed to help her pull her clothes together. "Eulalie, you're a woman now. You're not a little girl. Who's going to get you in trouble?" He handed her shirt over and watched as she put it on.

"You don't understand. I still have to live with my parents. If they put me out, I don't have any place to go."

Their eyes met. Before Vernon could tell her that she could stay with him, he remembered he had a surprise for her.

"Wait, I was going to make you breakfast." He moved to find his own clothes so he could get to the kitchen.

Eulalie narrowed her eyes at him. "*You* were going to make breakfast? Since when do you cook?"

Vernon smiled sheepishly. "I don't, and I'm not very good, but I had Al show me. I wanted to make something special for you."

Eulalie stopped putting her shoes on, and a smile grew across her face. She rushed over to him and planted a big kiss on his mouth.

"I can't stay. I've got to get back to my sister's house. But if you plan to court me properly, then I can't wait for breakfast. We'll have to do it another time."

He returned her kiss, and they finished dressing before he reluctantly walked her to the door. She'd insisted it would be better if she saw herself back to Cassidra's, so he left her with a hug and a promise that he'd see her soon.

25

Eulalie

Eulalie sat down in the chair at Ray's Café and tried to hide her grin. Leona and Cassidra settled into chairs on the other side of the table and looked at her expectantly. She'd refused to tell them anything until they were seated and comfortable. They only had a few minutes, and Eulalie wanted to tell them everything. Henrietta, Ray's waitress, brought them all glasses of water then disappeared to help another table.

"Tell me everything," Cassidra said.

Even though Eulalie knew she didn't completely approve, she was not going to be left out.

"Thank you both for being so understanding about all of this," Eulalie said. "I know it's not proper. You two are the only ones I can talk to."

"I understand falling in love with a man and letting him go too far. George and I certainly… weren't proper. But why Vernon Jackson? He's always been such a troublemaker. What do you even see in him?" Cassidra turned her nose up at the mention of Vernon. At least Eulalie didn't have to worry about one of her sisters having a secret crush on Vernon.

"You don't know him like I do, but I'm hoping you will. He's warm and caring and has always looked out for me."

"So what happened?" Leona asked.

"We went to his house and... you know." Eulalie blushed. Even though her sisters were understanding, she didn't need to spell everything out.

"Was it good?" Leona asked.

Eulalie nodded, still trying to keep herself from smiling. "I enjoyed it very much," she admitted.

Cassidra sat forward as much as her belly would allow. "Of course you enjoyed it. From what I've heard, he's certainly had enough practice." She took a sip of water and rolled her eyes at Eulalie.

"Oh, stop it, Cassidra. Besides, it's probably better than someone like Samuel, who looks like he's only been kissing his mother," Leona teased.

Henrietta walked over to the table, and the conversation stopped. They gave her their orders and resumed talking once she was far enough away from the table.

"So is he going to marry you?" Cassidra asked.

"He said he wants to court me first."

"Of course he does. What does this courting look like? You coming to his house in the late hours of the evening or actually taking you out on the town? You've already gone too far. You may as well make it official."

Leona shifted in her seat but didn't say anything. Eulalie studied her sisters, feeling the air at the table shift.

Cassidra reached across the table and patted Eulalie's hand. "I'm not trying to give you a hard time. I just want you to think about some things. I certainly understand that love makes us blind, and I want you to see what we see. The fact that you had to sneak out to meet him should tell you everything you need to know."

"I only have to sneak out to meet him because Mama and Daddy don't like him."

"That should tell you something too. Daddy is a preacher. Why wouldn't he like him if he wasn't a troublemaker?"

Eulalie huffed. "He's not the same man he was when we were teenagers."

"Did you look around his house?"

"Yes."

"And did you like what you saw? Could you see yourself living there?" Cassidra asked.

"There would certainly need to be some updates. He needs new furniture. His room still looks like it belongs to his parents. I could take care of that." Vernon certainly hadn't done it, and she didn't trust his taste.

"Does he have money to update everything, or will y'all be living hand to mouth, just happy to have a roof over your heads?" Cassidra asked.

"Well, we don't all have doctors for husbands, Cassidra, so we all won't be living like kings. Some of us have to find happiness elsewhere." Eulalie's retort was sharper than she'd wanted, but she couldn't help herself. She knew her sister was only trying to be helpful, but she didn't like the way she was taking licks for no reason. She hadn't even spent any time with Vernon, especially since they'd grown. They were all different.

The ladies chatted until hot food sat in front of them. Eulalie tried to dig into the smothered pork chops and gravy but found she couldn't taste a thing. She was chewing through the over-cooked meat when the bell on the front door sounded.

"What did you do? Did you know about this?" Cassidra hissed through gritted teeth.

Eulalie turned to see Vernon sauntering toward their table, carrying a bunch of freshly cut flowers. He'd traded in his usual brown pants and white cotton shirt for a navy-blue striped suit. His hair had been cut short and his face clean-shaven. He looked like a different man from the one she'd seen earlier. Eulalie liked that. He looked so handsome.

She'd mentioned to him that she'd try to get her sisters out to lunch, and it would be nice if he could come meet them. But she hadn't expected that he would actually show.

Vernon threaded his way through the tables to the ladies. Eulalie could only pray that her sisters wouldn't give him as hard of a time as they'd given her. The women stood as Vernon approached the table. He stood closest to Leona, who couldn't contain the excitement on her face. She opened her arms for a hug, and Vernon bent down and obliged. He stepped around to Cassidra and offered her a polite hug, which she allowed with a smaller, less ostentatious smile. He handed Cassidra the flowers then walked around the table to stand next to Eulalie.

"Do you ladies mind if I join you?"

Leona all but tripped over herself welcoming him to the table.

"Thank you for the flowers. Do you want to order something?" Eulalie asked.

Vernon shook his head.

"I'm only here to enjoy y'all's company. It feels good to be in the presence of such beautiful women. I think I might've died and gone to heaven."

The sisters laughed as a relaxed air fell over the table. Vernon asked about Cassidra and her pregnancy, which made her smile. As Cassidra launched into a story, Vernon rubbed Eulalie's thigh under the table, causing a firestorm in her belly. She'd never thought the day would come. She was seated at a table with Vernon and her sisters, and everyone was laughing. Eulalie couldn't remember being so happy. His touch ignited her memory of the passion they'd shared.

"So what are your intentions with our dear Eulalie here?" Cassidra asked, cutting down to brass tacks. She was the type who was going to be cordial for only so long before she got down to business. Cassidra kept her eyes focused on Vernon, seeming to refuse to make eye contact with Eulalie.

"I'm proud to say that I'm in love with your sister. I've been in love with her for our entire lives." Vernon smiled easily. He grabbed her thigh tightly under the table, and she let her hand rest on top of his.

This was just the first step of many. If she could get her sisters on Vernon's side, they would help convince Mama. If all the girls were on their side, Daddy couldn't help but agree.

"How do you plan to take care of Eulalie?" Cassidra asked.

"I will do whatever it takes. I'm no stranger to working the fields, if that's what I have to do." He moved his hand from under the table and rested his arm around her shoulders.

Pleased by the embrace, Eulalie leaned into him.

"Oh my God, no," Leona muttered.

"I'm sorry. I didn't hear you," Vernon said to Leona, but her eyes were trained on the front door.

Samuel walked in and looked around. He locked eyes with Eulalie and made his way straight to their table.

"Hello, ladies. Eulalie, what are you doing here?"

She could feel Vernon remove his arm and turn to face Samuel. It wasn't lost on her that he hadn't spoken to Vernon.

"How did you know we were here?" she asked, avoiding his question.

"I just returned and went to your house. Your mother said you were here eating with your sisters but didn't mention anything about him."

"What do you mean, Samuel? Am I not allowed to have lunch?" Eulalie pasted a smile on her face that didn't feel real.

"You shouldn't be eating lunch with any other man than your fiancé. I won't stand for you running around town, doing whatever you want."

"I told you I didn't want to be married. I don't think we should be talking about this here and now." Eulalie's cheeks warmed as everyone in the diner turned to look at their table.

"No, I want to talk now," Samuel said. "Tell me what you're doing here with him when we're supposed to be engaged." Samuel stood over her, his voice rising with each syllable.

Eulalie frowned and looked past him, seeing the ten other patrons staring back at her and the table. The diner had gone completely silent, everyone interested in what was happening.

"She said she doesn't want to talk right now. She's trying to enjoy her lunch. Maybe she'll come find you later." Vernon stood and pushed his chair back with a loud squeak.

Samuel turned his attention from Eulalie, finally allowing himself to make eye contact with Vernon. He puffed out his chest and squared his shoulders. "You think I'm afraid of you? I'm not. You're nothing but a poor, local troublemaker who likes to prey on innocent women. I've heard all about you, so I'm not surprised you've tricked these women into being here with you."

Eulalie could feel the heat rolling off Vernon in waves. She was seated between them, but the two men inched closer together with each word. To her left, Vernon's fists were opening and closing involuntarily. To her right, Samuel's chest heaved.

"Why don't you come over here and say that to my face?" Vernon said coldly.

"I'll always speak the truth, especially when it comes to the woman I love. I don't care who's in the way," Samuel said.

Eulalie pushed back her chair and stood between them. She turned her face to Vernon and pushed Samuel back with her right hand.

"Please don't do this," she said to Vernon, trying to get him to look at her. He shrugged off her words and stared at Samuel, shooting daggers at the shorter man.

"Don't worry about him. I think we should all just leave." Eulalie looked over at her sisters, who sat unmoving on the other side of the table. Leona's mouth could have held an entire bushel of berries for how far it was open.

"Help me," she mouthed.

Cassidra rubbed her belly and shook her head. Leona seemed to be stuck in a trance, her eyes moving back and forth between Vernon and Samuel.

"I don't know what's going on over here, but I can't have all that yelling! Y'all need to kiss and make up or take that shit outside!" Ray screamed from inside the kitchen, but he didn't move away from the grill. If there was someone in the eatery who hadn't been watching, they certainly were now. Noises rushed around her, but all Eulalie could hear was the whooshing of blood in her ears.

"Keep your hands off my girl, or I'll whoop your ass," Samuel said finally. He winked at Vernon then pulled Eulalie's hand down from his chest and captured it in his.

Vernon moved so quickly Eulalie didn't even see it happen. He spun around her, lifted his clenched fist, and punched Samuel square in the jaw. Time stood still. For a split second, the world moved so slowly that Eulalie could see everything.

Regret painted Samuel's face as he processed what had happened. Anger flowed off Vernon in waves. Shock covered Leona's face, but Cassidra's was nothing but a mask of fear. A cacophony of emotions surrounded Eulalie, and there was nothing she could do. Samuel wavered on his feet before finally falling to the floor, breaking the delicate bubble of the frozen tableau.

Henrietta screamed when Samuel's body slumped to the floor and pulled everyone out of their frozen state. Walter Gibbs, a man who'd been sitting at the counter, rushed over to Vernon and pulled him away from the table.

"Whoop my ass! I want to see you do it!" Vernon called roughly to Samuel's writhing body.

Walter pulled Vernon away and rushed him out the door as Cassidra and Eulalie moved to hover over Samuel, who moaned as they helped him sit up. Eulalie watched Vernon walk out, yelling as he exited. Then she turned her attention to Samuel.

"Do you think we should take him to see George?" Leona asked.

Cassidra shook her head and moved closer to Samuel. She took his chin in her hand and studied both sides of his face.

"No, he's going to be okay. His cheek will be a bit swollen for a while, but nothing else is broken."

When his eyes were clearer, Eulalie reached out to help Samuel stand.

"Come on, everyone. Let's pay and go home." Cassidra walked to the front to pay at the till.

Eulalie wrapped her arms around Samuel and walked with him toward the door. Leona followed then stopped to grab the bunch of flowers that still rested on the table. Eulalie kept her head low, refusing to meet any of the other diners' eyes. There would be talk.

She was sure of it. She could do nothing except keep her shoulders straight and her chin proud.

****

Once the girls made it back home, Samuel said he would call on Eulalie later and left the three of them standing on the porch. He walked away sheepishly, without turning back to look at her.

"Jesus, Eulalie. Are you sure that's what you want?" Cassidra asked.

"Don't use the Lord's name in vain, Sidra," Leona remarked.

Cassidra cut her eyes at her baby sister then turned her attention back to Eulalie. "You know exactly what I mean. Vernon is unstable and just as wild as when we were kids. Nothing has changed."

Eulalie didn't answer her sister. Instead, she watched Samuel walk down the street alone and felt sorry for him. As much as she wanted Vernon, something pulled in her.

"You can't marry him, Eulalie," Cassidra said.

"Just leave it alone, Cassidra. I'll figure it all out!" Eulalie screamed, pinching back tears.

26

Vernon

"You know Pearl's beside herself, right?" Al straightened his tie in the mirror. Seeming unsatisfied with the way it looked, he undid it all and started over again.

Vernon sat on the bed with his face in his hands. They were in Al's bedroom, getting ready for the wedding. All Vernon wanted to do was go home and stay there, but he had to be there for his best friend and sister. It was their special day, and no matter how much people talked about him, he had to show up.

"Birdie needs to take a deep breath and relax. I ain't gonna do nothing to ruin her day."

"You don't have to tell me that. I'm not worried about 'my wedding.'" Al dragged "my wedding" out in a high-pitched voice, obviously mimicking Pearl. "I thought she didn't even want a big wedding, and now here we are." Al fussed with his tie until it looked appropriate. Then he tucked his shirt in, pulled it out from the band of his pants, and started again. "Tell me what happened."

"The man came into Ray's with his chest puffed out. He was talking loud to Eulalie and being rude at the table in front of her sisters. Then he said he was gon' whoop my ass, so I clocked him in the jaw." Vernon gave a slight shrug. *What else was I supposed to do? Sit there quietly and let the man scream at everyone?*

"Well, he is her fiancé. If I found out someone was taking Pearl out and having lunch with her, I'd puff out my chest too."

"She told me she called the whole thing off. She said she wasn't engaged to him anymore."

Al inhaled sharply, but he didn't say anything. He stopped fumbling with his clothes and turned to face Vernon instead of looking in the mirror. "When's the last time you saw Eulalie?"

"Last weekend, when it happened. Walter had to walk me out of there. I was so mad my fists were shaking. I didn't get to say anything to her."

"You know the Hopewells will be here today. That won't be a problem, will it?" Al turned back to the mirror and started fiddling with his shirt again.

Vernon shook his head. He wasn't sure if Al didn't see or just chose to turn back around.

"Do yourself and me a favor and stay away from Eulalie. At least for today but maybe forever. Find someone else to fool around with who doesn't have a preacher for a daddy."

Vernon huffed. He didn't want to talk about Eulalie anymore. "Alfred, listen. I know Pearl is my sister, but I have to ask you. Are you sure you want to do this?" His voice cracked. He was stuck in the middle of the two, Pearl as his sister and Alfred as his best friend. If Al didn't want to get married to his sister, Vernon was going to support him and figure out how to somehow pick up the pieces of his sister's broken heart. There was no use getting married if he didn't really want to be.

Al smiled widely at himself in the mirror. "What are you going to do if I say I don't want to?"

"If I'm truthful, I'll probably take a swing at you, too, for break-ing my sister's heart," Vernon said with a smile.

Al laughed along with him. "Pearl means the world to me. I should have married her a long time ago. Besides, I thought you said you was going to be on your best behavior today." Al fixed his shirt one last time then turned toward Vernon with his arms out. "Do I look all right?"

Vernon stood and swept Al into a brotherly hug. Had it been anyone else, Vernon would have spent the afternoon talking about how they were losing their manhood that day. He'd had jokes pre-pared about wives ruining their spirits, but as he watched his best friend get ready, nothing seemed funny.

Vernon was overfilled with love and respect for his friend. He'd taken the mature route and was ready to make an honest woman out of his sister, the woman who'd been there for the both of them. Vernon's heart was so full he could have shed a few tears. Instead, he helped Al into his suit jacket, dusted off his shoulders, then put his own suit jacket on.

Later on in the church, Vernon sat with Al in one of the back rooms, waiting. Al paced nervously as Vernon stood next to the window. The murmur of guests broke through the thin door. From his position, Vernon looked out on the back of the church. A white tent had been set up, where all of the community would have dinner and fun after the wedding. Women hustled in and out of the church, working to set everything up. Mother Edith shook her hand at someone Vernon couldn't see. He wondered if it was Eulalie. *Is she out there hustling around, trying to make sure every-thing's nice? Is she thinking about me the way I'm thinking of her?*

The door squeaked open, and Reverend Hopewell walked in. He was dressed in his long pastoral robes with a small red cross on the right breast. The older man cleared his throat and walked over to Al.

"I'm going to go check on the bride. I'm supposed to be walking her down the aisle." Vernon shook Al's hand and walked around Reverend Hopewell. He didn't want to take away from Al's day and was certain the reverend had heard of the kerfuffle that happened in Ray's.

As Vernon entered the nursery, Pearl turned around to face him. She was a beaming beacon of light dressed in a white gown covered in lace. Vernon took in the beauty of his sister, who looked so much like their mother that he felt his breath catch. Her long veil floated around her.

"Whatever you do, don't touch her. We spent hours getting ready," a sharp voice called from her side. Pearl's best friend, Loretta, crossed her arms over her ample chest and frowned at him.

Loretta was about half as tall as Pearl, with voluptuous curves in all the right places.

"Shut it, Loretta," Vernon said with a wink as he made his way closer to Pearl.

Carefully, he pulled Pearl into a hug and gave her a light kiss on the cheek. "You look beautiful, Pearl, just like Mama. Al's gonna fall over when he sees you." He'd paid to have her dress custom made, his gift to her. She looked like a dream, with full sleeves and beading work.

Pearl beamed at his compliment. She gave a small nod of thanks then waved her hand in front of her face to keep from crying.

"Pearlie, I know it's a little late, but I just want to make sure. Are you certain you want to do this? You don't have to."

Uncharacteristically sweet and calm, she answered, "I'm sure, Vernon. Thank you for checking."

A knock sounded at the door. Mother Edith walked in and cooed over Pearl and her dress. "Everyone is seated and ready for you to make your grand entrance."

Vernon extended his arm, and Pearl tucked her hand into the crook of his elbow.

"Let's go get married," he said as they walked to the entryway of the church.

Loretta followed. Once they were at the door to the sanctuary, she looked over Pearl's dress one more time before spreading the dress and veil to trail. When Pearl was as perfect as a picture, he squeezed her hand. Loretta opened one door to the sanctuary, Mother Edith opened the other, and Pearl and Vernon stepped forward.

The church was crowded with congregants and friends alike. Vernon smiled hard as he escorted Pearl down the aisle in careful, measured steps. The organ played the powerful wedding march as they made their way closer to the beaming Al. Vernon looked at his friend, who only had eyes for Pearl.

Vernon was about halfway down the aisle when he saw Eulalie. She was seated on the left side of the church, his side, and he looked up and locked eyes with her. He smiled before he could stop himself. She stood on the end of the row, toward the front of the church, next to her two sisters and her mother.

Eulalie broke their eye contact, turning forward without smiling back. Vernon focused all his attention on getting Pearl down the aisle. When he passed Eulalie's row, his body swirled with an unregulated heat. At the end, he shook Al's hand, helped Pearl forward, then took his place. He couldn't worry about Eulalie at the moment. There would be time to talk later.

27

Eulalie

Watching Pearl walk around in her wedding dress made Eulalie want to cry. Emotions bubbled within her. She thought Pearl was the most beautiful bride she'd seen since Cassidra got married.

Pearl and Alfred seemed to genuinely love each other. When Daddy declared them husband and wife, Alfred pulled Pearl close to him and gingerly placed a kiss on her mouth. Most people shied away from watching the new couple's first kiss, but Eulalie couldn't take her eyes off them. From a few pews back, Eulalie could plainly see how much they cared for each other. The two of them turned to the crowd as the congregation cheered, and Pearl glowed. Eulalie tried to tamp down the jealousy rising in her throat but found it was making her choke. She wanted the love and peace that surrounded the two of them—wanted the excitement and happiness that the community was pouring on the newlyweds. She wanted her daddy to marry her and wanted him to be proud of her husband.

A tear formed in her eye. She tried to blink it away, but it trailed down the side of her nose.

"Oh my Lord, girl, are you crying?" Leona asked.

Eulalie nodded. "It's just so beautiful," she lied. Even though the wedding *was* beautiful, it wasn't why she was crying. She wondered if she would ever have a wedding like theirs. As it stood, Eulalie was probably never going to get married.

Pearl and Al walked down the aisle toward the back of the church, with Vernon trailing behind. Her eyes locked on Vernon's face, but he refused to glance her way, instead keeping his eyes trained on the retreating couple. He'd looked at her on the way to the front, and she hadn't been able to hold his gaze. Now, she stared him down, hoping he'd acknowledge her again.

She watched Vernon's tall frame walk past her, and her body ached to be wrapped in his arms. His suit fit extremely well, the dark fabric complementing his gleaming brown skin. She watched him as far as her eyes could see without turning around then moved her attention back to the front. She glanced up to see her father staring at her. Eulalie's face burned, like she'd been caught sneaking, but she kept a small smile on her face. Eulalie hadn't done anything wrong. She couldn't help how she felt for Vernon, no matter how much her father disapproved.

Turning, she followed the crowd from the pews into what was surely going to be a long evening.

****

Eulalie stepped out into the warm summer evening amid the joyous sounds of celebration. Neither Pearl nor Alfred had much family, but the community had shown up to celebrate nonetheless. Churchgoers gathered, giving hugs and greetings like they hadn't seen one another in years. They couldn't have picked a nicer afternoon.

The smell of cooked meats filled the air. A line formed, snaking around tables and chairs that had been set up for the celebration. Instead of standing in line to get food, Mama greeted each person with kisses and a smile. Eulalie and Leona waited at a table in the back.

"Is Samuel going to be here tonight?" Leona asked.

Eulalie shrugged. "I haven't heard from him since he left our house."

Leona nodded. "I guess I wouldn't show my face either."

"He doesn't really know many people in town except the few he works with. I don't think he's ever met Pearl or Alfred."

"Looks like Vernon is going to play music," Leona said.

Eulalie followed her sister's gaze toward where Vernon stood with the band. They were setting up their instruments, laughing together.

"Have you spoken with Vernon?"

"No, I haven't." The truth was that Eulalie was afraid. He still held a soft place in her heart, but watching him hit Samuel had scared her. She'd never seen two grown men physically fight.

Eulalie watched the men until Loretta LeMieux sidled up next to Vernon and let her hand rest on the small of his back. Loretta said something to the men without moving her hand from Vernon, which made them all burst into laughter. From where she stood, Eulalie could see Loretta's dress was too tight around the hips and low cut in the bust. When Vernon looked down the front of Loretta's dress, Eulalie had to turn her back. She refused to stand there and watch him take in the sultry woman's features. Standing there in her prudish dress, Eulalie let her shoulders sag.

The girls stood in the line to get food and eventually sat at a table with Mama, Cassidra, and Dr. George. Daddy waited until everyone else had gotten a plate before joining the family at the table.

When everyone had eaten, Vernon stepped to the front of the band, calling everyone's attention to him.

"Thank you, everyone, for being here to celebrate my sister and best friend's wedding. If you don't mind, we'd like to play a little music."

The crowd gave a roar of approval, making Vernon smile. The band burst into a lively round of ragtime. Al led Pearl out to the front of the tables, where the band played. He spun her with one hand and dipped her low, eliciting cheers. Pearl blushed and waved her hand nervously.

Vernon pulled the trumpet from his mouth and shouted, "We need someone to come up here and sing! Who's got the best pipes around?"

A murmur spread across the celebrants, each one pointing at someone else. Eulalie was enjoying the show until Ray Jenkins stood, pointed at her, and responded, "Let Eulalie sing. She has the most beautiful voice."

Eulalie shook her head in protest, but the more she said no, the louder everyone became.

"Go on up, Eulalie. Let them hear you sing," Mama said.

Eulalie stood up and wobbled her way through the dancers to where Vernon and the band were standing. She moved next to Vernon without looking at him and smiled at everyone watching her.

"This song is for Pearl and Alfred. May you have many happy and healthy years together." She took a few cleansing breaths before letting out the throaty first notes of "Amazing Grace."

Much to her surprise, the crowd hollered appreciatively. She finished the rendition to a hearty round of applause.

"Do you know any love songs?" Vernon asked.

Eulalie nodded without looking at him. With only an arm's distance between them, she could have sworn she could feel his breath on her.

"I… looove… you," she sang with a dramatic flair.

Vernon and the rest of the band played alongside her as she sang about her lover's lips. Pearl and Al danced slowly to the music, focused only on each other. Eulalie knew she sounded great. She had perfect pitch and a voice that could carry to the heavens. The heady music surrounded her and wrapped her in a cocoon. The romantic lyrics had her feeling like love was real, like it could overcome and transcend anything.

Eulalie finished the last notes of the song, and the band played a few beats further, punctuating the end of the song like a sentence. When it was all done, the crowd clapped fervently. Ray put two fingers in his mouth and whistled loudly.

"Take a bow. You deserve it," Vernon whispered in her ear.

She felt his hand on the small of her back. Her body yearned for more, but all she could do was meet his eye then nod.

Eulalie took a deep bow. Before she could stand up straight, her mother let out a bloodcurdling scream.

****

All eyes turned to the table in the back, where Eulalie had been seated with her family. Daddy was slumped over in his chair, his chin touching his chest. From where she stood, all she could see was the top of Daddy's head.

"Someone please help me! He won't wake up!" Mama screamed. She pushed him hard on the shoulder. Instead of looking up at her, he started to fall off the other side of his chair. She grabbed him by the shoulders to steady him then screamed again.

Dr. George, who'd been dancing with Cassidra, rushed to Mama's side. A group started to form around Daddy, blocking Eulalie's view.

She dashed away from the band toward the table, pulling gawkers out of her way. She ran to stand next to Leona, who had large tears streaming down her face.

"Everyone needs to take a step back! I can't help him with you all crowding around," George yelled. He laid the slumping reverend on the ground.

As George put his head down to Daddy's chest, Vernon and Al ran up to help hold back the crowd of onlookers. George yanked off his suit jacket, tearing a long gash in the sleeve. He pushed down hard on Daddy's chest in long continuous pumps. "He's breathing, but it's very shallow." He ordered a few men to help, making them jump in response.

Mama took one look at Daddy lying on the ground, with George pumping his chest, and let out another wail. Eulalie's eyes filled with tears as she left Leona's side to pull Mama away.

"This can't be happening! This can't be!" Mama shrieked. "William, please wake up."

Mamie Jackson took Mama in her arms and rocked her from side to side.

"Orlene, you can't carry on like this," Mamie chided her. "You're scaring your girls. Come on. We're going to pray to the Most High for complete healing." Mamie pulled Mama's head to her chest and muttered a few words in such a low voice that Eulalie couldn't hear them.

"Come on, girls. Gather around and join hands."

Mamie kept one hand on Mama and waved other women over to her. Eulalie joined hands with Leona on one side and Cassidra on the other. Mother Edith and Mamie joined hands on the other side of Leona, and the women formed a small circle around Mama. Other women moved closer to join the prayer circle as Mamie prayed fervently.

"Precious Lord, we stand before you today, praying for the health of our dear leader. Heal him, Lord. You can make a way out of no way." Mamie spoke with authority amid all the hustle and bustle that surrounded them.

Cassidra squeezed Eulalie's hand hard and whispered, "Eulalie." Eulalie tried to keep her eyes closed in respect to the prayer offered, but Cassidra crushed her hand again.

Eulalie looked over at her sister, whose eyes were as wide as dinner plates. "What is it?"

"My water," Cassidra said. Beneath her, the ground was soaking wet, as if a rain shower had passed right beneath her feet. The hem of Cassidra's dress was wet, and long strands worked their way up the fabric as the liquid set in. Cassidra squeezed Eulalie's hand again. That time, her face scrunched hard along with it.

"Oh my God, Mama!" Eulalie screamed.

Mama's eyes popped open. She started to fuss, but once she looked at Cassidra, the anger melted into panic. Mama pulled away from Mamie to run to Cassidra's side.

"She's having her baby," Eulalie explained.

"My baby. Sweet Jesus, why is this all happening now?" Mama wailed. She balanced Cassidra with her arm.

"Mama, calm down. The baby won't be here for a while," Cassidra said through choppy breaths. She scrunched up her face again as another wave of pain coursed through her.

Even though Eulalie's heart was racing, she jumped into action, while everyone stood frozen. "Mama, you get Cassidra home. She can't have that baby out here in the yard. Leona, go with them and make sure to find the midwife. I know George wanted to be there, but he's busy. I'll stay here with Daddy and make sure he's okay." Eulalie punctuated her words with a wave of her hand, and all the women scattered. Eulalie pushed her way through the group of men and found they were hoisting her daddy onto a wheeled cot.

"Where are they taking him?" she asked. George was occupied, trying to direct the men, so Vernon stepped forward.

"They're going to move your father to where he can be more comfortable. They have to carry him to the hospital because he can't walk on his own," Vernon said.

Tears filled her eyes, and she put a hand over her gaping mouth. "Is he going to be okay?"

"I'm not sure." Vernon pulled her into a warm embrace and held her until her breathing steadied.

"Vernon, Pearl wants to speak to you. She wants to know what's going on." Loretta stood behind Eulalie.

"Let me go check on my sister. Will you keep me updated about your father?" Vernon dropped his hands from around Eulalie's shoulders and stepped away.

Al held Pearl in his arms. They stood off to the side, obviously not wanting to be in the way.

Eulalie nodded and turned to follow the men carrying her father away.

28

Vernon

"Are you going to be all right to get home?" Al stood next to a running automobile. The crowd had cleared out from the church after the melee. Both Reverend Hopewell and Cassidra had large groups of people who'd followed them to their respective destinations. Everyone else had congratulated Pearl and Al then moved to either help clean up or go home. The band had packed up and moved out, leaving Vernon there with the bride and groom.

"Alfred, I'm not ten years old anymore. You don't have to follow me home. Go enjoy your wedding night." Vernon clapped Al on the arm.

"I don't know that either one of us is in the mood to celebrate. We had a lot going on, and Pearl isn't feeling great after everything that happened," Al muttered.

"I'm sorry your wedding got all messed up," Vernon said, not that he'd had anything to do with the antics. He was glad he wasn't the center of attention, the one who'd caused a ruckus. He couldn't get the images of Eulalie's crying face or her father lying on the ground out of his mind. He and the reverend hadn't had the best relationship, but he didn't want to see the man dead.

Vernon stuck his head into the car to smile at Pearl. She'd waited patiently for Al and Vernon to finish their conversation.

"I love you, Birdie, and I'm proud of you. I hope y'all are married for a hundred years."

"One day, we'll do all this for you. However, without all the extra medical issues. I sure hope Reverend Hopewell is all right."

Vernon reached over and kissed Pearl on the cheek. "Don't y'all wait on me to get married. You'll be waiting the rest of your lives. Enjoy your wedding night. I'll check with Eulalie and let you know what's going on later."

Al got into the driver's seat and pulled into traffic. Vernon waved until they'd driven down the street. Then he picked up his horn and turned to walk home.

****

Instead of heading home like he should have done, he found his way to Lucky's Juke Joint. He didn't want to be alone. Watching Al drive off with Pearl made him feel sad, though he should have been happy. Before he'd even sat down, Jarvis, the bartender, brought him a small glass of gin and set it down in front of him.

"I didn't even get a chance to order anything," Vernon said.

"I know what you want. Besides, isn't your sister getting married today? It's a celebration, so this one is on the house."

"Drink with me, Jarvis. It's been a hell of a day."

Jarvis poured himself a sip of the gin and set it on the counter in front of Vernon's drink. Together, they picked up the glasses and threw the contents back in one quick gulp.

Lucky's was one of the nicer places a man could go to get a drink. It wasn't like those random barns out in the country that put a few gas lamps out and served moonshine out of an old bathtub. Prohibition had come, drying out most of the county, except for those with enough money to line the pockets of the politicians.

Lucky's was one of those places. It had a proper wood bar and cushions on the barstools. Wood paneling ran along the ceiling, and the walls had been painted with a fresh coat of white paint. A pair of shelves sat on the wall behind the bar, showing off all the different liquors that had been imported from all over the world. Vernon looked at his bottle sitting on the lower shelf, his chest puffing with pride.

Mr. Stuart, Lucky's owner, had taken a chance on him, and Vernon liked to pay him back by patronizing the establishment whenever he could.

"Is Alice working tonight?" Vernon asked.

"Naw, she has the evening off. Can I get you something else to drink?" Jarvis poured what Vernon asked for then moved off to help another man.

"What are you doing here, Mr. Jackson? Do you mind if I sit with you?" came a sultry voice from behind him.

Vernon turned to see Loretta standing behind him. She was still wearing the pink dress she'd been wearing at the wedding. She smiled sweetly and batted her eyelashes at him.

"Loretta, what are you doing here? Are you by yourself?" He looked around to see if anyone else was there with her, but she stood alone. He patted the seat next to him, and she hopped onto it. "Jarvis, get the lady whatever she wants, and put it on my tab."

Loretta was beautiful. Even Vernon had to admit it. Her skin was the color of a ripe summer peach with subtle hints of brown. Her slick hair had been pulled into a bun at the top of her head, but after the day, small pieces fell around her face messily, curling around the edges. Her hair and round cheeks gave her an air of innocence, which was a direct contrast to the sultry sway of her body. She had a full bosom, a small waist, and curvy hips. As Vernon sat next to her, his mouth went dry. She was the type of woman who could turn his entire life around with the crook of her finger. He wouldn't even know what had happened to him.

"Thank you, Jarvis. This looks wonderful," she drawled before turning to Vernon.

"Can you believe everything that happened today?" he asked.

"All this wedding stuff has me thinking about my own," Loretta admitted. She took a sip of her drink then set the glass back on the bar.

"I don't ever see you getting married. You don't seem like that type of woman."

"Now, why do you say that? I'm a woman. Of course I want to be married."

"You just don't seem like being married would make you happy. I can't see you waiting at home for your husband to arrive while you cook and clean." Vernon sipped his drink. "I don't mean to offend you. I just never thought I'd see you get married."

Loretta pursed her lips before turning them up into a sly smile. "What about you? When will the great Vernon Jackson get married?"

"I'm not great."

"What makes you think you're not great?" She smirked, and Vernon could see how a man could fall for her.

She was smart, pretty, and wittier than most people he knew. He wasn't sure whether he was lonely or the alcohol was getting to him, but Loretta's smile was drawing him in, something that had never happened before.

As soon as he realized he liked Loretta's smile, Eulalie's face flooded his thoughts. He thought of how frustrated he'd been when he'd seen Eulalie and she hadn't spoken to him. They'd been at the wedding all afternoon, and they hadn't said a word to each other. When she'd stood next to him and sung like an angel, it almost knocked him off his feet.

"Can I get y'all another drink?" Jarvis pulled him away from his thoughts.

Vernon nodded. He indicated that Loretta's glass should be refilled also then drained his drink. "Eulalie, I'm not great. I'm just a regular man. You know I'm just trying to be a good man. I shouldn't even be drinking like this, but today was a bit too much."

"My name is Loretta. And of course I know you're a good man. That's why I'm here with you."

"I'm sorry. I know your name is Loretta. I don't know why I called you that." Vernon shook his head, trying to clear it. Loretta didn't resemble Eulalie at all. Eulalie was browner, taller, and sweeter than Loretta. For some reason, he couldn't stop thinking of her perfect face.

"You love her, don't you?" Loretta asked with a laugh.

Vernon shifted uncomfortably but sat with her question for a moment. Had anyone else been asking, he would have tried to avoid the question. But Loretta was so earnest, her face so hopeful.

"Yes, I think I love her. It doesn't matter, though. Her family will never accept me. I'll probably never get married, and now you know why."

For an hour, they sat drinking to pass the evening. They talked about the wedding and what had happened in Ray's Café.

When the conversation ran dry and the drinks were finished, Loretta stood, her legs wobbling. "Will you walk me home?"

"Of course I will." Vernon paid his tab then followed Loretta out of the loud bar, into the dark night.

<h1 style="text-align:center">29</h1>

<h1 style="text-align:center">Eulalie</h1>

"Orlene? Where are you, Orlene?" Daddy rasped.

A wave of relief washed over Eulalie, but for some reason, her eyes filled with tears. She was so glad to hear his voice. They rushed down her cheeks so fast she could have filled a bucket. Eulalie had been seated next to her father's bedside for hours since they left the church. She was alone with him in the small hospital, since Dr. George had left hours ago to be by Cassidra's side. Neither Leona nor Mama had stopped by, so Eulalie had no idea if the baby had been born yet or what it was.

Eulalie wet a towel and wiped Daddy's face with it. "I'm here, Daddy."

"Who's that?"

"It's me. Eulalie. Mama's at Cassidra's house. She's having her baby. How are you feeling, Daddy?"

"Sweet girl." He tried to sit up, grunting.

"No, Daddy. Dr. George said to lie here and try to rest. He thinks you had a heart attack. We didn't know if you would—" Eulalie couldn't finish the sentence, and it didn't matter anyway. He'd woken up, so there was no sense in harping on the worst thing that could have happened. When George left, he'd given her the instruction to send for him if something else happened, but there was nothing for her to do. Either Daddy would wake up at some point, or he wouldn't. Eulalie had spent the next few hours at her father's bedside, praying for his recovery.

"Bring me some water, sweetheart."

Eulalie jumped up obediently. She helped him sit up just enough to be able to get a few sips of water in him without spilling it all down the sides of his face. When he was done, he settled back in. Eulalie pulled the covers up to his shoulders and fluffed his pillow.

For her entire life, Daddy had seemed so strong, so much larger than life. He wasn't much taller than her, but he'd seemed so big. He'd always had a big voice, someone used to projecting to be heard by a crowd. Lying there in bed quietly, her father seemed fragile. Even the large belly he led with seemed a bit deflated, like it wasn't carrying as much air.

"Can I do something else to make you feel comfortable?"

"No, sweetheart. Just let me lie here until this knot leaves my chest."

"Are you hungry? Maybe you just need to eat something."

"No, I just want to rest. Tell me about Cassidra's baby." He closed his eyes and rested his hands on his chest. She couldn't tell if he was in pain or not.

"I don't know anything about the baby. I've been here with you. If I had to guess, I'd say it's a girl because of the dramatic way she wanted to make her entrance."

Daddy smirked at Eulalie's joke but didn't laugh. That was how she knew he wasn't feeling well.

"I'm so proud of that girl I can't even say it. She's so smart and beautiful, and she married so well."

Eulalie froze. He was right—she was perfect. She was the perfect sister, wife, and daughter. She'd done everything exactly correctly.

"Leona, well, she's trying the best she can. She's a little too smart for her own good, but she'll be all right. Now, you, Eulalie, I'm worried about you." Daddy let out a little wheeze and had to stop talking to clear his throat.

Eulalie thought her heart might stop.

"Daddy, just try to get some rest. We can talk about this later." She wasn't in the mood. She hadn't slept enough.

"I may not be long for this world, child. That's why you need to hear it now," Daddy rasped. "If the Lord sees fit to call me home, I want you to know how I feel."

Please, God, don't say anything mean. Please just leave me alone. She prayed fervently that Daddy would switch course, but he seemed intent.

"Eulalie, you've always been my favorite daughter. Cassidra is too much like her mama, and Leona is too interested in her books. You are the one who has taken her smarts and made something of herself."

"Daddy, I thought you didn't care for me being a teacher. I thought you wanted me to be like Mama."

"Don't interrupt. Let me get it out." He cleared his throat then took a deep breath.

Eulalie tried to give him a sip of water, but he pushed her arm back. She set the glass down then tried to focus.

"Cassidra will be an easy wife, and so will Leona. You, on the other hand, have always been headstrong. You have always thought you were right and wanted to do exactly what you had a mind to do. What I'm trying to say is that you need to be very careful who you marry."

At that point, Eulalie didn't feel like she was ever going to get married.

"Daddy, don't worry about me getting married right now. Just focus on getting better. We have plenty of time for this conversation."

"That's the problem, child. We may not have much time. I'd like to see you settled before I—before I pass. I want to marry you just like I did your sister. Now, I'm not telling you who to marry. I'm just asking you to consider Samuel."

"Don't say things like that," she interrupted, but Daddy shook his head.

"Listen. I understand it may not be a love match, but it doesn't have to be. A man like Samuel will take care of you for the rest of your life. He will keep a roof over your head and keep your children fed. Please, Eulalie. I need you to do this. I can't pass knowing you're still out here messing with the likes of Vernon Jackson."

"But, Daddy, what if Vernon could give me all those things? He has a home, and I know he will care for me for the rest of my life."

"Eulalie, listen to me. I know you like him. I don't know why, but I understand. If you can get that man to marry you, I will marry you tomorrow. But he's not that kind of man. I know men like him. He cares about himself and no one else. Please just think about Samuel. Samuel is a good man, and he cares for you very much. Just think about it."

"I will" was all she could say.

The room door creaked open. Eulalie had to stop herself from running to see who it was. She'd been up all night worrying about Daddy, sleeping upright in the chair next to his bed. And there he was, talking about getting married, saying that marriage was about duty and honor, that love came second. She felt she was going to be sick, but nothing came up.

A weary Mama padded into the room. Her high heels clicked across the floor as she made her way to the bedside.

"William, are you all right?" she asked.

"I'm fine, Orlene. Tell us about Cassidra." Daddy's voice was weak but had a glimmer of hope in it.

"Baby girl Ophelia is here. She's seven pounds and ten ounces, born at five after five this morning. Cassidra and Ophelia are doing just fine." Mama ran her hands over Eulalie's crown and kissed her forehead.

Eulalie turned to Daddy and said, "I told you," which made him wheeze with laughter.

Now that Mama was there, Eulalie could let her take over.

****

Eulalie pushed open the door of Cassidra's house. They were taking too long to greet her, and she didn't want to wait. She'd already been up all night, so a few more hours of staying up to get what she wanted didn't matter.

"Sidra. George. Leona. Where are you all?" she called down the well-lit hallway, but no one answered. Eulalie left her shoes in the front before moving to explore.

A tinny baby whine called out from upstairs, making Eulalie almost burst into tears herself. She knocked on the closed bedroom door and entered only when invited in.

Inside, Cassidra lay in the bed like she hadn't had the longest night of her life. Her sheets were neat and clean, with a pristine coverlet laid over the top. She had bathed recently, her hair still wet and plaited down. In her arms, a little bundled baby wiggled, shaking a fist free from the thin blanket.

George, Cassidra, and Leona waved Eulalie over, their faces full of questions.

"Eulalie. How's Daddy?" Cassidra asked as Eulalie made her way to the edge of the bed.

"He's awake, but he still sounds bad. He needs to rest." Eulalie sat next to Cassidra on the bed and held out her arms. "How are you?"

"It was the worst thing I've ever gone through, but now that she's here, it was all worth it. Look at her little nose. She looks just like George." Cassidra passed the wiggling bundle to Eulalie.

Eulalie pulled the blanket back to peer at the tiny baby. Baby Ophelia scrunched her face at the feeling of new arms but didn't cry. Eulalie's chest heaved with emotion, and for what felt like the tenth time in the last twelve hours, she started to cry. The minute she locked eyes with her niece, it was love at first sight. Ophelia blinked slowly as she tried to focus on Eulalie. She was only a few hours old, and Eulalie couldn't see any features that belonged to Cassidra or George, but she was wonderful all the same.

"Sidra, she's perfect, and I love her so much already. Can I keep her, and you can just make another one for you?"

Everyone laughed, shaking their heads.

"You know, if you just got married, you could have one of your very own."

"No, you make beautiful babies. I only want yours." Eulalie sat holding Ophelia until the baby cried, looking for her mother's milk.

Eulalie reluctantly passed Ophelia back to Cassidra. Nestled in her mother's arms, Ophelia quieted immediately.

Leona sat on the bed next to Eulalie. Both sisters watched Cassidra bare her full breasts to bring Ophelia close to her.

"I'll leave you ladies to it," George announced before walking out.

"I think it's about time for us to go home and let the new mama deal with her baby. We'll be back to check on you, Ophelia." Leona reached over to kiss both Cassidra and Ophelia then looked at Eulalie.

All the sisters had been up all night. Now that a new day had broken, they all needed rest.

Eulalie and Leona bid George goodbye then made their way out of the new family's home.

"Are you sure Daddy's okay?" Leona asked. She looked tired, pushing her glasses up on her nose.

Eulalie shrugged. He'd woken up, and that was all she knew.

"I'm sure Mama will tell us when she gets home," Leona continued. She turned to head home, but Eulalie had other plans.

"Actually, I have another stop to make. I'll meet you there."

Leona stopped walking and turned to face Eulalie. "Where in the world could you possibly have to go? It's seven o'clock in the morning, and our family just had one of the wildest evenings. You need to go home and go to bed." Leona was all but shouting.

"Just go on home. I'll be there shortly."

"No, tell me where you're going."

Eulalie looked down the empty neighborhood streets, trying to decide how honest she wanted to be. She wasn't in the mood to fight with her sister and didn't want Leona to follow her. Eulalie bit her lip and decided to go with the truth. "I'm going to see Vernon—"

"Why? Why are you bothering? I thought we all talked about this." Leona waved her arms up and down in frustration.

"Daddy said he wanted to see me married before he passed."

Leona stood stock-still as if trying to process the words. "Is he dying?" she finally asked.

"I don't know, but he's awake and said he wanted me to be settled. I'm sure he's fine. Please don't worry."

"And Daddy said he wants you to marry Vernon Jackson?"

"No, he said I need to find a man who will always take care of me. If that means marrying Vernon, then he would do it. And I know Vernon will always take care of me. I know he will."

"I can't let you go over there and ask that man to marry you. It's embarrassing, and it's not how things are done. If he wanted you, it wouldn't have taken so long."

"You don't understand. You never have. How was he supposed to court me with Daddy saying no at every turn?"

"Fine. If you want to ruin your life, go ahead. I can't stop you. Just remember I told you so when it all goes to hell." Leona stomped away, leaving Eulalie standing on the street corner alone.

Eulalie turned toward Vernon's house. She just needed to have a quick talk, and then, only then, could she go home and rest.

30

Vernon

Vernon rolled over in his bed, wanting to get a few more hours of sleep. Daylight seeped into his room, through the curtains, but he pulled the covers over his head and tried to will himself back to sleep. His head throbbed. His eyes felt like they were going to fall out. He was still fully clothed. When he heard something crash in the kitchen, he jumped from the bed and ran to the other room. He should have stopped to get a weapon, but his brain wasn't quite awake.

He rushed into the doorway to find Loretta standing before the lit stove.

"What are you doing here? What the hell is going on?" Vernon tried to keep his tone light, but he was shocked. He tried to remember the previous night, where they'd been, and what they'd done. He remembered drinking in Lucky's and being with Loretta but had no recollection of her returning to the house with him.

"You drank too much last night." Loretta's dry tone didn't match her sunny smile.

"What does that have to do with you being in my house?"

"I couldn't just leave you alone. Anyone could have taken advantage of you." She dropped a few eggs into the skillet.

The sizzle seemed too loud and made his stomach turn. He wasn't in the mood for eating. Nor was he in the mood for an exchange of words with her.

She scrambled the eggs, and he became aware of her femininity. She wore only one of his nightshirts, which fell to her knees. From where he stood, her bare legs and feet were out to be gazed upon, but he forced his eyes upward. He looked over his own attire, the same fancy shirt and slacks he'd worn for Pearl's wedding. His tie had been long forgotten. The first few buttons had been undone, but for the most part, he was still dressed.

"Loretta, I want you to know that I didn't invite you here to take advantage of you."

"Darling, I would never let you take advantage of me. And you didn't."

"I didn't what?"

"Take advantage of me."

He wasn't sure how he could bring up the subject of lovemaking without being vile. Surely he hadn't drunk so much that he'd crossed the line with Loretta.

"What are you sweating about, Jackson?" Loretta pulled the scrambled eggs from the pan and dropped them onto a plate. She walked around the kitchen like she owned the place despite visiting very little, even when Pearl had lived there.

"I'm not sweating. I'm concerned that we may have gone too far. You know, we made some choices that we shouldn't have."

"Like making love?"

Vernon swallowed a mouthful of air. "Yes, like making love." His voice cracked. He'd never been hawkish about being with a woman. *Why am I letting Loretta get under my skin?*

"We didn't."

"We didn't what?"

"Make love," she said with an exasperated sigh. She handed him the plate and pushed him outside the kitchen to the dining room table.

"How do you know we didn't make love?"

"Because, darling, I promise, if you ever made love to me, you would never forget it. Also, all you talked about the entire way home was how much you loved Eulalie Hopewell and how beautiful she looked. You were supposed to be walking me home, but when we stood outside your house, I had to come inside. You were in no condition to get to my home, and I didn't want to go in the dark myself." Loretta stood in the doorway separating the dining room from the kitchen. She waved the dirty spatula at him, pointing at his plate.

"We didn't even sleep in the same room. I slept in Pearl's old room. I hope that was all right. Now, eat your eggs before they get cold. I'm going to get dressed and go home now that you've woken up and it's light outside."

"Thank you. For the eggs." Vernon still wasn't hungry, but at least he could relax. Loretta was beautiful, but he didn't like her in that way. He'd always seen her as one of his sister's friends.

He pushed the eggs around on his plate, smiling at the memory Loretta had recounted. Even when he'd been drinking, he still thought of Eulalie. Not wanting to hurt Loretta's feelings, he took a small bite of the eggs. Salt spread across his tongue, making his mouth water. He wavered between wanting to spit them out and forcing himself to swallow. His instinct overrode thought, and he spat the eggs back onto the plate. Loretta was sweet, but there was no way he could eat them. She must have dropped the entire shaker of salt in the skillet. Jesus Christ, at least she'd only wasted two of his eggs.

He waited until she closed Pearl's bedroom door before taking the plate to the kitchen. He scraped the uneaten food into the refuse then left the plate in the sink. He would wash it and the rest of her mess later.

Vernon took two steps back toward his waiting bed, then a frantic knock sounded at the door. He paused, mentally deciding whether or not to open it. He really wasn't in the mood to deal with Ricky or Big Mike. Pearl and Alfred were probably busy and would have just come in instead of knocking. When Vernon thought it could be Mr. Winston from next door needing help, he relented and walked to the door. The last person he'd expected was Eulalie.

She pushed past him, forcing her way into the house, a blur that streaked past him. Even if he'd wanted to stop her, he couldn't. His hands hadn't moved fast enough. She shook as she moved, making Vernon jittery. He tried to shake the cobwebs from his mind, but his thoughts lagged. Loretta was in the other room, and Eulalie moved with fury.

Eulalie paced the middle of the living room, like the lack of furniture had been set up specifically for her. She took four steps, turned in front of the old settee, then marched toward the fireplace on the opposite end.

"How's your father?" Vernon folded his arms and tried to relax. He genuinely wanted to know how Reverend Hopewell fared but couldn't get his mind off the other woman redressing in his sister's room.

"We have to get married, Vern. My daddy is insisting on it. He woke up and said he would marry us."

Vernon hesitated. "Eulalie, I've had a long night, and I'm not in the right mind to discuss this. You mean right now?" His mind swam with the consequences.

"I thought you wanted to marry me. Isn't that what you said? You pulled me into your bed and said you wanted to be with me."

"I also said I wanted to court you properly. I do want to marry you, but we've all had a long evening. Your father fell ill. Your sister had a baby. I'm still wearing the suit from last night. Now is not the right time to force a marriage. Are you sure your daddy was even in his right mind?"

Eulalie stopped mid-pace. A sneer crossed her face before she furrowed her brow. "Are you saying my father lost his mind?"

"I'm not saying that at all. I wasn't there, and I don't know how he is. Eulalie, the man passed out at a wedding and had to be carried out. Surely he doesn't mean to marry us today, right now."

"He may not make it, and he wants to see me settled."

"That doesn't mean we can barge in on his deathbed and demand that he marry us. It's not right, Eulalie. We can't." Vernon tried to hold his hand out to steady her pacing, but she pushed past his outstretched arm.

"Do you not want to marry me?"

"Yes, I do. But not like this. This is crazy. Look at you. You're pacing like the devil and won't sit down. You look like you haven't slept. I had a long night, and I know you have too. Just let me think about all this. Can I call on you later? Please?"

Vernon reached out and pulled Eulalie's hand. Facing the fireplace, he brought the back of her hand to his mouth and kissed it gently. Eulalie's eyes locked with his. He moved to pull her into an embrace, but the door behind him creaked open.

"Good Lord, Vernon, did Pearl take all of her clothing with her? There's nothing in here to change into, so I have to go home wearing the same dress I wore last night." Loretta's footsteps tapped across the wood floor.

Vernon didn't bother turning around. Eulalie's face said everything he needed to know. He thought she'd be angry. He expected her to yell. Instead, her shoulders dropped, and the corners of her mouth turned down. She looked from him to Loretta then back again, taking in each of their outfits.

"Eulalie, you don't understand. I know how it looks, but it's not what it seems." He waved his hands between himself and Loretta. "I drank too much last night, and she walked me home." Vernon's pulse thundered. Even that sounded feeble to his ears.

Loretta, with all her sass and spunk, for once, didn't say a word.

Eulalie bit the corner of her lip. She pivoted without a word and marched to the front door.

"Eulalie, wait. Please." Vernon chased her and grabbed her wrist as she stepped across the threshold.

She caught his gaze and said, "I should have known," before yanking her arm away to break out into a full run. He wanted to chase her. But perhaps that time, it was better to just let her go.

Vernon turned around to find Loretta's eyes filled with fear.

"I'm so sorry. I would never have interrupted had I known it was her. I thought Pearl and Alfred were here." She wiped away a few of the tears that had started to run down her cheeks. "I would never do anything to hurt you or her. I didn't mean for any of this to happen."

"Don't worry about it. Everyone just needs a bit of rest." He wanted to give Loretta a hug to reassure her, but it didn't feel appropriate after what had just happened.

"I'll talk to her. I will. I'll tell her everything."

"I will talk to her when the time is right. For now, just let her be." Vernon stood stiffly, waiting for Loretta to leave.

As if taking the hint, she walked to the door, but she stopped before stepping out. "I'm sorry, Vernon." For the second time that morning, a sniffling, sad woman left his home.

31

Eulalie

Eulalie zipped away from Vernon's house, hustling until she couldn't breathe anymore. When she was ten blocks away, she slowed to a stop, allowing herself to let out the full cry she'd been holding in. The hot tears wet her warm cheeks. As much as she wanted to pull herself together, she couldn't stop. *How many different ways can he show me he doesn't want to marry me?* He'd taken her innocence when they were younger, and she didn't have good-enough sense, because she'd let him do it again as an adult. Everything he'd told her was a lie. She walked and cried until she ran out of tears. Eventually, she was going home, but there was one more stop she had to make.

Eulalie turned onto First Street then walked down Greenwood Avenue until she stood outside of a small business building. White painted letters were drawn across the front picture window. Inside was a simple one-room layout. A long row of chests of drawers ran along the wall, with one desk in the back and another closer to the door. Empty chairs surrounded the desks, waiting for people to meet to discuss their finances. It was Sunday morning, and no one could be expected to be there working, but Eulalie stepped forward and banged on the door.

Samuel opened the door slowly, his face showing his surprise to see her. Like many other business owners, Samuel lived in an apartment above his small office. Eulalie had never seen his living space but had no doubt the furnished apartment was just as neat and organized as the office.

"Hello, Samuel. I'm sorry for how I treated you. I should never have gone to Ray's with that man. Will you still marry me?" Eulalie asked.

****

Two weeks later

Eulalie sat in front of her vanity mirror, staring at her reflection. Though it wasn't the first time in the last few weeks that she'd wanted to cry, it was the first time she'd told herself to pull herself together. All the hubbub and mess going on around her didn't matter. In a few hours, she was going to be a married woman. Vernon hadn't come to see her, and Samuel had stepped up.

Despite everything that had happened, Samuel was still agreeable to marrying her. Eulalie had spent the last week mourning what life could have been like before she let herself think about the future. Thoughts of Vernon still stung, but every day that passed found her breathing slightly more easily.

Mama opened the bedroom door slowly and shut it with a quiet click behind her. Eulalie didn't bother looking up. From Mama's careful intrusion, she knew it wasn't going to be good news. If it were, Mama would have come in cheering. Instead, she didn't say anything.

"I certainly wish you would do something different with your hair. Are you sure you don't want Clara to style it?" Mama fiddled at the nape of Eulalie's neck. Her voice was scratchy and tired.

"My hair is fine, Mama. It's not something to worry over."

Clara and Mama had wanted a complicated monstrosity on the top of her head, including ribbons and curled hair, but Eulalie remained steadfast on her hair being slicked back and pinned. There would be no flowers or decorations, no frippery or frills. It needed only to be simple. It didn't matter anyway. No woman remembered what her hair had looked like when she got married.

"Just let me know if you want Clara to do something special. We have a few hours, since..."

That must be the real reason her mother was creeping around. Eulalie wished she would just come out with it. "Since what?"

"Since Delores is still working on your dress," Mama finally admitted.

"It's my wedding day. I'm getting married in four hours, and my dress is not done?" Eulalie's words lacked any energy behind them. They'd been to a fitting the week before, and the dress had been mostly ready with the exception of a few hems and cinching. *How did a week pass without it being completed?*

The last couple of weeks had been trying. Eulalie's unfinished wedding dress was one of the final nails in a very large coffin. Daddy, who'd been the founding pastor of Greenwood Baptist Church, had been replaced when he couldn't get out of bed the Sunday following the Jackson wedding.

He'd been unceremoniously displaced by one of the deacons, who'd not so much as preached a sermon to a group of children. Half the church members were in an uproar at Deacon Rivers stepping up to the pulpit without a vote from the other members.

He'd preached the last two Sundays and didn't appear to want to stop despite there not being any official handoff.

After hours of back-and-forth, establishing which path the church would take, decade-long friendships had been splintered. The Hopewell family, who had been the first family for so long, stayed home, away from the proceedings, to care for their beloved patriarch.

Half of the church's women's group cycled in and out of the Hopewell household, trying to help Mama care for Daddy. At times, he was awake and alert, and other times, he murmured for hours, lost in his own thoughts.

Baby Ophelia developed colic, making Cassidra's house one filled with tears. Eulalie tried for a bit of respite at Samuel's office but found herself bored and in the way. Samuel worked quietly without talking to her, only offering a wan smile when she made any noise.

Mama ran constantly between home and Cassidra's, fitting in wherever she could. Leona helped keep Daddy company but holed up in her room with her books and projects.

Eulalie and Samuel planned for a quick wedding as soon as his family could take the train down from Chicago. She wouldn't have anything close to the celebration Pearl had had. Only his family and hers, something small, so as to not disturb everyone else in the family.

It's not about the wedding, Mama reasoned. *It's about the marriage. I don't even remember who came to my wedding.*

Vernon hadn't bothered to come talk to her. Nor had she gone to seek his company. That ship had sailed, no matter how jagged she found the memories.

Now, her hair was plain, her dress unfinished, and her household was in shambles. She didn't know what kind of mood Daddy was in or if he was able to even perform her wedding that afternoon.

Mama sat on the edge of the bed and let out a long breath, like she hadn't exhaled all day. "I'm sorry this wedding isn't working out very well. Maybe we should just postpone everything."

Eulalie sucked in a breath, and her head spun. She wasn't excited about getting married, but that wasn't what the wedding was about anyway. She turned to face her tired mother. "There's no sense in delaying the inevitable. The sooner I move to Samuel's, the sooner you have one less person to worry about."

"I will always worry about you, darling, just like I worry for Cassidra. It doesn't matter how long either of you are married. You will always be my babies. Even when you move to Samuel's, you are always welcome to come home."

"Do you think Daddy will be able to marry us?" Eulalie asked tentatively.

Mama nodded, but her eyes said otherwise. "We're only going to the backyard. He'll get up for you. You know he'll do anything for you."

As Mama rose and moved to leave, a sonorous knock sounded from the front of the house. Mama sighed, but Eulalie jumped from her seat.

"I'll see who it is. It's probably Delores with my dress. You can go check on Daddy."

There was no use ruminating on all the things going wrong. She could answer the door and get a bit of fresh air.

Eulalie moseyed down the steps then crossed the entryway to pull the door open. When she found Samuel standing on the porch, wearing a plain pair of pants and a simple cotton shirt, she inhaled sharply.

"I'm sure you weren't expecting me. At least not this early," he said. His clear voice was deep and confident, such a difference from her mother's.

"Samuel, this is a pleasant surprise. I'm glad you're here." Eulalie smiled. She stepped onto the porch with him, closing the door behind her. She looked down at her plain dress. The brown fabric was faded from overuse. Standing with Samuel, she didn't feel overly concerned about her appearance. He didn't seem to notice when she wasn't dressed up. Strangely, she felt comforted in his presence, like she could be herself, however she was packaged.

"Will you still be glad of my presence when I tell you the bad news?"

"Oh Lord, more bad news. I don't know if I can handle it."

"Will you take a walk with me?"

Her head swirled at the implications of what he was going to tell her. He smiled easily, waving her forward.

"Of course I will."

Eulalie followed Samuel down the few porch steps and away from the house. She tried to enjoy the day as much as she could but couldn't shake off the impending sense of sadness that fell over her shoulders. A bird chirped in a tree as they passed, its song of happiness grating on her nerves.

"What is it you wanted to tell me?"

"My family won't be able to make it."

"I don't understand. Why not? Do they not support this marriage?" She hadn't met any of his relatives, and he hadn't mentioned any issues before today.

"No, it's not that. Their train derailed in Saint Louis. I got a wire this morning saying it's a mess. There's dead cattle, luggage strewn about everywhere, and even a few hurt people. My family is all okay, praise the Lord, but they won't be able to make it until next week."

Eulalie digested his news and let out a cleansing breath.

"I have something to tell you as well," she said with a small smile. "My wedding dress is not finished either. Delores was supposed to have it delivered yesterday, but it's still not here." She paused and grabbed his hand, which was warm under hers. "I'm sorry to hear about your family. I'm glad they're all fine."

She reached out her arms to hug Samuel and stepped closer to accept it. Eulalie felt the warmth of the late-morning sun on the back of her neck as well as Samuel's arms wrapped around her and the languid pat he gave her back. But there was nothing else. There was no burst of excitement or fire growing in her underthings at his touch. She was safe.

"Do you think we should postpone the wedding? It truly doesn't matter the day we get married. We don't have to plan anything. We can do it the day your family arrives." It surprised her how comfortable she was to say the words. Earlier, she'd insisted to Mama that they stick with the plan. But in light of Samuel's news, fate seemed to be telling her she should wait.

Samuel started to walk again, making Eulalie continue behind him. He scratched the back of his hand then crossed his fingers. "What would you say if I suggested we not get married at all?" he asked.

"I would ask why you don't want to get married."

"I *did* want to get married, and I still will if you want to. Only I've come to the realization that we don't truly suit. I thought we would. You're an educator and very smart. I'm very smart and work hard. I thought since you were a preacher's daughter, you would want a man who works hard and is successful to take care of you. That you would want to have children and be there with them." He paused to take a breath.

Eulalie wanted to speak, but she stood silently, letting him finish.

"We should get along perfectly, but I'm finding you don't seem to take any pleasure in my touches. You make too much noise when I'm working, and I like a quiet home. You seem to want things that I can't give you. So I think it best we call it off." He looked out over her head, his eyes unfocused.

Eulalie stopped on the sidewalk in front of the Williamses' house, realizing her relationship with Samuel was over. His words stung, but ultimately, she knew he was right. She'd known theirs hadn't been a love match but thought they'd grow into a peaceful understanding. Eulalie had known passion that would carry her for the rest of her life. Passion had also given her the highest highs and lowest lows. She didn't need any more passion, only the peace of understanding.

"Would you hate me, Samuel, if I said I agree with you? I don't think we suit either." Eulalie had thought she'd run out of tears, but there she was, crying again.

Samuel neared Eulalie again and pulled her into another embrace.

That time, she stayed there, allowing herself to release all the expectations that had been placed on her and all the tears she still had. Her body shuddered as she let the tension fall from her shoulders. At some point, she would have to explain to her family what had happened. With the church community in such an upheaval, her broken engagement would be an anthill on the side of a mountain. She would have to return to the community as a single woman, one with no real prospects. For the moment, all she could do was cry.

Once she felt like she'd stood there long enough and taken up enough of Samuel's time, she allowed him to release her. He wiped the last of her tears with the pad of his thumb. His eyes were unreadable, but he gave her a small smile.

"Okay. Then I believe we will consider ourselves no longer engaged. Please know it was the honor of my life to be your fiancé, and I wish you the best." He kissed her on the cheek then turned to walk her home.

"I hope you find happiness, Samuel. You are the best of men, and you deserve it."

32

Vernon

"Vernon, what are you doing here? I thought you'd be out drinking somewhere." Al looked up from the sizzling skillet on the stove. He'd been stirring so intently Vernon hadn't been sure his friend had heard him come into the hot kitchen.

"I figured I'd get here early to practice one of the pieces of music I'd been working on. I want to hear how it sounds out there in the dining room. Thought I might get something to eat if I was lucky. What should I be drinking about?"

Al looked around the empty kitchen of the supper club like he was trying to find someone else, but no one appeared. He took a deep breath. "Pearl should probably be the one to tell you this, but…"

"Tell me what, Al?"

"We heard Eulalie's getting married today. At least I think it's sometime today."

"You must have heard wrong. I just walked past the church, and no one was there. If she was getting married, I'd be able to smell the food cooking all the way over here. They'd be putting up ribbons and pulling out all the stops for one of the Hopewell daughters." Vernon shook his head at Al. When he'd walked past, the doors had been shut, and there wasn't a hint of activity.

Al shrugged. "Maybe I could have it wrong, but I don't think so. I think they're doing it at her house, since her father is still—I don't think he's well."

Vernon set his trumpet case down then leaned his back against an empty wall. He needed the support to help him think. Al had mentioned Eulalie, and Vernon didn't trust his legs to hold him up. For the last two weeks, he'd thought of nothing but her. He wondered how she'd been or if she'd ever speak to him again. He hadn't done anything with Loretta. Nor did he have any interest in Loretta.

"What are you going to do?" Al asked, pulling Vernon from his thoughts.

"I ain't gonna do nothing. It doesn't have anything to do with me. If she wants to be married to him, I'm happy for her, and I wish her the best." More than a few times, Vernon had thought of going to see her, wanting to talk to her and explain. Every time, he'd talked himself out of it.

Al narrowed his eyes in disbelief. He looked like he wanted to say something but instead turned back to the simmering meat on the stove.

Vernon closed his eyes then launched into the story of how Eulalie had found him and Loretta at his house the morning after the wedding.

"She wouldn't let me say anything to her. Her eyes popped out, then she turned and walked out. Didn't say another word to me."

"Did you and Loretta do something?" Al didn't bother looking up that time.

"Man, if I wanted to do something with Loretta, I would have had her in my bed years ago."

"That don't answer my question."

"Naw, I haven't done anything with Loretta. I never kissed her, touched her, or let her touch me. Loretta is a hussy, and I don't like hussies. I would never date my sister's friend like that anyway." Now that Vernon's mouth was running, he couldn't stop.

"What's wrong with dating your sister's friend?" Al crossed his arms, leveling his gaze at Vernon.

Vernon stood up straight. "You know what I mean. I'm not trying to say nothing about you. Don't worry about Loretta right now. I'm not studying her. What would you do about Eulalie if you were me?"

"Me personally? I wouldn't have let her go."

"That doesn't help, and you know it." Vernon bent over to pick up his horn. He didn't need a lecture from Al. For years, Al had run the streets with Vernon, chasing women all over town. Now that he had two weeks of marriage under his belt, Alfred Harris was a scholar on women and marriage all of a sudden.

Vernon didn't want to fight with his best friend, and he wasn't in a great mood. Now that Al had pointed out Eulalie's potential wedding, he couldn't think of anything else. All he needed was to sit down and play his horn for a while. That would take his mind off everything. He'd started to leave the kitchen, headed for the dining room, when Al called from behind him.

"I guess I didn't realize you were a quitter."

"Come on, Al. Don't do that. I'm not in the mood." Vernon pulled his hand into a tight fist. He didn't want to fight Al, but the man was nearing dangerous waters. It wouldn't be the first time Vernon had swung on Al and probably wouldn't be the last.

"Naw, you need to hear it. All you've been talking about is how much you've changed and how grown you are. How you've been taking care of your responsibilities and being a good man. If you're such a good man, why don't you reconcile with the one woman you love?"

Al's tone deflated Vernon's anger. He was absolutely correct. Still facing the dining room, Vernon asked, "What if she's already married? What if it's too late?" He turned to look at his friend, whose face was hopeful.

"If it's too late, then at least you tried. At least you told her the truth and how you feel. It may not be too late, though."

****

Vernon banged on the Hopewells' front door. Instead of waiting for someone to answer, he stepped down from the porch and walked across the grass to get to the backyard. There was a chance he wasn't too late. His throbbing pulse made his feet run faster. Vernon couldn't stop her from marrying another man, but she needed to know exactly how he felt about her. He couldn't live with her thinking he didn't want her or that Loretta had been a part of his life. She needed to know that he would love her forever, no matter how their lives moved forward.

He burst into the backyard, preparing himself to make a scene, but he found nothing. There were no guests, decorations, or food. The clothesline blew lazily in the wind without even so much as a towel hanging on it. Vernon stopped, forcing his pulse to calm down.

On the way over from Al's, he'd worked himself into a frenzy, thinking of all the things he had to tell Eulalie. He hadn't stopped to consider that perhaps Al didn't have all the information. Feeling silly, he turned to walk away but bumped right into Eulalie standing behind him.

She squawked as she fell back.

Vernon jumped, surprised at her presence. "Oh my God, Eulalie, I didn't hear you back there." He reached out and helped her up from the grass.

She brushed off her dress and straightened her skirt. "It's all right. I probably shouldn't have walked so close to you. What are you doing in my backyard?"

"I was checking to see if you were getting married. Someone said… They said you were getting married today."

Shame heated his face. Saying the words aloud made him feel like a child again, trying to explain why he'd had a box of snakes.

"And if I was getting married, what difference would it make?"

"It makes a difference because I love you, and I can't live without you. I don't want you to marry Samuel. I want you to marry me."

Eulalie crossed her arms and furrowed her brow, taking a step back from him.

"I know how it doesn't look good, Eulalie, but I promise you I am not and never will be involved with Loretta."

Eulalie exhaled loudly and nodded. "I know. Loretta stopped by the house, and we had a conversation. She said all you could do was talk about how much you loved me." She smiled sweetly.

"Why didn't you come see me and tell me?"

"Why didn't *you* come see *me*?"

"I was scared you wouldn't believe me. I was afraid you wouldn't speak to me again. I want you so bad I'm willing to punch anyone who disrespects you. But, Eulalie, I also want you to be happy. If your family doesn't want us to be together, if you don't want to be together, then I respect your decision."

Eulalie's eyes filled with tears. "Oh my Lord, I've been crying so much in the last few weeks I didn't think it would be possible to cry any more." She wailed, and Vernon's heart broke.

He moved closer to her and pulled her into his arms, savoring the feel of her body.

"Please don't cry. I don't want to upset you. Tell me what you want, and I'll give it to you. If you want me to leave, I'll leave. But if you want me to stay… if you say you'll marry me, I'll never leave you again." Vernon's voice wavered, but he continued, "Tell me I'm what you want, and I'll give you everything you want."

"I want to be married to a man who loves me. A man who will clean up his life and take care of me. I want a responsible man. Can you be those things?"

Vernon wiped the tears from her face. "I will spend the rest of my life proving to you that I can be that man. Please say you'll marry me and that you want me."

"I want you. You're all I've ever wanted." Eulalie's lips parted slowly, beckoning him forward.

He took the opportunity and pressed a small kiss to her lips.

Excitement overtook him, turning the small, chaste kiss into a barn-burning, fire-starting one. He feasted on her lips, tasting her tongue like it was the last time he'd ever see her. There, under the shadow of her father's house, Vernon held Eulalie, swearing to himself he would never let her go.

33

Eulalie

Eulalie led Vernon by the hand through the front door of the house, her heart pounding. She moved timidly, like she was creeping through a dragon's lair instead of her own home. In the split second she'd spent in the back with Vernon, she made her decision. She was going to be with him. It didn't matter what anyone in her family had to say. She'd known since she was sixteen years old that she loved him. It had taken her almost ten years, so she wasn't going to let any more time slip past.

They went down the front hall and into the kitchen, where Mama waited, her head resting in her hands. Eulalie had already delivered the news of her breakup with Samuel. Mama had cried and forced Eulalie to come to the kitchen for a warm drink to calm her nerves.

"Who in the world was knocking on the door?" Mama asked without looking up from the table.

Vernon cleared his throat.

Mama jumped at the masculine sound, taking a minute to adjust her eyes to the visitor. When she realized who was there with Eulalie, her hands flew to her chest, covering her heart. "Oh my Lord, what is happening now? My heart can't take no more."

"Mama, don't panic. Everything is fine." Eulalie wished her voice sounded as strong as she felt. She was throwing her mother's world topsy-turvy, but it was time to stand up for herself. Had she done that weeks ago, she would never have accepted Samuel's proposal in the first place.

"Vernon and I are going to be together. I love him, and we're going to be married. I hope you and Daddy will accept it and him into the family." She gripped his hand tighter and pulled him closer.

Mama stood slowly and made her way toward them. She held out her arms, forcing Vernon to step forward and accept her hug. "Welcome to the family, then. Would you like something to eat or drink? I've got tea and an apple pie just waiting to be cut into."

"I would love a piece of pie, Mrs. Hopewell. Thank you for taking this well. I love your daughter and will take care of her until my dying day." Vernon pulled Mama tight then released her.

"How about we sit down and talk while Eulalie goes upstairs and talks to her father? They will probably need a few minutes." Mama pulled Vernon deeper into the kitchen, luring him with the promise of all the food his belly could hold.

He gave a sneaky wink and followed, letting Mama talk his ears off.

Eulalie recognized an order when one was given and turned toward her parents' bedroom.

****

Eulalie sat next to her father's bedside without a sound. He looked up from his Bible, waiting for her to speak.

"Daddy, I have something to tell you, and I don't want you to be mad."

He didn't say a word but put his Bible down to indicate he was listening.

The sooner she said the words, the freer she would feel.

"Samuel and I have decided to end our engagement, and I'm going to marry Vernon Jackson instead. I would like your blessing."

Daddy gave a wheezy chuckle. He sat up further in bed and leveled his gaze at her. "I should have known this would happen. As much as I worked to fight it, it appears man truly can't out-plan God."

Eulalie didn't know what was happening. *Is this the same man who spent my entire life telling me to stay away from Vernon?* This was the same man who'd preached a Sunday sermon about the devil dressing up as someone you knew, someone who was coming for your children. He'd talked about wayward children and making good decisions. Something had happened to her daddy, and Eulalie wasn't sure how to take it.

"I'm not sure you heard me. Vernon Jackson and I have decided to be together."

"I heard you just fine. You're twenty-six years old, Eulalie, and it's time for you to start making decisions for your own life. If he makes you happy, then that's all that matters. I'm sorry I spent so much time trying to keep you two apart."

"That's a great point, but why did you do it? I know he was a bit of a wild boy, but he's no different from all the other knuckleheads running around here."

"There's something I need to tell you. It's not really my story to tell, but I want to talk to you about it. If your mama is okay with you marrying him, then I guess I'll be okay with it too."

Daddy fiddled with the covers, seeming to be stalling for time. His eyes softened and he started. "Believe it or not, there was a time before you were born when your mama and I were just as young as you are. I wasn't always fat and old."

They laughed together for a few moments. Eulalie's heart was so full she reached out and held Daddy's hand just to feel nearer to him.

"I'd seen your mama around town and thought she was the most beautiful woman I'd ever laid eyes on. I spoke with her, and she was so kind and lovely. I asked your grandparents for permission to court her, and they agreed, then I asked her to marry me." He pursed his lips. His eyes turned serious, making Eulalie lean in closer.

"Everything was perfect until Joe Jackson showed up to town from Mississippi. He took a liking to your mama, and to tell you the truth, she liked him too."

Eulalie gasped. Her mind whirred with Daddy's words. *Mom's lover Joe was a Jackson?*

Daddy saw her wheels spinning and saved her from her imagination. "Yes, Jackson. Vernon's father. He wasn't Vernon's father at the time. He was just another young man in love with Orlene. We went through so much. I went through so much. One minute, she was going to marry me, and the next, she wasn't sure what she wanted to do. I almost lost her, and I was heartbroken. I don't know why she chose me, but she did. And here we are, with you beautiful girls and this happy home. I suppose you can imagine my surprise when Vernon Jackson started making eyes at you. I couldn't believe it. Here was another Jackson man coming for one of my girls. I thought I could keep you from going through what your mama went through and what I went through. If I'm being honest, I had to work through a lot of jealousy. I'm sorry for letting my story affect yours." He patted Eulalie on the hand.

"How come you didn't tell me?" she asked, trying to keep her emotions to herself.

"Sweetheart, when was I supposed to tell you that you couldn't date the son of the man your mama almost married? The only thing I could do was protect you the best way I knew how. I hope you get that."

Eulalie nodded. Her father had been hurt and, in turn, wanted to protect her. She didn't agree, but she understood. Eulalie pulled her hand back and reached over to hug him.

When she stood, she said, "Vernon is here, and he's going to want to speak to you, if that's all right."

Daddy nodded and told her to send him up.

✷✷✷✷

"I need to talk to Mama. Privately."

Mama and Vernon looked as cozy as old friends. She hated to interrupt their bonding, but she needed to get Mama's side of the story.

Vernon must have seen the seriousness in her face, because he jumped from his seat. He offered her the chair and stood before them. "Do you think your father will be all right if I go speak to him? We need to have a conversation."

"Please, young man, go speak to him. I'm sure he's been waiting to see you since the minute Eulalie stepped out of his room."

Eulalie gave Vernon the directions to the correct room then sat down with her mother. "Why didn't you tell me?" Even though they were alone, Eulalie still whispered. For some reason, she didn't want to frighten her mother off.

Mama gave her an easy smile. "I suppose Daddy told you who Joe was?"

Eulalie nodded. She had so many thoughts running through her mind, so many questions she had for her mother now that she understood. *Is Mama happy? Does she feel like she made the right choice? Would she have done the same things if she had it all to do over again?*

"That night in my room, you told me to make a good choice. I thought you were telling me to choose Samuel." Eulalie let out a cleansing breath.

"Then, my dear, you weren't listening. I didn't hint that you should choose Samuel. I asked you to think about what you wanted from your life and who you wanted to be with, because when it's all said and done, you are the one who has to live your life."

Eulalie sat back, digesting her mother's words. She was sure in her heart that she wanted to be with Vernon.

"If you had to do it all over, would you still make the same choice?" Eulalie's heart pounded in her throat as she waited for her mother's answer.

Mama smiled and nodded. She opened her arms wide, beckoning Eulalie forward. Eulalie stood and pulled her mother into a long embrace.

She whispered, "I would have chosen Daddy time and time again. But I'm proud of you and the choice you've made. I hope you'll be just as happy as I've been."

****

"Eulalie, go get your sister. We're going to need a witness." Daddy shuffled into the kitchen, where she and Mama were huddled around the table.

Eulalie dropped her fork then looked at Vernon and her daddy, who looked to be complete opposites.

Daddy was only a few inches taller than her. Vernon stood tall and strong, like a steady oak tree. Eulalie took her time looking between the two men until she realized Daddy was wearing his preacher's robes.

"What do you mean?" Eulalie asked, a smile growing across her face.

"We were supposed to have a wedding today. Unless I'm mistaken, I have two young people here before me who are ready to get married." Daddy tapped the cover of his Bible on his thigh.

Eulalie met Vernon's eyes, and his face broke into a wide smile.

"What do you think? Are you ready to be married?" Vernon asked.

She nodded and ran to find Leona.

****

At half past four in the afternoon, Eulalie Ann Hopewell pledged her love and undying devotion to Vernon Eugene Jackson. The happy couple waited just long enough for Cassidra, Dr. George, Ophelia, Leona, Pearl, and Alfred to convene at the Hopewell household.

Since her wedding dress wasn't ready, Eulalie asked her mother if she still had hers. Mama let her try on the dress, which was horribly out of fashion, but Eulalie couldn't have cared less. She felt like a queen, and Vernon only had eyes for her. While he was away from the house, Vernon changed into a clean gray suit and stopped to buy flowers and a thin gold band for his bride.

When they joined their hands together, standing in front of their families, Eulalie couldn't remember ever being happier.

"Therefore, what God has joined together, let no man tear asunder. I now pronounce you husband and wife. Vernon, you may now kiss your bride." Daddy had said those words many times before, but now, they resonated with Eulalie.

Vernon stepped forward, brought her into a loving embrace, and placed a gentle kiss on her lips. "I love you now and forever-more."

34

Samuel

Samuel knew he shouldn't have come to this godforsaken town. He should never have listened to the man who told him Greenwood was going to be a colored haven just like Chicago. The man had been right about one thing—the weather. Everything else had been a disappointment. He hadn't grown up in the neighborhood, so he didn't know any of the people who all seemed to know one another.

When he met Eulalie, he'd been so taken with her sweet smile and polite countenance. Between dinners with Eulalie's family and his work, he'd managed to stay busy. Now, he had nothing else to do. The woman he'd been courting for the last couple of months was no longer interested in being around him. He'd spent the last eight weeks between his office and small apartment, intentionally working long hours to save money. He'd wanted to buy a large home and fill it with all the things that made Eulalie happy. He hadn't had a sip of liquor, instead focusing all his attention on work so that one day, he could slow down and enjoy life.

Now that he was no longer engaged, all of that was about to change.

Thank you so much for your support. It means the world to me. Follow my journey at:

MarissaMcQueen.com